She bit her lip an this man's friend. As ____ s and falls of his face, _____ and-some than any m_____ ____ roud, incredibly male, and, the good Lord help her, she had never felt more female.

Sadly, he was also the exact sort of person her step-uncle would forbid her from.

Perhaps it was this that triggered that latent spark of rebellion, and she asked, "Sir Eagle, tell me. Do Indians kiss?"

If he were startled by her question, he didn't show it. Instead, he stepped toward her. He answered calmly, "Of course."

"But I mean, do they kiss, lips to lips, like the English do?"

"I believe" he muttered, as he placed his arm against the tree, "that the English cannot claim complete ownership over something so common as a kiss. All human beings enjoy much the same thing."

As he spoke, his head had descended so closely to hers that she realized she could read his thoughts; it was an unbelievably intimate feeling, as though he had become a part of her. He wanted to kiss her. She knew it as surely as the fact that she wanted to be kissed.

# BLACK EAGLE

## GEN BAILEY

BERKLEY SENSATION, NEW YORK

**THE BERKLEY PUBLISHING GROUP**
**Published by the Penguin Group**
**Penguin Group (USA) Inc.**
**375 Hudson Street, New York, New York 10014, USA**
Penguin Group (Canada), 90 Eglinton Avenue East, Suite 700, Toronto, Ontario M4P 2Y3, Canada
(a division of Pearson Penguin Canada Inc.)
Penguin Books Ltd., 80 Strand, London WC2R 0RL, England
Penguin Group Ireland, 25 St. Stephen's Green, Dublin 2, Ireland
(a division of Penguin Books Ltd.)
Penguin Group (Australia), 250 Camberwell Road, Camberwell, Victoria 3124, Australia
(a division of Pearson Australia Group Pty. Ltd.)
Penguin Books India Pvt. Ltd., 11 Community Centre, Panchsheel Park, New Delhi—110 017, India
Penguin Group (NZ), 67 Apollo Drive, Rosedale, North Shore 0632, New Zealand
(a division of Pearson New Zealand Ltd.)
Penguin Books (South Africa) (Pty.) Ltd., 24 Sturdee Avenue, Rosebank, Johannesburg 2196,
South Africa

Penguin Books Ltd., Registered Offices: 80 Strand, London WC2R 0RL, England

BLACK EAGLE

A Berkley Sensation Book / published by arrangement with the author

PRINTING HISTORY
Berkley Sensation mass-market edition / May 2009

Copyright © 2009 by Karen Kay Elstener-Bailey.
Cover art by Robert Papp (Lo Res).
Cover design by George Long.
Cover hand lettering by Ron Zinn.
Interior text design by Kristin del Rosario.

ISBN: 978-0-425-22818-0

BERKLEY® SENSATION
Berkley Sensation Books are published by The Berkley Publishing Group,
a division of Penguin Group (USA) Inc.,
375 Hudson Street, New York, New York 10014.
BERKLEY® SENSATION and the "B" design are trademarks of Penguin Group (USA) Inc.

PRINTED IN THE UNITED STATES OF AMERICA

10  9  8  7  6  5  4  3  2  1

*For Michael Badnarik, author of the book*
Good to Be King *and*
*the step-father of the Constitution*
*who first taught me that*
*we are all kings and queens*
*here in the land of the free*
*and the home of the brave.*

*And for my husband, Paul Bailey,*
*whom I love with all my heart.*

# Acknowledgments

A special thanks goes out to the following very beloved people, who are Gen Bailey's Warriorettes. You have not only my appreciation, but my respect and admiration.

| | |
|---|---|
| Francis Miller | Debra Guyette |
| Cathie Morton | Lori Barnes |
| Janet Hughes | June Phyllis Baker |
| Diana Tidlund | Rebekah Elrod |
| Jane Squires | Heather Bennett |
| Sheila Lawson | Diane Dicke |
| Sharon Crumper | Tami Bates |
| Katherine M. Kakegamic | Melinda Elmore |
| Dena Walton | Jennifer Johnson |
| Beth Reimer | Deanna Fullbright |
| Terry Stuart | Sonja Dimitrovski |
| Emma L. Metz | Dianne Westbrook |
| Kristy Centeno | Malana Whited |
| Catherine Abernathy | Linda Barnes |
| Denell Wieczorek | Monica M. Carter |
| Melissa Keith | Kathy Lynn Reed |
| Amy Lytle | Jean Paquin |
| Raeann Williams | Robin Priddy |
| Arlene Jones | Debbie Mercer |
| Marilyn Wigglesworth | Tressa Thorp |
| Jenny Cooper | Donna Bratton |
| Kimberly Rouleau | Deidre Durance |
| Katherine Edgar | Carla Corless |

Lilian Gilliers                    Paula Willhoite
Vickie Batten                     Pepper Cash
Kristen Waxler            Michele Rose Sonnenberg
Sarah Wendt                    Debbie Cosentino
Heather Wentz                  Tamara Miranda

# Author's Note

For my brother-in-law, Robert Bailey.

Your warmth, your humor, your kind-hearted encouragement, as well as your presence in my life will never be forgotten. In all things, save one final moment, you never let me down.

Thank you for the time you were here in my life. I am better for your presence.

With love,
Gen Bailey

# Prologue

*It is a time of unrest. Both the English and the French are battling for control of the North American continent. Both seek the support of the strong and invincible Iroquois confederation. Deprivations are extant on both sides of the quarrel, the French and Indians of Canada against the English and the Mohawk of the Americas.*

*As always, in any time of dissension, there are those who seek to profit from the ruin of others.*

The Territory of the Mohawk Indians
The Keepers of the Eastern Door
Iroquois Confederation
Lake George area in what is now upper New York State
*Saskekowa Moon,* September 1755
Early evening

Flintlock in hand, with powder horn thrown over his shoulder, bow and quiver full of arrows strapped across his back, the lone runner's feet flew over a bloody path that wound through the forested valley of the Adirondack Mountains. As he jumped over a barrier of branches blocking his path, he caught his breath. Offshoots from tree limbs and debris cracked as his foot hit against them. But he didn't fall. It was simply not an option.

With barely a miss of a beat, the young warrior, Black Eagle, brought himself back into pace, continuing onward, ever pushing himself faster. *I will be swift as the eagle,* he repeated to himself silently. *Since the life of my good friend, Sir William Johnson, depends on my speed, I dare even the West Wind to be faster than I.*

Behind Black Eagle and in the distance, shots and cannon fire, from the battle that was still waging, echoed against the quiet of the forest. It was a strange comparison. Particularly so, since the fighting would likely carry on throughout the remainder of the day. But for Black Eagle, the battle had ended. His friend, William Johnson, lay wounded from the battle and now required help; assistance that Black Eagle and a few of the chiefs were determined to provide in the form of a medicine man and the Water-that-runs-swift.

*There is no doubt I will be successful. No creature, not even the eagle, himself, is faster than I. I will save my friend.* With this thought in mind, Black Eagle picked up his speed.

"Did ye send him?"

"We did."

"Did ye tell him it was for me?"

"We did."

The officer let out a pent-up breath. "Then it is certain I am that the lad will be successful. How long will it be taking now?" asked former trader and Indian agent William Johnson. He grimaced as he tried to sit up.

"If Black Eagle meets with no resistance, we should rendezvous with him by nightfall at the Water-that-runs-swift." It was White Hair speaking, an aged warrior from the Oneida tribe.

Johnson fell back against the sturdy tree that sheltered him. "Good," he said. "Good. 'Tis glad I am that ye sent Black Eagle, for I could not be liking a young man more if he were my own son. Indeed, while possessing the wily wit of a Mohawk, Black Eagle yet has the manners of an Englishman. Havena I seen to that myself?"

"He is also the fastest runner in all the Mohawk Nation," said White Hair.

"That he be. That he be. At least we won the skirmish

this day, thank God." Again Johnson grimaced in pain. "Where is Dieskau, the French commander?"

"He has been taken to your bed, and your surgeon is with him now."

"Dieskau will also need to journey with us to the Water-that-runs-swift," said Johnson. "I fear that if we leave him behind, upon our return, we may find him scalped."

White Hair frowned, then said, "If you tell the warriors to leave the commander alone, they will do as you say."

"And can ye be promising me that?"

White Hair hesitated a little too long.

"No," said Johnson. "The French commander will come with us. The Water-that-runs-swift shall help him, as well as myself. Are the others with ye ready to take us there?"

"They are," replied White Hair.

"I thank ye for yer friendship," said Johnson. "Where is my good friend and yer chief, Henrick? He should have met me here."

"Has no one told you of the great sachem?"

Johnson frowned. "No."

"Forgive me for being the one to bring you the sad news that Henrick fell into a group of women, wives of the Abenaki Indians allied to the French. It is they who killed him. They stabbed and scalped him."

Johnson shut his eyes and placed his head in his hands. At length, he said, "I shall be missing him." Lifting his gaze, he addressed White Hair and said, "It is a sad ending for the gallant sachem that he was. When this business is done here and we are back in yer camp, we will speak words of condolence to his relatives and to those others who will mourn him."

"It will be so."

"And my brother-in-law, Matthew Farrell? . . ."

White Hair remained silent.

"Was he, too, killed?"

White Hair's silence spoke better than words could have. Johnson, who had raised himself up onto his elbows during this short exchange, fell back to the ground. "'Tis a dreadful business we do here. I fear my sister, Catherine, young Farrell's wife, will ill abide these sad tidings." Johnson breathed in heavily. "But come," he continued, "we must see to those who be still alive. Be it a long journey to the Water-that-runs-swift?"

"Not long," said White Hair, "but arduous for you and the Frenchman, since it will pain you both to move."

Johnson nodded. "And yet it must be done."

White Hair bent his head in agreement. "If our friend and brother Johnson is to remain well, it must be done."

Again Johnson nodded. "Then let us be doing it. How many men will be carrying us to the water?"

"There are five of us, but I will ask more to help since we must move the Frenchman, as well. Are you ready?"

Johnson looked deeply into the red-painted face of this native-born warrior, a Mohawk fighter. Inhaling quickly, it did not escape Johnson's notice that these odd-looking natives were the truest of friends.

On a deep sigh, he said, "The very air here smells of gun powder, blood and death. Bad business, it is. Bring Dieskau here to me so that I might explain what it is that we do."

"It will be done . . ."


Black Eagle continued to fly along the narrow path that had seen more battles than he cared to recall. The very woods echoed with the departed spirits of his countrymen. That such a beautiful ground should bear great strife was to be lamented, and Black Eagle couldn't help but consider that Hiawatha and the Peacemaker of the Iroquois confederation would be unhappy to learn of the number of wars that had come to their country . . . and in the name of "peace."

Such thoughts, however, were a waste of precious energy. The white man's war was here, and whether the Iroquois people liked it or not, their homeland was situated between the two fighting nations.

Passing quickly through a stream, Black Eagle set his

pace again and turned his thoughts to other matters, to the woods that greeted him on every side of the path, and to the sounds and scents of the forest. It was a beautiful time of year, trees and bushes wearing their orange, gold and red leaves, as though they would announce their departure from this world with beauty and vigor.

Black Eagle couldn't help but be aware of the comparison between himself and his people to these trees. So much better it was to leave this earth in the full glory of battle, than to cower and hide in fear. Such was the Mohawk spirit.

Brown, red, gold and green leaves littered the path as he ran onward, the musky scent of the leaves filling his nostrils and causing him to recall other times when he had enjoyed their fragrance. Those past times were happy days, filled with harmony and sunshine, times that were in deep contrast to the present.

Johnson, who was a staunch friend of the Mohawk long-house of the wolf, must live. For his sake, for the sake of the Iroquois. With Henrick taken in the day's battle, Black Eagle could only surmise that Johnson would become more and more important to the Iroquois.

It was probably safe to say that, though few white men had ever earned the love and respect of the Mohawk people, Johnson had accomplished it. Not only were his dealings as a trader honest and fair, his knowledge and adherence to Mohawk tradition was without fault. The fact that he had also married a beautiful Mohawk maiden had sealed his acceptance, causing him to become a person who was much loved by the Mohawk people.

But he was particularly special to Black Eagle. Because of Johnson, Black Eagle had attended a white man's school—at least for a year. Because of Johnson, Black Eagle had come to an understanding of what the white man was about.

It was probably safe to say that Johnson was as influential to him as an uncle or other member of his clan.

He must be saved. By now several of the Mohawk warriors should be carrying Johnson to the place where the water runs fast—a location known to the whites as Saratoga. It was well known amongst his own people that the water there was special—it was healing . . . and it would particularly be so if a medicine man could be persuaded to accompany Black Eagle there.

Thus, since Black Eagle was acclaimed as the fastest runner amongst the warriors—both Indian and white—it had been put upon him to run to the nearest Mohawk village, a village called *Canajoharie*. The medicine man there was renowned. It was hoped that with persuasion, the medicine man would accompany Black Eagle to the Water-that-runs-swift.

Black Eagle frowned; the hour seemed late. There in the western sky, he could discern traces of the pinkish orange rays of sunset.

Had he run so long? It had been late morning when he had started on this journey.

But what was this, ahead of him? Was it sunlight streaming into the dark forest? Was his journey almost at an end?

With leg and thigh muscles that felt burned from his hourslong exertion, Black Eagle sped forward, bursting from the forest only minutes later. Immediately he was engulfed in the neat, clean fields of the three sisters, corn, bean and squash, and his heart rejoiced. At last, he thought, he was amongst the civilization of the Mohawk, the village of *Canajoharie*.

But he was not from this village. He could not simply storm into it.

"Our people have been so much put upon by other tribes, and by the white man, that it is difficult for a man to be able to distinguish enemy from friend. Therefore, if you ever wish to visit a village that does not know you, you must sit and smoke a pipe of peace before entering the village. If you do this, a messenger will come to you."

So had spoken a sachem from his tribe.

Producing a pipe, Black Eagle sat and smoked, and soon, he was met by a scout from the village.

"Brethren," said the scout as he approached Black Eagle, "I see by your clothes and the tattoo on your arm that you are of the wolf clan of the confederation. Brother, I see also by your actions that you come in peace."

"It is so," Black Eagle returned. "But I come bearing news on the war that has been waged nearby here."

"Did you fight in this battle?"

"*Nyoh*, yes, I did."

"Then the news that you bring is good news?"

"It is both good and bad. The French have been defeated, but our friend William Johnson has been hurt, and it is feared that he may not recover. Several warriors are carrying him to the healing place of the Water-that-runs-swift. I have been sent here to *Canajoharie* to seek the assistance of your medicine man. I have this wampum belt to show your sachem my sincerity." He pulled the belt from a bag that hung from his shoulder.

The messenger nodded. "It is good. We are close to the Water-that-runs-swift. Come. Welcome to our village. I will take you to our medicine man at once. But before I do, let me inquire if you have had an evening meal."

"I have not," said Black Eagle.

"Then please honor me by seeking my longhouse first. My wife will set a meal before you that is quick, but nourishing. Then we will speak to the medicine man."

Though still urged to hurry, Black Eagle ignored the feeling, and nodded. "I thank you for your hospitality. I will follow you."

And so it was done.

**William Johnson's camp near the
Battleground of Lake St. George
Nine days later**

William Johnson was positioned in his tent, on his bed. At his side was Black Eagle, who had only just returned with Johnson and the other warriors from the healing waters.

Said Johnson, "Black Eagle, ye did well for this heart of mine. I cannot begin to thank ye, son, for what ye and the other Mohawk's have done. I know I speak not only for myself, but for the French commander, Dieskau. It is my hope that he will fare well enough that he will leave this country."

Black Eagle nodded. "It is a good plan. It is well that you captured him in battle, and have sheltered him from harm, when others might have chosen to do differently."

"Aye," said Johnson. "I am certain we both will recover well because of all ye and the others have done. Now, come close to me, son, come close," continued Johnson, clutching at Black Eagle's shoulder. "Yer feet are quick, yer mind is bright, and I fear I will need your assistance yet again."

Black Eagle didn't speak. Rather, he bent toward the Irishman.

Said Johnson, "Would ye carry these messages to Albany for me?"

"I would be honored."

Johnson nodded. "I thought as much. Now, permit me to tell you what it is that I require. This message"—Johnson pointed to the sealed note in his hand—"be a letter to my wife and sister to make our home ready to receive the French commander. This other 'tis a letter to Governor Shirley, the devil take the man. A more disagreeable person I have never met. Yet, word has it that he has replaced Commander Braddock, who died in battle recently, God take his soul."

Black Eagle nodded. "Is it your intention, then, to remain here, instead of returning to Albany?"

"Aye, that I shall do. I fear that I am destined to construct a fort here to show the French that the English intend to remain. Otherwise the French may think they have liberty to force the entire valley to adhere to their command. 'Tis my duty to inform the commander-in-chief, Governor Shirley, of what I do, though I fear no good will come of it."

Black Eagle nodded. "It is to be regretted that you must

remain here, and that the Governor thinks more of his status than he does of winning battles," he said.

"Aye," said Johnson. "That it is." He clutched at Black Eagle's hand. "I fear my wife's face swims before me. No mistake, I miss her, especially after all this business here. Now, son, here are the letters. Be fast."

Again Black Eagle nodded. "Your home, Johnson Hall, is well known to me, and I should have no trouble delivering the first letter. But where will I find Governor Shirley? Is he in Albany?"

"Aye, that he is. Governor Shirley is stationed in the home of John Rathburn, a well-known financier. He lives near the southern end of Albany. Do ye think ye can find it?"

Again, Black Eagle nodded.

"Take these notes to their destination, lad, as quickly as ye can and tell Governor Shirley this for me: 'A fort is required here to show the French that we mean to stay, and that we will not tolerate French presence on land that is claimed by King George.' Tell the governor that I will be staying here to oversee our new fort's construction."

"I will." Black Eagle frowned. "Is it your belief, then, that the war between yourself and the French has not ended?"

"I fear it has barely begun."

"Then there will more fighting." Black Eagle spoke as though to himself. "Tell me, why do the English hate the French so much?" he asked. "Would it not be better to stop this fighting and try to live as neighbors?"

"Do ye forget what all yer people have suffered at the hands of the French?"

"I do not forget. Imbedded in my memory is the massacre of my people by Champlain. But it will not be an easy victory if the war does not stop here. Relatives of the Mohawk, who are allied to the French, may fight with the French, and I fear if this war continues, the Mohawk will yet witness brother pitted against brother."

Johnson scowled. "It is the French who started this war."

Black Eagle grimaced. "Is it? My relatives in the North tell me that the French say the English started the war."

Johnson cleared his throat. "Now don't ye be forgettin' the covenant chain yer people hold with mine."

Black Eagle remained silent. The covenant chain, a simple agreement between his people and the English, tied the Mohawk to the English.

"Son," continued Johnson, "much depends on this message yer bringing to Shirley. Yer the best that I have. Can I depend on ye?"

When Black Eagle didn't reply at once, Johnson paused, and it did not escape Black Eagle that Johnson's look took in his measure.

"I know ye have already run a good distance in these last few days, but ye are rested now," continued Johnson. "Can ye do it?"

Black Eagle nodded.

Johnson relaxed. "Thank God that ye are here and that ye are willin' to do it," said Johnson as he handed over the note. "God speed."

# One

Gasping, Marisa Jameson awoke suddenly. Sitting up, she coughed, breathing in swiftly and wheezing as she dislodged whatever it was that seemed intent on choking her.

With eyes wide, she wondered if it were only this that had disturbed her sleep. Or was it something else? A dream perhaps? She searched her memory. She couldn't remember.

Sighing, she reached for the cup of milk that was resting atop her nightstand. But as she clasped her hand around what should have been a cup, it met with nothing but air. She frowned, then lifted her brows.

Oh, yes, she recalled it now. She had asked Sarah to take the distasteful milk back to the kitchen, and good riddance to it. It had been sour, something Marisa could barely tolerate.

Marisa sighed, and throwing back the coverlets of soft wool and cotton, she sat up. Casting her legs over the side of the four-poster bed, she plunged her feet into the slippers that had been positioned there especially for her.

As she stood, the soft beaver felt that lined the slippers warmed her feet. But she barely took notice of the convenience. Luxuries were too commonplace for her to contemplate their origins, or sigh over their costs, be those costs financial or of a more life-giving nature.

Grabbing for her sleeping jacket, she pulled the linen material of it over her chemise and padded toward the pitcher of water Sarah was certain to have set out on the nightstand. Not bothering to pour the liquid into a cup, Marisa took a sip of the water from the ladle.

That's when she heard them. Footsteps and hushed voices. Outside her door.

Her heart skipped a beat, and her head came up. Was she in danger?

She held her breath.

No, thank God. The footsteps were fading into nothing; the creaking of a door being opened and closed at the end of the corridor announcing that whoever was out there had no intention of disturbing her.

But it was odd. It was the middle of the night. Could her step-uncle, John Rathburn, be entertaining at this hour? Or was it Governor Shirley?

Perhaps it was Shirley, since the Governor had made the Rathburn house the center of his command. Was the Governor liaising with someone at this hour? With an officer of the militia perhaps?

Marisa drew out a long breath. War. What could be more inconvenient?

She frowned as a thought crossed her mind. It was doubtful that whoever had disturbed her was the governor, since his quarters, which were situated alongside of her step-uncle's, were stationed in the west wing of the Rathburn residence. Marisa's rooms, on the other hand, were located in the east wing, far away from the governor or any other male member of the household.

Then who was it? What was it? She had not imagined those footsteps . . . or had she?

Marisa stirred uneasily. She supposed she would have to be the one to discover if it were phantom or human being that had passed by her door, otherwise she would worry over the possibilities the night through.

If only Sarah's rooms were situated closer to her own.

Again Marisa sighed. Because there was a chill in the house at this time of year, Marisa opened her chest of drawers and grabbed hold of a dressing gown. Shoving her arms through its long sleeves, she tied the ribbons, which held the robe in place, around her neck in front.

Her hand reached for the candlestick holder. But half-way to it, she hesitated.

No. That wasn't wise. If there were a clandestine meeting occurring within this wing of her home, a light, any light, would only serve to announce her approach. Besides, she could see well enough without a stream of light, since her eyes were already accustomed to the dark.

Slowly, she pulled open the door to her chamber, and tiptoed out into the corridor. She turned to her right, since it seemed that the footsteps had faded in that direction. Cautiously she swept forward.

Further along the corridor she saw it at last, a shaft of illumination quivering beneath the door jamb of the far-thest room in the east wing. Barely daring to breathe, she stole toward that door, plodding one careful footfall after another, until she had come so closely up to the door, she could hear the muffled voices in the room beyond.

Pressing her ear to the door, she recognized her step-uncle's voice at once:

"Ye will be required to dress as the Indians do," he was saying. "Are there those amongst ye willing to shave their head so that they might resemble the Indians more closely?"

"Aye, Gov'nor. For what you be paying them, this be no problem. No problem a'tall."

Marisa didn't recognize the ownership of that low and gravelly voice. She pressed in more closely to the door.

It was her step-uncle speaking once more. "The town is just across the Pennsylvania border. 'Tis a Dutch village, which ye will find . . . right here."

The men paused, and Marisa could only surmise that her step-uncle was pointing to a map.

"Over here, to the south and the west," he continued, "are the tobacco fields, which should be barren at this time of year. They had a good crop this year." There was the sound of the map being rolled together. Then her step-uncle continued, "Now here be the plans: Ye are to set the entire area to flame, do ye understand? Nothing is to be spared. Town and fields are to be burned so that nothing is left standing."

"I understand, Gov'nor," said that unusually low voice. It was strange, thought Marisa, because no emotion was echoed in the voice she heard, as though the man were being asked to do no more than walk the dog. But the man was continuing, and he said, "What I fail to grasp, beg pardon, is why."

"'Tis not yer place to understand why I ask this of ye. Are ye not being paid enough to make the act worth yer while?"

"But I need tell the men something," that low voice insisted, "if they are to destroy everythin' there, there must be a reason."

A long pause followed, then, "Very well," said Rathburn. "If ye be insisting on telling them something, tell them that certain of the Dutch colony molested a young girl. That should set their sense of duty afire."

"Aye, Gov'nor. That it should. But pardon sir, is it the truth? Did someone from the colony molest a maiden?"

"Of course 'tis not true. But I'll not be having ye force me to speak the truth to yer men."

"But ye will tell me? The truth?"

"I will, provided I have yer word that it goes no farther than this room." Rathburn paused.

"Ye have it."

"Very well," said Rathburn, and Marisa, still listening at the door, could easily envision her step-uncle's self-satisfied smile. "Suffice it to say," Rathburn continued, "that the destruction of the Dutch homes and their fields will cause their loans to be called in, which the townspeople will be obliged to pay to me."

"Aye, Gov'nor. But if all the Dutch land is destroyed, how will they pay ye what they owe ye?"

Rathburn laughed. "'Tis a problem, indeed." Again Rathburn hesitated. "Perhaps the land will have to be confiscated as payment."

"Ah," said the unknown voice. "'Tis a means by which to extend your influence?"

"Exactly," agreed Rathburn. "Their fields will be ready to bear more tobacco within a year or perhaps two, and the Dutch will be obliged to work the fields, which will then belong to me."

"Ah, now I understand."

"Do ye? Do ye grasp it in full, then?"

"I believe so, Gov'nor. Ye will own the land. The profit will be all yers."

"And the people," added Rathburn. "Don't forget that the people and their labor will also be mine."

"But they is white people, a free people. If ye own them, then . . . What you speak of is . . . it's slavery, ain't it, Gov'nor?"

"Perhaps. At least it will be so for five years."

"Five years?"

"The amount of time it will take the people to work off their obligation, I think."

"Ah! I understand. 'Tis indentured servitude that ye seek from them."

"Yes. And the profits will be quite . . . shall we say, profitable?"

"Aye! That's right smart, Gov'nor."

"Indeed."

There was a pause. Then the two men laughed.

However, on the other side of the door, Marisa frowned. Was there something innately intelligent about the destruction of others' livelihood and property?

But then, perhaps, she was too naive to understand it. Mayhap such deeds as this were commonplace amongst the wealthy, a means by which fortunes were made. But if this were so, did she approve . . . ?

It wasn't as if she *cared* about a people she didn't even know. It was only that the scheme seemed to be pure trickery, stealth.

Footsteps sounded on the other side of the door, nearing her position. Marisa panicked.

*She mustn't be discovered.*

Taking a quick step backward, Marisa spun around on her heel and fled. She knew her escape required her ability to be as noiseless as possible, but as her nightgown swished out behind her, and her slippers whispered over the hardwood floor, she doubted her success. Her white chemise and dressing gown billowed out in back of her, adding to her discomfort and causing her to feel much like a phantom.

It seemed to take forever to run the distance of the corridor, but at last her door loomed before her. Reaching out to turn the doorknob, it swung easily open, and she stepped into her room none too soon. Footsteps echoed along the corridor in her wake, and Marisa leaned against the door, gasping, praying that she hadn't been seen.

The footsteps came closer and closer. Was it her imagination or were they loud? As if her uncle and his guest, the unknown gentleman, had no care that they might awaken the single resident of this wing.

The two men paused outside her door, and Marisa's heart stopped in reaction, then it suddenly raced headlong. She shut her eyes and prayed to the Lord that she should remain undiscovered.

Perhaps it was the prayer that did it. Though she could

feel every beat of her pounding heart in her throat, nothing untoward happened. The footsteps wandered on past her door until her step-uncle and his bully were well out of earshot.

Still Marisa barely dared to breathe.

Alas, she was still leaning heavily against her door when it occurred to her that this entire episode couldn't possibly be real. It simply could not be. How could her own step-uncle be involved in a plan to destroy the lands and livelihood of an entire village? Worse, with further plans to enslave every soul within that village?

It simply couldn't be.

Marisa forced herself to breathe in deeply, then out again. But the calming effect of the action did not materialize. Far from being consoled by her late-night discovery, Marisa was alarmed.

Coming away from the door, she wondered what she should do with this knowledge? Should she perhaps seek out someone of authority?

Not likely. She had no proof of any wrongdoing, and since she was herself under the jurisdiction of her step-uncle, she could not legally give witness against him. Nor did she wish to do so.

Though John Rathburn might be an indifferent guardian, he was still her only relative, her parents having perished long ago during the journey here to America. Luckily, Marisa was not remembering the particulars of that journey. After all, she had been little more than a babe.

One thing was certain. She couldn't stand here the night through. Propping herself away from the solid oak of the door, she began to pace her room. What to do? Should she try to forget the entire episode? After all, what was a town of Dutch settlers to her? They were faceless people.

Besides, were the Colonies not already at war? Was it not true that lives were already being spent? Besides, no lives in that Pennsylvania town would be at risk . . . or would they?

Might they not try to save their property?

*Thou shalt not steal. Thou shalt not kill.* The Commandments from the Scripture streamed through her mind.

What to do? What to do?

As she trod down the length of her room and back again, Marisa gradually drifted toward her bedside table, where the basin and pitcher of water still stood, placed there at the start of the evening by her own dear friend Sarah.

*Sarah.*

Sarah, her maid. Sarah, her friend. Sarah, who was more like a mother or a big sister to her. If anyone would know what to do, it was Sarah. Heaving a sigh of relief, Marisa felt better almost at once.

Feeling calmer, Marisa wondered if perhaps she might yet be able to find some sleep this night. In preparation, she removed her dressing gown, as well as her sleeping jacket, and lay them at the foot of her bed. Crawling between the covers, Marisa at last settled in, knowing that on the morrow, she would tell Sarah about the entire episode.

But sleep was not to be the restful pleasure that she sought, for her dreams were far from pleasant, and when Marisa awoke much too early the next morning, she discovered that her head, particularly there at her temples, was pounding.

No amount of rubbing her forehead eased the headache, either, and at last arising and grabbing hold of her sleeping jacket, she went in search of Sarah.


Sarah Strong listened to the concerns of the young woman that she had come to love as though she and her young charge were related by the bond of blood, rather than by a mere friendship. Because Sarah was ten years Marisa's senior, she could easily recall the day when the captain of the *Wayflower*, the ship that had brought Marisa's family to the New World, had brought Marisa to this very home.

Tragically Marisa had been the only one of her family

to survive the hard and long journey to the New World. She'd had a father, a step-mother and an elder brother, Sarah recalled. However, none but Marisa had lived to tell of the journey, not that Marisa had ever talked of it. In truth, Marisa never mentioned the incident.

At the time, Marisa had been four years of age, and Sarah fourteen. That had been fourteen years ago now. It had been a difficult and troubling time, Sarah's first year of servitude at the Rathburn estate. Because Sarah's own parents had acquired a debt to John Rathburn and had perished in a fire shortly thereafter, it had been Sarah's fate to live to pay off her parent's debt.

Six years more was all that remained of that obligation now. Six years and Sarah would be free of this house. But free to do what, she wondered?

She was twenty and eight now, too old to marry. By the time she earned her freedom from the Rathburn estate, she would be thirty and four, well past the age where a respectable man might seek her hand . . . unless that man were a widower who had been forced to seek an older woman in marriage, that she might care for his children.

Sarah sighed. How different her life would have been had her parents never acquired their liability to John Rathburn. But now was not the time to bemoan her lot in life. She would endure this for the sake of her parents. In the meanwhile, the young woman whom Sarah regarded as fondly as if she and Miss Marisa were sisters, was upset.

Sarah fixed a smile upon her countenance before saying, "There, there, it cannot be all that bad, can it?" Sarah arose from the stool where she had been sitting, to pace toward the bed where Marisa sat. Seating herself alongside Marisa, Sarah laid her hand atop her friend's. "I am certain that it cannot be as terrible as it might seem to you now."

"I hope you're right, dear Sarah. For 'tis bad. Very bad."

Sarah nodded in understanding. "Then tell me about it. I will listen."

Marisa exhaled and swallowed hard, before she began, "It happened in the middle of the night last evening. I was

awakened by what I know not, but I heard footsteps outside
my door, and I decided to investigate . . ."

"Yes?" Sarah encouraged. "And what did you find?"

Marisa fidgeted. "T'was my step-uncle and a bully," she
began, and though she stumbled often in the telling of it,
eventually Marisa related the entire incident to Sarah.

At the tale's conclusion, Sarah hardly knew what to say.
Words failed her at the moment, and all she found herself
able to do was frown.

"What should I do?" Marisa asked.

Sarah's frown deepened. "You say your uncle—"

"He is my step-uncle, Sarah dear, and you know as well
as I that he cares nothing for me. He is obligated to raise me
only because of my step-mother. But beyond that, there is
nothing to tie us. As you know my own mother gave her life
giving birth to me, and the woman that I called 'mother'
for many years was not my own blood relative. She was
kind, I believe, though I was too young to remember it well
now. But by blood, I am not tied to John Rathburn."

"Yes, of course," said Sarah. "Sometimes I forget."

Marisa nodded, then stared at Sarah. "Dear Sarah," she
said, "tell me, what is your impression of these goings-on?"

Sarah hesitated. "What was it that your uncle said to
this unidentified man?"

"My uncle gave the man leave to hire others, who were
to be instructed to burn the fields and all the concerns of
a Dutch town, which name I do not know. Nor do I have
knowledge of where that town is located. Not exactly."

"And you say that these Dutch people are in debt to your
step-uncle, and he means to lay title to their fields as well
as to their livelihood?"

"Yes."

Sarah gulped. Despite herself, a sickness was already
invading her soul, and she wondered if her breakfast would
long remain where it was. She said, "And your step-uncle
means to bring the people in that town into servitude to
him?"

"Yes."

It was too much. Sarah lay her free hand across her stomach, her fingers clutching at Marisa's hand. The feeling of nausea could barely be ignored. At first, she bent over at the waist, trying to stave off the nausea, and removing her hand from Marisa's, she placed it over her forehead.

"Sarah, are you all right?" Marisa's face loomed largely in front of Sarah's vision. "Sarah?"

"I am certain that I am all right," said Sarah. "'Tis only that I feel suddenly very ill. Would you excuse me that I might go to my bed?"

"Of course, but, Sarah, there is more that I—"

"Would you like to accompany me to my own room, then, where we might speak of this some more?"

"Of course. I am sorry that you do not feel well."

"It is nothing; nevertheless, let us retire to my own quarters where, God willing, if you are interested, I will tell you a story of my own."

Marisa frowned. "You have a tale that you have never said to me?"

"Aye," said Sarah.

"But I thought we shared everything."

"And so we do . . . mostly. But it has seemed so unnecessary to relate this tale to you, for it is not a pleasant one. But perhaps I have been wrong to withhold it from you all these years." Another wave of nausea shook her physically; beads of perspiration formed above her lip. "Excuse me, dear Marisa, but I fear I must obtain my own quarters at once, for I suddenly feel worse than I did only a few moments ago."

"Yes," said Marisa. "Yes. By all means, let us go there at once."

Sarah arose to stand by the bed, but Marisa remained seated, and she said, "Has this story of yours anything to do with my step-uncle?"

"It does, for you know, I am here in servitude to your uncle—"

"He is my step-uncle. And you were saying? . . ."

"The things that you have said to me are troubling—"

"I am sorry."

"Don't be. 'Tis only that this tale of yours is very similar to one that I know all too well. The only reason I am here in your step-uncle's employ is because *my* parents were indebted to him, and they perished in a fire, leaving only myself to recompense the debt."

"No! Sarah!"

"'Tis true."

"But this is incredible. Then it would appear that my step-uncle has done this before?"

"Excuse me." Sarah jumped away from the bed, and fled across the room, arriving at the chamber pot with barely enough time to empty the contents of her stomach into it.

"Oh, Sarah, I am so sorry, I should not have bared my soul to you and told you what I have."

"You most definitely should have," said Sarah as soon as she was able. Straightening up, she wiped her mouth upon her apron before rising up to her feet. "'Tis only that—"

Just as quickly as she had stood up, she flopped down again, turning back toward the chamber pot as another bout of nausea swept over her. Again, she heaved, and the rest of what had been in her stomach took leave of her.

Glancing up toward Marisa, Sarah noted that Marisa looked truly alarmed. "Sarah," said Marisa. "Come with me. I will escort you to your room, where I shall insist that you remain for the rest of the day."

"No," Sarah protested, "there is too much work to do."

"I will hear no more about it. You are too sick to attend to your duties today."

Sarah sighed. "A few hours of sleep might help me, perhaps."

"I shall insist that you take the rest of the day for yourself."

Sarah shrugged. "We shall see," she said. "At present, however, I do believe that I should like very much to take to my bed."

"Then come with me. I will escort you. Was my step-uncle cruel to you?" asked Marisa, as she took Sarah's hand into her own.

Sarah was reluctant to say anything.

"Sarah, was he cruel to you?"

"It was all so long ago, that . . ."

"He was, wasn't he?"

Sarah didn't reply, her silence making her answer evident.

In due time, however, Sarah said, "For years I have lived in fear of John Rathburn, in fear that he might repeat . . ."

"That he might repeat what . . . ?"

Sarah couldn't say more. It was beyond her to do so.

"Did he . . . take advantage of you?"

Sarah bit her lip.

"He did, didn't he?"

Sarah turned away.

"You needn't say it. I can tell from your expression that he has taken advantage of his position."

"As many men do," said Sarah. "Most men believe it is their right."

"I suppose that's true, but I still cannot champion the practice of demanding physical tribute from a maid."

Sarah nodded. "If it makes you feel any better, I should tell you that once you came here, the practice ceased. Though I admit that the circumstance that brought you to this house was not a happy one, it is true that your being here has lent me much support."

Marisa shook her head. "Sarah, I had no idea."

"The worst of it happened long ago, at a time when you were much too young to know anything of it. But come, do not fret over my situation in life. What is more important is that your step-uncle is planning to do to others what he did to my parents." Sarah's voice caught. "To lose everything, home, livelihood, way of life. 'Tis enough to be the death of one. That one man should have leave to inflict such unhappiness upon so many."

Marisa's head came up and her gaze seemed to catch onto something in the distance. "You are right," she said.

"'Tis unbecoming of my step-uncle. Do you suppose we might be able to stop him?"

Sarah shook her head. "If there be a way, I do not know it."

"Nor do I, dear Sarah. But there is one particular that I cannot forget."

"And that is . . . ?"

Marisa, however, didn't answer. Instead, she said, "I shall confront him with this knowledge. Perhaps if he be made to understand that others are cognizant of his plans, he might restrain himself."

Sarah breathed in noisily. "You mustn't do so. Your uncle is capable of anything." She placed her hand over Marisa's. "Please promise me that you will not do this."

Marisa hesitated before she said, "Perhaps you are right. But someone, somewhere has to say 'no, 'tis not right' to the man. Perhaps that someone is me."

"No," said Sarah.

But when Marisa said nothing more, Sarah shook her head. She had a bad feeling about this.

# Two

"You say he bears a field message from Johnson?"

"Yes, sir."

"Then show him in at once. What did you tell me is his name?"

"Black Eagle, sir. He is from the Mohawk."

Governor Shirley nodded. "Send him in."

Coleman, the Governor's aide, opened the door and motioned Black Eagle to enter. "Come this way."

Black Eagle strode forward, his tall figure dwarfing the Englishmen who stood beside him. Quickly Black Eagle took stock of the room, memorizing little details about it; the grand fireplace, the Governor's desk, the rug that softened one's footfalls, the gun rack filled with muskets, which he noted were primed and ready.

The Governor, himself, held an air of suspicion about him that Black Eagle noted at once. Moreover, there was a scent of tobacco about his countenance and a slight odor of the white man's whisky on his breath. But the man was not the least bit intoxicated. His eyes were brilliant with intelligence even if, at this moment, his attitude toward Black Eagle were less than friendly.

Speaking first, the Governor broke into Black Eagle's thoughts, and said, "I am told that you come bearing messages."

"That is true, sir," said Black Eagle, his voice strong, steady and deeply baritone.

"Well, bring them here, young man. Bring them here."

Black Eagle stepped farther into the room, pacing across its width. He stopped directly in front of the Governor's desk.

"They are here," said Black Eagle, as he reached into a bag that hung from around his shoulder. He presented the letters forthwith to the governor, who took them at once.

"Ah," said Governor Shirley who scanned the papers. "Ah, I see. Victory was ours today, but that incompetent Johnson was injured, though I see that he writes that he is almost well now."

Black Eagle frowned. Both men seemed to hold the other in contempt. Perhaps within their own ranks, the English were not as invincible as one might suppose.

Black Eagle, however, remained silent, alert.

"How is it that Johnson is almost well?" Governor Shirley asked as he eyed Black Eagle as though the bearer of the news were to blame. But to blame for what? For Johnson's speedy recovery? Black Eagle quietly noted another peculiarity that did not fit the general picture the English liked to present to the Mohawk sachems.

However, all Black Eagle said was, "The Water-that-runs-swift is healing."

"Is it?" Governor Shirley's look at Black Eagle was skeptical. Then, with a note of condescension, he added, "I thank you for delivering these papers to me. I suppose that I am indebted to you, and so I ask, is there anything that I can do for you? Anything that you need?"

"Some food and water would be welcome," said Black Eagle.

Governor Shirley might be many things, including a prude, but it was obvious to Black Eagle that Shirley dared not break with the convention of giving aid to one who has executed a service. Therefore, he said, "It will be done. Mr. Coleman?" he called to his aide.

"Yes, sir?"

"Take this scout to the kitchen and see that he has a good meal."

Coleman saluted. "Yes, sir." Then, barely missing a beat, Coleman turned to Black Eagle, "This way."

Black Eagle acknowledged Shirley with a nod, and followed Coleman out the door.


The delicious aroma of food being cooked announced the kitchen long before Coleman and Black Eagle attained its inner sanctum. With every footfall, the air surrounding them became warm, and filled with an enticing fragrance.

There was a feel in this area of the house that boasted of the best that the white civilization had to offer, and as Black Eagle stepped into the kitchen's inner chamber, he was surrounded by the bustle of several different women. The moist heat that radiated throughout the place, which he supposed was created by the various stews that were cooking over the fire, was pleasant. He relaxed.

"Stay here," said Coleman as though he addressed an idiot, instead of a grown man. He then left Black Eagle standing at the room's wide entrance, while he trod farther into the room. Black Eagle could see the Englishman trying to capture the attention of one of the cooks, noted with pleasure that Coleman was not having an easy task of it. Black Eagle breathed in deeply and took in the scene before him more fully.

A few of the women had hiked up their skirts to tie around their waists, although several of the younger women wore no more than a simple shift of white, most likely to avoid accidents from the fire, Black Eagle surmised. Two windows served as lighting for the room, while tables—and there were several—boasted various brass pans, funnels, wooden bowls, many skillets and kettles. Several dressers against the walls held dishes, and adorning those walls were pans, which were all sorted out by their different shapes.

It was a busy environment, and Black Eagle felt as though he were intruding on a domain that was exclusively feminine. For a moment he experienced a notion of being ill at ease, until someone brushed past him, leaving in their wake an arousing scent of the fresh outdoors and femininity.

Black Eagle's attention was immediately caught, and he gazed at the back of the exquisite creature who had ventured into the bustle of the kitchen. Her dress was different than that of the other women in the kitchen. It was made of an elaborately decorated material, and it was full, particularly at the sides of the waist, a style that Black Eagle had disdained when he had first seen it on the white woman.

But on this creature, it was impeccable. The dress was fashioned in a soft shade of aqua, a color that the women of his village valued. The young woman's hair was piled up high on top of her head, while silky ringlets of reddish-colored curls fell down over one shoulder.

"Mrs. Stanton?" The beauty's voice was delicate, barely audible, yet the cook acted as though the woman had shouted, for the cook immediately stopped what she was doing to give attention to the young lady.

"Yes, miss?" said cook.

"Mrs. Stanton, my maid, Sarah, is quite ill, and I beg you to see if we might have some baking soda or other remedy here in the kitchen that might settle her stomach."

"Yes, miss," said Mrs. Stanton. "One moment, miss."

"Of course," said the vision of loveliness. As the elegant creature waited, she turned halfway around, so that Black Eagle was presented with her profile. Her jawline was strong, her cheekbones were delicate, her nose dainty and not overly long, and the outline of her lips was full. All at once, and without any warning, Black Eagle's stomach plummeted, and his body reacted in a strong and distinct, yet entirely male, fashion.

She was beautiful, she was delicate, the sort of creature that a man would treasure his whole life through, if he could but have her. Moreover, there was a quality about her that would cause a man to wish to please her, if only to see the glory of her smile. A smile that was at present missing from her countenance.

A desire to jest with her, to witness the wonder of her favor overtook him. But he suppressed the longing. There was little purpose in speaking to her in any manner whatsoever, since little would come of it. They were of two different worlds, worlds that held little, if anything, in common.

He gazed away from her, but only for a moment. Soon, Mrs. Stanton approached the young lady.

"I have some freshly made chicken broth," said the cook, "which has been cooked almost the day through. If anything will settle Miss Strong's stomach, it will be my broth. Shall I take it to her?"

"Yes, please," agreed the dainty creature. "She is in her room. Do you know of it?"

"Yes, miss," said Mrs. Stanton, who was an older and heavy woman. Taking hold of a pot of stew, the cook immediately left the kitchen.

And that's when it happened. The beauty turned in full toward him. She did not acknowledge him. In truth, it appeared that she was searching for something and did not even see him. Black Eagle, however, watching her, found himself unable to resist the impulse to make himself known to her, perhaps to even see if he could cause the enchantress to smile.

Addressing her, he said, "Rarely have I seen a woman who could with a mere glance make a man's heart sing."

The beauty's gaze rose up to take in Black Eagle's measure. And though her look was less than complimentary, she did reply to him, saying, "Did you speak to me, sir? And without an introduction?"

"I did," replied Black Eagle at once, "but you must forgive me for doing so. I may never again have the honor of looking upon you, and the desire to witness your smile might make a man forget all else."

Under his compliment, the beauty's lips twitched, but she turned away from him, only to swing back in a moment, to say, "Did you tell me that your heart sang?"

"I did," he responded. "Upon taking a mere look at you,

my heart told me that all the happiness there was to be found was possessed here, in this delicate figure of a woman."

"Sir!"

"Naturally," he went on to say, "if I were a white man, I might never put this observation into words. But I am not a white man."

"Indeed!" she said. However, her glance again took in his countenance. "Your English is very good for an Indian."

He nodded. "A result of various black robes and the Scotsman, who is an English trader, Sir William Johnson."

She nodded briefly. "You are the first Indian who has ever spoken to me," she said, "though I have lived here most of my life through."

"Have you? I regret that I am only now making your acquaintance. And I apologize for my people."

Again her lips twitched, but no full smile was to be witnessed upon her countenance. She said, "Excuse me. I must bid you farewell, for a friend awaits me."

Black Eagle nodded. However, as she turned away, he found he couldn't let her go yet, and he said, "Miss?" repeating the name that Mrs. Stanton had called her.

"Yes?" she replied, bestowing upon him yet another look that took in his appearance.

"Could you not spare this poor heart of mine a tiny smile? Something that he could take with him, to recall at leisure, or perhaps during times that are less than pleasant. After all, the countryside is at war and a man never knows what might become of him upon the morrow."

Her glance at him was considering. She said, "You speak very elegantly."

"A result of practice, I fear, since one must express himself well if one is to become a sachem for his people."

"You wish to become a sachem?"

"Or perhaps a Pine Tree Chief."

"A Pine Tree Chief? I believe that is the first time I have heard of this kind of chief."

"That is to be regretted, for they are important amongst

my people," he said. "And now I beg you, could you not spare me a smile?"

She turned away from him. "I could not," she said and made to pass by him.

"You! Indian!" It was Coleman vying for Black Eagle's attention. "I have your breakfast prepared. This way!"

Black Eagle nodded at Coleman, then said to the lady, "A brief smile from you would help this weeping heart of mine, and it would cost you little."

"Has this man been bothering you, milady?" asked Coleman as he approached Black Eagle and the beauty.

"He has," said the vision.

"I am sorry to hear that, milady," said Coleman. "Shall I take the whip to him?"

"Oh no," the enchantress said, and turning slightly toward Black Eagle, she smiled at him, showing delicate, white teeth. Then she added, "I hope that this will spare your heart the expense of breaking." And before Black Eagle could grin back at her, she swept away, leaving the kitchen and Black Eagle's devotion behind her.

He watched her departing figure until he could see her no more. Coleman grabbed hold of him, but Black Eagle made no motion to extricate himself from Coleman's grip.

"Come along," said Coleman gruffly. "You are lucky that Lady Marisa chose to spare you. For what you have done, you could easily be whipped."

"Is that her name? Lady Marisa?"

Coleman was silent.

But Black Eagle was beyond reproach. "She smiled for me," was all he said, then he grinned, and without the slightest protest, he allowed himself to be led to the promised meal.


Marisa shook her head slightly as she made her way toward Sarah's quarters. Savage though he was, that Indian was dangerous, she thought to herself. The young man possessed a golden tongue, something that could prove to be dangerous to a feminine heart, if a lady so desired to take his words at face value.

No doubt, the women of his village vied with one another for his favor. And why not? He was certainly a handsome man, his figure slim, yet commanding.

Tall, but not too tall, his body was well formed and strong. He had worn leggings and a shirt, which formed a short kilt of white. A red blanket, decorated delicately with beads, had been thrown over one of his shoulders and held there Roman-style. The typical breechcloth of which the Indians were fond had been worn between his legs, and upon his feet had been moccasins, which had been decorated, as well.

He had been heavily armed, she had noted. Ammunition pouches had been thrown on a strap that was supported over his shoulder. On a belt around his waist had hung a powder horn with a tomahawk tucked into that belt. In one of his hands, he had held a musket.

Yet, though heavily equipped and a stranger to her, she had been far from frightened of him. Indeed, fear was not an emotion one might connect with the young man.

In essence, she thought, warming to her thoughts, his was a handsome countenance, despite the fact that he wore his hair cropped close to his head, with only a tuft of longer hair sitting atop his head in a style her fellow Englishmen called a Mohawk. Personally, she preferred the longer-haired silhouette of a gentleman. But there was definitely something to be said for hair cropped close to the head, and long hair falling over his shoulders. At least it was so on this particular young man.

An odd feeling of excitement swept through her, and without consciously willing it to be so, her step became a little livelier. There was also a thrill of awareness rushing through her veins, as though he had not been the only one impressed. Her breath caught in her bosom. Indeed. She feared she liked the man.

No doubt it was due to the young man's compliments. What woman's head wouldn't be turned?

Smiling, shaking her head, as though to dislodge the man's image from it, she hurried along the corridor. Sarah awaited her.

# Three

Sarah was not well.

Reaching out, Marisa smoothed back Sarah's blond hair, and removed the wet rag from Sarah's forehead. Gingerly, she touched her friend's face. Her skin was hot, much too hot. Biting her lip, Marisa dipped the sopping rag into cold water and reapplied it to Sarah's forehead.

As a feeling of helplessness overtook her, she wondered what else she could do. As the day had worn on, Sarah had gradually become worse, and Marisa, in her worry, had forgotten all about the Indian with the golden tongue.

Certainly Marisa had sent a servant in search of the family physician, asking the man to hurry to the house. But the doctor had given little advice, saying only that Marisa should keep Sarah quiet and warm. As if Marisa hadn't already been doing exactly that.

At present, Sarah was sleeping, though that sleep was fraught with whimperings and stirrings.

Marisa frowned. There must be more that she could do. But what? This was Sarah, after all; Sarah, her friend and confidant. Sarah, who had never wavered in her devotion to

Marisa. Sarah, who had taught her, schooled her, laughed with her, befriended her.

"No, do not leave me! Do not go in there!" Sarah sat up all at once. Her eyes were wide, yet unseeing, except perhaps for whatever was in her mind's eye. "Mother! Stay with me! Do not leave me!"

Marisa dropped to her knees beside Sarah's bed, and gently coaxed Sarah back into a prone position, but Sarah fought to be free, and sat up again. She said, "No, Mother, do not leave!"

Marisa hardly knew what to do, thus, she did the only thing that seemed natural. She took Sarah's hand into her own, and rubbed it.

How could Sarah have lived all these years with such pent-up emotion? And within terribly close quarters to the man who had caused her grief?

But then, Marisa reminded herself, until today, Sarah had not known that it was John Rathburn who was to blame, not only for Sarah's servitude, but for the deaths of her parents. Problem was, now that she knew or at least suspected the truth, how was Sarah to endure these next six years? Would not forced proximity to the man responsible keep the wound continually open?

"Mother! No!"

Instinctively aware that it was wrong to say too much around a person so ill, Marisa did no more than take Sarah into her arms, urging her back against the mattress and pillow. Tears, mirrored in Sarah's eyes, clouded her own.

It was unfair, nay it was terribly wrong, that Sarah should have to remain here, locked into a debt that was not of her own making, and to a man who had most likely caused the entire matter. Sarah's circumstance needed to change. But how?

Marisa had never had cause to give thought to concerns such as this. The only rule of law that she had ever known was the cold neglect of John Rathburn. Surely there was something *she* could do.

Perhaps there might be a sympathetic ear within Albany's administration of justice. Mayhap Sarah's servitude could be reversed. Who would speak for Sarah?

Certainly there were no witnesses from ten years ago who could come forward to accuse John Rathburn of wrongdoing. And even if such people did exist, what magistrate would believe them when pitted against the Rathburn wealth and reputation?

Only someone as wealthy as he could stand for Sarah. Only a person who's reputation was as well thought of as his . . .

As realization dawned, Marisa sat back on her heels. There *was* such a person. One person, who alone might be able to persuade John Rathburn to give Sarah her freedom.

That person was she, Marisa.

For a moment, Marisa's brow cleared as she considered her position. Not only might she hold sway over John Rathburn, she held an ace. Had she not last night heard him plotting the ruin and demise of an entire village of people? Was this not only unjust, but illegal?

"No!" Sarah cried, interrupting Marisa's thoughts. "Not my mother, my father! No, it cannot be!"

Marisa closed her eyes, letting a tear fall down over her cheek. Dutifully she pressed Sarah back against the bed's pillow, and bending, she dipped the rag that had been made hot by Sarah's feverish forehead back into cold water. Quickly, she replaced the rag over Sarah's forehead, then, picking up Sarah's hand yet again, Marisa plotted exactly what she would do, and what she might say to her guardian, John Rathburn.

She had much time in which to plan her strategy, as well, for it was well into the night when Sarah at last drifted into a restful sleep. Rising up onto her feet, Marisa knew what she would do, and she would do it yet this night.

Taking hold of the bucket of water, which by this time was warm, Marisa exited Sarah's room, glancing back once at Sarah before she gently shut the door.

*   *   *

Richard Thompson was not a man of honor. Quite the contrary, he was little more than a hired assassin. He was also an imposing man, a huge man with more than his share of flab, weighing perhaps three hundred pounds. Mousey-brown, tangled hair, thick jowls, yellow, broken teeth and a breath that might stagger the most stouthearted of men, he was not the sort of man to endear himself to any other soul, except perhaps those who had need of his services.

But this was exactly the impression he wished to present to the world. Such a look as he had was "business." Though Thompson was not the most intelligent of people, he was bright enough to know when he'd floundered into a good thing.

And his enterprise with John Rathburn was, indeed, a "good thing." Over the years, Thompson had hired out his services to Rathburn for the more delicate occasions when Rathburn required an opponent to be eliminated. True, Thompson might exude an appearance of being an oaf, but he was thorough in his work, and most importantly, he operated in complete secrecy.

Bad things were known to happen. It was a rough land here in America, a dangerous environment, a place where accidents were commonplace. And if at times, Thompson ensured that accidents did, indeed, happen, where was the fault?

Though constructed to be sturdy, the wooden steps quivered beneath Thompson's weight as he made his way to the front door of the Rathburn estate. He was under no illusions as to what was the purpose of Rathburn's summons. However, little could he have envisioned that on this one occasion, even he was to be startled.

"I's here to see Rathburn," he stated to the butler, who answered the ring of the bell.

James, Rathburn's butler, nodded succinctly. He did not extend his hand to take Thompson's overcoat as was customary. Instead James, the butler, backed up, away from

Thompson, sniffing indignantly as the fleshy odor of the
man permeated the hall. He said, "Mr. Rathburn is expecting you. This way, please."

If such rudeness were an unusual circumstance for
Thompson, he deemed not to show it. With barely a glance
at the butler, Thompson grunted out a response and followed the man into Rathburn's private office.

"Ah, there ye are, Thompson. Thank ye, James. We will
require a bottle of brandy, two glasses and complete pri-
vacy. No one, and that includes my niece, is to disturb us.
Do ye understand?"

"Clearly, sir," said James, who left posthaste. He returned
shortly thereafter, and set out the liquor and glasses on a
table. "Do you wish me to pour, sir?"

"No, James, that will be all."

James nodded and quit the room so quickly, one might
have thought an evil lurked there.

His hasty departure left an awkward silence in its wake.
To cover over the gap, Rathburn slowly poured the brandy
into the two glasses and offered one of them to Thompson,
who shot down the liquor as though it were no more than a
spot of warm tea.

Rathburn was longer in his enjoyment of the brew. After
some moments, he said, "Have ye ever considered a bath,
Richard?"

"What fer?"

Rathburn didn't answer, sighed instead, and continued,
"I have an unusual task for ye, Thompson."

Thompson grunted, nodding. "Who is it to be this time,
gov'nor?"

Rathburn didn't hesitate to answer, stating forthwith,
"My niece."

Thompson spit out whatever liquid was left in his mouth.
"Come again?"

"The person in question is my niece."

"Miss Marisa?"

"That's right."

"But I's met Miss Marisa." Thompson, for all that he

might be immune from that deterrent called scruples, was yet taken aback. "But she is young and . . ."

"My ward?"

"Bonny," said Thompson. "I was going to say bonny."

"That she is," said Rathburn. "She will also be heir to a small fortune, when she comes of age to inherit. A fortune, I might add, that I will lose to some young suitor in the near future, if I cannot convince her to marry the man of my choice."

"Then ye is jealous of her?"

"No," stated Rathburn. Rathburn strode to his desk, where he opened a drawer and removed a pistol. "But I fear she has become much too inquisitive and an embarrassment to me. She has made certain information about my business known to herself, and that information is . . . delicate. Further, she fears me not." Sitting in a chair pulled up behind his desk, Rathburn studied the pistol, before he proceeded to prime it. "I am afraid that her dangerousness to me has recently exceeded her worth."

Momentarily Thompson was silent. "But have ye not raised her from when she was a small child?" he asked.

"So I have," said Rathburn. He shrugged, then smirked. "The Lord giveth, the Lord taketh."

"I have never kilt a woman. Could ye not simply send her abroad? Perhaps to the nuns?"

"That I could. But she presses me now, and there is damage she could do to me before I am able to make arrangements to send her overseas. She has threatened me." He set down his pistol and spread his hands out over the desk. "Me."

It did not escape Thompson's regard that Rathburn's eyes burned momentarily with a fire of insanity. In reaction, Thompson, all three hundred pounds of him, quivered. Rathburn, however, was continuing. "She plans to take her maid east to Portsmouth, New Hampshire," he said. "'Tis a place where our family has often summered. There are friends there, who will welcome her. I believe my niece hopes to find her maid other employment there.

However, it is my intention that neither she nor her maid should arrive there . . . alive."

Thompson flinched. "The maid, too?"

"I am afraid so. It would appear that my 'dear' niece has shared her knowledge with her maid."

"Two women . . . Not one, but two," Thompson muttered. "I've never kilt a woman afore," he repeated.

"If ye feel ye cannot to do the job . . . Of course ye do realize, that I am paying double for yer services."

Thompson hesitated. Under his breath, he muttered, "The way through New Hampshire is through woods that are deep in Indian country, the Abenaki."

"Indeed, it is so," said Rathburn. "How fortunate. Many accidents could happen along the way."

Thompson pulled at his collar. "The Abenaki's are not friendly to England. Could I not save ye the trouble and expense of a journey, and do the deed here?"

"I should say not! T'would be an outrage. Why, the townspeople might question my ability to provide protection, might even doubt my worthiness to guardianship, which of course would include the loss of her fortune, should their doubts prove true. No, indeed," continued Rathburn, "an accident along the path north and east 'tis better."

Thompson, however, was not convinced, and he stalled further, saying, "What ye need is a scout, and I's no scout."

"Ye may have leave to hire one, though I doubt ye'll need one, since the deed could be done once ye are outside of Albany."

"But what if a chance to end it quickly does not prove itself in so timely a manner?"

"Then ye will need a map and a guide. An Indian scout would be best since any other might give witness against ye." Pivoting the pistol in his hand, Rathburn pretended to check its sights. "Of course, if ye decide the task is beyond ye to perform, the assignment is not an obligation."

Rathburn's statement was a veiled, unstated threat, and Thompson well understood it. He grimaced. Truth be told,

Thompson might be many things, a bully, an executioner, an assassin. But his "business" was typically conducted with stealth, and always under the cover of darkness. In truth, no threat to himself had ever presented itself.

This last was a pointed detail. For there was one particular aspect to Thompson's character that ruled his existence: He was an unprecedented coward.

He glanced once at the pistol that Rathburn so ungraciously handled; he wiped his lips, setting his mind to the fact that his future recommendations would hereafter include two women. Then, said Thompson, "Do ye have that map here?"

"I do, indeed."


"Oh, look!" said Marisa, as she dragged Sarah toward a merchant who was selling one of the largest pumpkins Marisa had ever seen. "I think we should ask cook to make us a pumpkin pie for our trip."

Sarah smiled and shook her head. "And how are we to transport a pie?"

Marisa pulled a face. "'Tis a fair point you make, since we will be traveling with only the three horses. Perhaps cook could bake the pie before we set out upon our journey."

"Perhaps."

"Come," said Marisa, as she pulled Sarah with her, threading her way through the crowd.

The Albany marketplace was bustling with humanity on this fine and warm autumn day. Scents of baked cornbread, stewing apples and pumpkin pie had drawn a large crowd to the market, and the ambience surrounding the patrons on this day was delightful, the air brimming with the hum of good will and camaraderie. Conversation and laughter buzzed around Marisa and Sarah as they shifted slowly through the crowd, while a young, male servant followed in their wake.

To their right, a small crowd had gathered around a juggler, who was, Marisa noted, quite a handsome gentleman. And in the distance straight ahead of them, actors were performing a puppet show, much to the delight of several children.

Both Marisa and Sarah paused to sample the delights of some baking apples and cornbread, sharing their find with the boy who accompanied them. In due time, however, they approached the pumpkin vendor.

"Are you not excited about our trip?" asked Marisa as they gathered 'round the vendor.

"Very," said fair-headed Sarah. "I admit that this journey comes at a fortunate moment, since the urge to leave Albany, if only for a little while, has taken hold of me."

"Yes," said Marisa, "although perhaps we might find the seashores of New Hampshire more to our liking, extending the length of our trip into something more permanent."

Sarah frowned. "Pardon?"

Marisa's gaze danced off Sarah. Had she said too much? In an effort to shield Sarah, Marisa had not mentioned her meeting with John Rathburn of a few days previous. Nor did she intend to do so now. In an effort to conceal her error Marisa rushed on to say, "Which one of the pumpkins do you think we should buy?"

"I think," said Sarah, after only a slight hesitation, "that we should buy two pumpkins. You pick one, and so will I."

"Yes. A good suggestion. I'll take that one," said Marisa, anxious to put the subject of their coming journey behind them. However, as Marisa reached out to hand over the coinage to the merchant, she caught a movement out of the corner of her eye. What was that? The image of a man? An Indian?

At once, her stomach dropped. Was it the savage? she wondered. The young man who had uttered such golden words to her?

Distracted, Marisa let the servant boy pick up the pumpkin for her, while she glanced to her left, so as to attain a better look. She caught her breath. It was a Mohawk Indian certainly. But it was not *he*.

The butterflies that had taken flight within her commenced to settle down, and Marisa inhaled deeply. What was wrong with her? she wondered. Had she lost all sense of propriety? How could she be reacting in such a positive manner to a man who was so completely beneath her station? Was she bored perhaps?

"I'll take this one," said Sarah to the vendor, not noticing that her charge's attention was devoted elsewhere. "Please," Sarah motioned the servant boy forward, "take these back to the cook, ask her to make a pie for this evening, and then return here. I'm certain we'll have more purchases." She smiled at him, and the boy, deeply impressed, hurried off to do as bid.

"Sarah," asked Marisa, "what do you think of the close-cropped hairstyle of the Mohawk Indians?"

Sarah gazed quickly at her charge, then toward the place where Marisa was staring, and after a brief pause, Sarah observed, "As long as it's closely-cropped and not bald, I think 'tis fine." Sarah smiled. "I must admit that I have a liking for their long hair in back."

"I, too." Marisa, who was still looking off toward the Indians, asked further, "Why do you think they shave their head?"

"I really don't know," answered Sarah, "nor have I ever given it any real thought. But now that you ask, I'd say that on some of the Indians, the style is attractive. On others . . ."

Marisa nodded. "Sarah, let me ask you a more personal question, if I may."

"You may."

"Do you think," continued Marisa, "much as the other colonists do, that the Indians are savage?"

Sarah drew her brows together and scowled at Marisa. "The Indians practice torture on some of their captives, and I believe that torture is a savage practice."

"Yes," said Marisa, "indeed, it is. But is our society any better?

Sarah paused. "Come again?"

"Have we not burned witches? Have we not drawn and

quartered our enemies, boiled men and sometimes women in oil?"

"True, but—"

"Should one judge all people in a particular society based on the actions of a few?"

Sarah gave her charge a considering glance. "You are most philosophical today," she remarked. "To what do I owe such uncharacteristic observations?" When Marisa didn't deem to answer at once, Sarah said, "My dear Marisa, in all these many years, I have never noticed you to be curious about either the Indians or their way of life. Why do you do so now?"

Marisa shrugged. "I wouldn't say that I'm curious. It's simply that . . . Take William Johnson, for instance, and Johnson Hall. He has made a strong alliance with the Mohawk Indians and I have heard that the Indians use his property at their ease. I have also gathered from various people that the Indians have made Johnson Hall the center of their government. And it is common knowledge that Johnson himself has taken a Mohawk wife, that the children from that union are strong and able-bodied, and . . ."

Sarah raised an eyebrow at Marisa. She said, "Has something happened to cause this sudden interest in ideology?"

"No . . . Well, perhaps. A young Mohawk warrior spoke to me the other day—"

"With or without introduction?"

"Without. But he was so admiring of me that I forgave him. He made me smile."

"Smile? What did he say?"

"He told me that my beauty had touched his heart."

"His heart?" Sarah paused, sighing. "Oh, my dear Marisa, beware."

"Why?"

"Because it appears to me that he might have captured your admiration in a fashion that even your own peers have not. Has he?"

"I am only curious about him."

Sarah arched a brow. "Do not become too curious," she

said. "It would not do to become infatuated with such a man as he is, since no earthly good could ever come of it."

"I speak of mere interest. Nothing more."

"I do hope so. Though we live side-by-side with these Mohawk people, one would not seek a husband from amongst them. Such an association could never be."

"A husband? Oh Sarah, please. Let me assure you that such a detail is not, and has never been, within my thoughts."

"I am glad to hear it. Beware, however, that when a man speaks to you of matters of the heart, he is courting you."

Marisa paused, and wide-eyed, she asked, "Do you believe it may be so? Do you feel he might have been courting me?"

Sarah shook her head, then cast a contemplative glance at the Indians. At length, she returned her attention to Marisa, and said. "Beware, Miss Marisa, unhappiness lies in that direction. Besides, with your fortune and your beauty, it may be said that you could have your pick of any man in this town."

"*If* my guardian will permit me to choose my husband without interference. Do you think he might?"

"Most likely not . . ." Sarah paused and, perhaps more philosophical now, said, "If your uncle has anything to do with it, I fear that you will be forced to . . ."

Silence. "Forced to what?"

"I fear I have said too much."

Marisa frowned. "I know that my step-uncle has an eye to the fortunes of men, but I believe he is awaiting a young man of good fortune and family name—someone whom I might fancy, before he demands I marry. It is true that to this day, he has only suggested alliances to older men, most of whom I could barely tolerate, let alone marry. It is also true that my step-uncle has intimated that when I marry, I should fill his coffers with gold. But I have always considered he was joking, although I think it is safe to say that, as regards my own marriage, I may likely have little say in the matter."

Sarah didn't answer, her silence telling.

"Perhaps it was only a dream, but it seems to me," continued Marisa, "that my step-uncle might have once lectured me, very long ago, about marriage, but . . ." As though her head suddenly hurt, she brought her hands up to it, her brows drawn together. "No," she said after a while, "I cannot recall it. Mayhap it was only a dream I try to recall, or maybe in my uncle's case, it might be a nightmare." Marisa grinned.

But Sarah's look was distant, and instead of returning the smile, she said, "Your uncle is who he is, and he is a financier. I fear that within a year, perhaps two, you will be expected to marry . . . and well. Therefore, it might be well that you seek to have amusement wherever you might find it, be that source Mohawk or English . . . providing it is innocent, of course." She nodded toward the Indians. "Shall we go, then, and speak to those young men? Ask them if they know where we might find your Mohawk suitor?"

"Sarah! We shall do no such thing! Why, the idea is vulgar, indeed."

"Then let us leave here. We have more shopping to do yet this day." Sarah paused. "Oh, do look, over there. Someone has made apple cider. Shall we go and sample their wares?"

"Yes," said Marisa, then again, "Yes."

So, with the subject tabled—at least for the moment— the two women picked up the chiffon material of their skirts and headed in the direction of the next vending stand.


Black Eagle would have had to be blind not to notice that the beauty he had so recently admired was here this very day. At present, she was strolling through the marketplace, arm in arm with another woman, who was almost, but not quite, as pretty as she.

The two women added to the beauty of the landscape, and Black Eagle noticed that they were drawing the eye of

many a fine young man. That none of those men solicited
the women's attention seemed unnatural to Black Eagle,
especially when such pleasure could be drawn from a mere
conversation with the object of one's adoration.

He wondered, was the Englishman too busy with his
own business to indulge in more than a passing glance?
Or was the reason something else? Were the white women
too heavily guarded by their relatives, that one dare not
approach?

Most likely it was the last, since no man in his right mind
would ignore the opportunity to indulge a moment's pleasure. That this also included him did not escape his notice.
Crossing his arms over his chest, Black Eagle leaned back
against a wooden post, that he might let his gaze roam leisurely over the beauty's figure.

She was small, although perhaps it was her waist that
made her appear so, since it looked to be uncannily petite.
A green ribbon, placed strategically at her breast brought
emphasis there, although the beauty of her face was not
paralleled. Her soft, green dress flowed over her curvy figure, and her reddish golden hair was caught up in an ivory-
colored net in back. A straw hat, complete with another
green ribbon tied around it, decorated her head. Although
he couldn't see them from here, he knew her eyes to be a
golden brown, and from within their depths a smile could
be coaxed.

Once again, the desire to tease the beauty, to witness
that smile and feel her response, overrode an inclination
to merely sit back and enjoy the show. He had come away
from the post where he had been lingering, and had already
taken a step forward, when he stopped short. Something
was preventing him from proceeding any further.

"Did ye hear me, boy?"

Black Eagle looked down at the hand that had taken possession of his own arm. Following that hand up to its owner,
Black Eagle grimaced. Where had this man come from? Had
he, Black Eagle, been so out of touch with the environment
around him, that such a man could sneak up on him?

It should not have been. Especially since the man's stench alone should have alerted Black Eagle to his presence. Ah, he thought. What a woman could do.

"I have spoken to several Indians this day," said the man whose breath seemed to be worse than his general odor, "and I have discovered from each, in turn, that ye is the best guide to be had in this country. I be goin' to Portsmouth, New Hampshire, into Abenaki territory, and I have need to hire me a damn good scout, since I intend to keep me scalp. What say ye?"

Black Eagle didn't even deem to answer. Instead, he gazed again at the place where he had last seen the beauty. He exhaled. She was gone.

Disgruntled, he turned his attention to the man who was so demanding of it. Said Black Eagle, "I am not interested in scouting for you. Seek out someone else."

"But ye havena even heard how much coinage I aim to be paying ye."

But Black Eagle had already made his decision. He disengaged his arm from the other man's hold.

"Now see here, ye young savage . . ."

Black Eagle turned, presenting his back to the man, and made to step away, when the brute, who must have been speaking to himself, said, "I reckon I'll have to tell Miss Marisa that we be delayed yet again."

Black Eagle paused. *Miss Marisa?* Had the beast's tongue actually spoken the name of the beauty?

Black Eagle turned back. Looking askance at the man, he said, "Miss Marisa? Will there be others traveling with you into Abenaki territory then?"

"Aye," said Thompson. "Havena ye been listening to me? I'll be escorting Miss Marisa and her maid to the east, toward the sea. But I'll be needing a guide to ensure our safe passage. I'm willin' to pay ye well."

Black Eagle glanced in the direction where he had last seen the enchantress, but as before, her figure was not to be seen. However, it mattered little. Her image was imprinted on the very recesses of his mind.

To be certain that it was the same person they were both speaking about, Black Eagle questioned, "The one you mentioned, Miss Marisa, and her maid? Who exactly are they?"

"They are financier John Rathburn's niece and her companion. Why be ye asking?"

Black Eagle didn't deem to answer the question. Instead, he said, "Have you a map of your destination so that I might determine where it is and estimate the danger involved?"

"I do. I have it with me here." The brute reached into the dirty inner workings of his leather coat. From there, he extracted a sheet of parchment, which he extended toward Black Eagle.

Black Eagle nodded, reaching out to accept the document from the man. Briefly, he unrolled the paper and scanned the markings on the map, then said, "What you say is true. Your journey will encroach upon Abenaki territory, and as anyone here will know, they can be a fearsome foe."

"Aye. Can ye escort us through there without a cost to life?"

"I can."

"Ye'll do it, then?"

Black Eagle nodded. "I will. When do you plan to leave?"

"In the next few days," said Thompson. "Can ye be ready?"

"I am ready now."

"Good," said Thompson, grinning. "Good."

# Four

Music from a fiddle, violins and a flute filtered into the Rathburn stables where Black Eagle was preparing the three horses—two roans and a dapple gray—for their journey. Checking over their cinches, to ensure that the leather was strong, Black Eagle was a stern critic, his eye catching perhaps what another might miss.

He was frowning; something was not right. It looked as if . . . Pulling hard against one of the cinches, the leather fell apart in his hand. *Hunh-uh!* He stared at the straps dumbfoundedly. Then he picked up another cinch, making the same experiment, then the third.

Each one was damaged in its own way, and as he studied them, he could only surmise that they had been broken at one time, then sewn and glued back together so cleverly, that the error remained undetectable. Was the white man so negligent, so unaware, that he hadn't seen this?

Or was there another reason for what should have been a simple repair? Certainly the white man could not be so frugal that he could ill afford the best straps available.

He examined the bits of leather, noting that the cuts

were not clean, which would make it appear that the damage was due to simple wear. But on all three?

Was it possible that the animals were not regularly used, so that the fault had remained undetectable until now? It was possible. However, Black Eagle's frown deepened.

Laying the damaged cinches aside, Black Eagle's thoughts raced, although outwardly, he set himself to mindless work. Picking up a brush, he began the long process of scrubbing the animals down for the night.

One thing was certain: New cinches would be secured or the horses would stay behind. Either way it mattered little to him, particularly since, from the start, Black Eagle had not been in favor of taking horses. Although it was true that a horse could run faster than a man, the animal could not travel as far as a man in the course of a day, mainly because of the necessity to rest every few hours. Plus, the animal was easy to track, required too much care along the way and announced their position to any enemy.

But, when the English had insisted that their women could not walk the entire journey, and that their "things" had to be transported with them, Black Eagle had given little resistance. It wasn't part of his plan to negate the judgment of the English. Besides, he wasn't altogether adverse to plodding a slower journey. If it meant a few extra days spent in the presence of the beauty, then he would acquiesce.

Again the strains of the music from the big house trickled into the livery and Black Eagle fought a desire to be there, to watch the beauty and mayhap if he were lucky, to speak to her again. But he would not do it. Not because of the peculiarities of the English dances, since he was well acquainted with these. Nor was it fear of criticism from the Englishman's condescending eye. Rather it was because *her* image haunted him.

He was fascinated with her, and this, he knew, would not do. He might admire the young lady, might watch her with longing, but he was well aware that there was no future in the flirtation; their worlds were too dissimilar to permit a union between their respective cultures.

As the wise sachems had often counseled, if marriage were not the intended outcome of an association with a woman, one should not indulge in it. One's heart—and hers—could be held in balance.

Still, as a delicate melody swept into the stable, filling each nook and cranny with the pulse of the English dance, he could little ignore it. The music was in three-quarter time, he noted, and the rhythm affected him in a way he would never have suspected it might. Unbidden, a desire to be there, to see her, to learn more about her, entered into his breast, and he could have sworn his heart ached.

Firmly, he set the matter of the beauty from his mind, but not so the cinches. He would go in search of Thompson and make his demands.

As he finished rubbing down the last of the three animals, he sniffed at the air around him. Was it the stables, or did he reek of horseflesh?

A stream, deep in the forest that skirted the Rathburn property offered a simple and easy solution, and he washed up there, donning the best clothing he had. After all, Thompson might be at the ball.

His other clothing he washed in the stream, hanging them in a hollowed out cavity in a tree. It was a very old and large tree, one he had taken special notice of as he had scouted the Rathburn property.

As he stepped back toward the big house, an airy melody washed over him, and Black Eagle sighed, reminding himself he was not attending the ball, he was looking for Thompson. Unfortunately, he was all too aware of the yearning of his heart.


As Marisa stepped with her partner in time to the music, she hid a smile. She was happy. Not for herself, of course, but for Sarah. Indeed, Marisa had succeeded; she had bested her step-uncle in a battle of wills. True, it had been a test of spirit, but she had persisted, had made it perfectly clear to her step-uncle that he was in the wrong, not only in regards to his future plans for a particular Pennsylvania Dutch settlement, but also as concerned Sarah's past.

This ball, which Rathburn had arranged in honor of Sarah and Marisa's departure, proved her success. Undoubtedly, the ball was a simple affair in many ways. Necessity had made it so, due in part to the fact that both she and Sarah were leaving forthwith—the very next morning. But, though there were probably no more than fifty guests in attendance this evening, no expense had been spared. Strategically placed torches and candles lit the room, while the scent of burning wax, of food—roast meat and freshly baked bread, cakes and pies—permeated the hall.

Gentlemen and ladies had adorned themselves in their best, causing the interior of the room to be awash in color schemes of pink and coral silks, as well as the hues of blue and gold. White wigs, with the required two curls at each side of the face sat atop the natural color of the hair. The orchestra was a simple affair, as well, a few violins, a cello, bass and flute.

Their music filled the hall now, lending the atmosphere a certain gaiety and a rhythm that kept the guests stepping around the floor to the music of a minuet; sweep, step, step, sweep, step, step, promenade forward, turn to face one another, step up, step back, bow, curtsy.

Her partner coughed, and Marisa smiled at the gentleman whom she had favored with the dance. The young man, who was of medium height, with a wave of sandy hair that peeked out beneath his wig, was most likely the handsomest man in the room tonight. But though he smiled at her adoringly, Marisa was not so easily impressed. Indeed, not.

For years her heart had remained untouched. There was no reason for it to be different tonight. Indeed, for all she knew, it might always be so.

But why? Though there were young men of whom she was fond, her affections had never progressed farther than mere attraction. Truth be known, Marisa had never been kissed; not by a man, a boy, a relative . . . no one.

Again, why?

Was it because she had never met a man to whom she might shower her devotion? Or was it most likely due to the reality that, as she had recently told Sarah, she might likely have no say in the matter of her own marriage?

Marisa frowned. If the latter were the case—and she did suspect it was true—why did she think this?

As if asking the question brought on the memory, a recollection, long looked for, but much forgotten, flashed in her mind. For a moment, she was distracted. She trembled, and daintily smiled at her partner to offset a feeling of being ill at ease. But like a book that once opened, refused to be closed, her mind replayed a scene from her past:

*Marisa had been a shy child of seven years of age when John Rathburn had summoned her to his study. Expecting the best of such a beckoning, Marisa had been overjoyed. Perhaps, after three long years of living within the Rathburn household, Marisa's step-uncle was at last ready to lavish her with the love Marisa craved.*

*Sarah had ensured that Marisa looked the epitome of fashion, in her sack dress of ivory silk, adorned with the white of her petticoat. True, she had still worn the back-fastened bodice, so common for her age, but this dress was her best, and it gave her confidence. As the butler had ushered her into the Rathburn inner sanctum, the lace edging of Marisa's cap had fluttered delicately around her face, making her feel feminine and pretty.*

*The scent of mildew was the first detail she recalled, then came the memory of the room, itself, which was lined wall-to-wall with books. At first her gaze had settled onto her step-uncle, who could have been the embodiment of British conservatism in his white-powdered wig and black tailored coat. Her step-uncle had always appeared to her to be a cold, foreboding and condemning sort of man, and on this day it was no different. However, there was an extra appearance of bitterness about him at this moment. Indeed, there had been an expression of disdain so great that it had set her knees to trembling.*

*Instantly, Marisa's joy had fled, replaced instead by an overwhelming feeling of inadequacy. Under Rathburn's censuring glance, she had shifted uneasily from one foot to the other.*

*"Stop that!" Rathburn had ordered, but Marisa couldn't stop. In truth, beneath his anger, her fidgeting became more pronounced.*

*"Sit!" Rathburn had said with disgust, gesturing toward a chair that looked to be three times bigger than she was. Marisa had dutifully obeyed the command and had sat back in the seat, her feet out straight in front of her.*

*"Yer parents are dead."*

*Marisa gulped and straightened her shoulders at this seeming attack. Did her uncle think she was unaware of that fact?*

*"Therefore ye come under my rule. Do ye understand?"*

*Marisa nodded.*

*"Good. The age of seven deems ye old enough to know of yer duty in this household. And it is yer obligation to me that bids ye to me this day."*

*Marisa had only stared at Rathburn with a wide-eyed look.*

*"Now, yer first and foremost responsibility is to bring no disgrace to our family name. There'll be no childish display of emotion in this house. No tantrums, no temper, no anger, and certainly no childish giggles are to echo within these walls. Do ye comprehend this?"*

*Marisa nodded yet again. Had she committed some wrong of which she was as yet unaware? In her mind's eye—perhaps in self-defense—the room and her uncle took on a dreamlike quality.*

*"Additionally," her uncle was continuing, "ye are to present yerself as calm and poised as long as ye are a part of this household. And though it might seem a trifle early to speak of it, let me detail yer duty in the marriage bed."*

*Marisa gazed down at her lap, embarrassed, but she otherwise remained quiet.*

"*Ye have been seen playing with the servant boys, and this t'will never do. Understand now that yer keep is not inexpensive to me. Ye shall repay me when ye are of age, by bringing honor and fortune to the family when ye marry. Bloodline and fortune will have out, and part of the Rathburn familial obligation includes that only the 'right' classes shall be united. So do not be giving yer attention to the servants, lest ye fall in love with a lad unworthy of the Rathburn name. As God is my witness, ye will do yer duty to me when the time comes for yer marriage. Do ye understand?*"

Again, Marisa nodded.

"*Now speak up, lass. I would have yer word on this.*"

*Marisa opened her mouth to utter what she realized must be her complete agreement, but though she tried to find her tongue to say the words, her mouth simply refused to do her mind's bidding.*

*Watching her, John Rathburn grunted in revulsion. Marisa was at once shamed. But still she couldn't speak.*

*Waving his hand at her, Rathburn said, "Ah, ye be too young. If not in age, then in disposition. 'Tis a waste of time, ye are. Now go! Leave me at once!"*

*Marisa, not needing to be told twice, jumped to the floor and, ignoring Rathburn's warning of propriety, ran out the door and back to Sarah's waiting arms. She had cried and cried, until at last she had drifted to sleep.*

Though her steps in time to the music had not faltered, Marisa was shaken. She had truly forgotten the incident. In essence, at the time, so embarrassed had she been over her seeming inadequacy, she had not even had the courage to relay the details of the incident to Sarah. Marisa had instead cried until there had been no more tears left to be shed. Even then she had hiccupped through most the night.

By the next morning, however, the entire occurrence had seemed to wash away, to trouble her no more. Or so it had appeared. However, it looked as if the incident had in fact receded into the dark recesses of her memory, where it had remained buried and unheeded until now.

But why was she recalling it now?

As Marisa looked up, her gaze fastened onto the silhouette of a man who stood amongst the guests, there toward the back wall of the ballroom. Yet he might have been directly in front of her for all that her attention clung to him.

It was he, the Mohawk Indian. The one who had so impressed her with his oratory and admiration. Her stomach somersaulted.

Step forward, step back, turn, swing up and exchange places, step up, step back, promenade. It was as though her feet knew the dance, for her mind was far away from the minuet's requirements.

Her handsome young partner coughed, bringing her attention back to him. The cough was soon followed by another in kind, then a bout of hacking. Putting a hand to his throat, he coughed again and said, "So sorry. Would you please excuse me?"

"By all means." She nodded. He retreated, and she was ready to step out of line, as well, when his place was suddenly filled by another man. She gazed forward. Her eyes rounded.

"You!" It was the Mohawk.

"*Nyoh*, yes, 'tis I. Forgive me," he replied in his deeply baritone voice, "but I can hardly be expected to remain long as a spectator when the most beautiful creature in the hall has need of a partner. Would that I fill that role."

"Sir!" She might have protested, but being swept up in the rhythm of the dance, whatever she might have said perished on her lips. Clasp hands, swing forward, step back, then advance, exchange places. She couldn't fail to note that, though he were Mohawk, his knowledge of the dance was without fault.

"Once again," she said as they promenaded, "you dazzle me with your knowledge of our English manners and culture. Pray, tell me, did you also learn dancing from the monks?"

He smiled at her. "English traders," he said simply. "And perhaps the influence of William Johnson who insisted that one day I would need the skill."

"Yes, William Johnson," she said. "I have heard of

him. He has been quite influential amongst the Iroquois, I believe."

"He has," said the Mohawk.

Though he was obviously dressed in his best, the Indian was an odd man out here in this hall, she noted, where the powdered wigs, the *justaucorps* and waistcoats of the Englishmen were the rule. By comparison, the Mohawk was wearing black from head to foot, though a streak of white appeared at his neck. His apparel seemed to consist of a tunic, belted at the waist, that looked to be a combination shirt and kilt. Skin-tight black leggings and high-topped moccasins completed the outfit. Over one shoulder, worn Roman-style, and draped around his waist, was a red blanket, heavily adorned with shell beads of white.

"Have you met him?" asked the Mohawk.

"Who? William Johnson? Yes, he was a guest here at Rathburn Hall once."

With their hands still clasped, the Indian stepped toward her, she followed suit. They both stepped back, forward again, then they turned round, clasping hands once more.

The music softened, ending in a long drawn out chord that allowed the dancers to bow and curtsy to one another. A round of applause followed. However, while the others were engaged in the act of clapping, Marisa faced the Mohawk instead, and she asked, "Have you a name?"

"Black Eagle," he supplied.

She nodded. "I thank you, Sir Eagle, for coming to my rescue on the dance floor." She smiled at him before saying, "And now I must leave you." She spun around to step away from him, only to find that he had laid a hand at her elbow, there where her sleeve ended in lace. Her nerves there tingled.

"A moment of your time, please. There is something I would say to you, something I would ask, if you would permit me."

Whether she had it in her mind to agree or protest was a moot point: He had placed his other hand upon the small of her back and was leading her toward a set of French doors that opened up onto a veranda, overlooking a parklike reserve of the Rathburn estate.

"Sir," she managed to utter at last. "I must protest. I am without a chaperone."

"It is not my intention to take you away from your party or those who would protect you. In truth, I have come here tonight in search of the man known as Thompson."

"He is not here."

He nodded. "Then might it not be possible to find a quiet spot along the side of the room where we might engage in a moment's talk? There is a matter of concern that I must relate to you."

Marisa shook her head. "I'm afraid that I . . ." She paused and glanced over her shoulder toward the ballroom, looking to her right, to her left. Although her step-uncle was not to be seen at present, her gaze found and centered on his henchman, James. The butler's frown at her spoke adequately for him, and Marisa knew she was being warned to act in a manner befitting her position. Moreover, if she didn't perform as expected, James would, indeed, carry tales.

Something within her rebelled. As a little girl, Marisa might have once submitted to the butler's unspoken threat. But she was a woman, full grown. Perhaps it was the memory tonight that caused her to resist, maybe not. But it is perhaps well to observe that there is not a being alive who will not, from time to time, protest the bars of his or her imprisonment. For Marisa, that time was now.

Tilting her chin upward, she stared at James, though she spoke to the Indian, when she said, "There is a path through the garden, Sir Eagle, that is quiet and will serve us better than trying to raise our voices above the noise of the ballroom. Shall I show that path to you?"

He nodded. "If it be your pleasure, I would be most honored."

Still holding onto James's stare, Marisa placed her gloved hand atop the Indian's. "This way, please," she said.

# Five

The moon was full, with no cloud cover to eclipse its glow, which by comparison caused the stars overhead to dim their brilliance. The moonlight was ethereal, a mere airy reflection of light that cast a shimmering, silvery glow over everything it touched, the trees, the grasses, the landscape . . . him. Odd how handsome he appeared beneath the misty beams of moonlight.

She studied him for a moment. The night and the misty beams were said to be a woman's territory. However, an exception should be made for this man, she thought.

His features were strong, yet pleasing; his cheekbones high, his lips full and sensual. Glancing at him now, an odd feeling washed over her. He was handsome, yes, but there was also an indefinable quality about him that made her feel as though she were safe, protected.

Unlike most Mohawk men, his head was not bald. Instead, he wore his hair cropped close. True, the ever-present strip of longer hair sat atop his head in true Mohawk fashion, but it was tempered by the outline of his natural hairline. And in back, a section of his hair was kept long, flowing over his shoulders.

His manner of dress was unusual, and it occurred to her

that he was most likely clothed in his very best. His tunic, belted in at his waist, fell to midthigh, resembling a kilt, and it was black with only a hint of white peeking out from beneath it, there at his neck. Perhaps it was because of this tunic, but his manner of dress reminded her of the Scots, except that in this man's case, his leggings reached high up beneath that kilt. The blanket draped around his shoulders did not detract from or hide his strength, rather it emphasized his shoulder's width.

Her gaze dipped lower, toward his waist where a wide belt held an assortment of weapons. She looked lower still, toward the apex of his legs, and realizing where her thoughts were leading her, her glance skipped off of him, coming to rest on the deciduous trees of maple, oak and elm, which lined the pathway.

She inhaled, and the musky scents of autumn flooded her senses, magnified in the cool, evening air. It brought to mind the pleasant images of corn husks, pumpkins and apple pie. Dry leaves, crunching beneath their footfalls, scattered over the hard-packed earthen track where they trod.

Overhead a dove cooed, accentuating the serenade of the crickets and the locust. So, too, did the soft music of the violins provide a welcome backdrop. The wind, which blew from behind them, ushered in other sounds, the sighing of the trees beneath Nature's breath, a nighthawk's squawk, high in the sky.

"Sir Eagle," she said at length, as she turned toward him to come directly to the point, "you mentioned that there is a something specific that you wish to say to me."

"*Nyoh*—"

"What does that word mean?"

"Yes," he answered. "It means yes. There is a matter of some concern that I need to say. Yet, even while I know I should speak of it, I am distracted from my duty by the moon and the starlight. If I had thought you beautiful in the light of day—and I have—it pales in comparison to how you look under the influence of the moonlight."

She sighed. Beneath his compliment, which seemed to

be quite sincere, she softened. It would not do, she thought, to take out her frustration with James and her step-uncle on this Mohawk man, who seemed to continually lift her spirits. She said, "Again you are most flattering to me."

"No flattery. I speak but the truth."

She held up a hand, as though to hold back whatever else he might take into his mind to say. "Sir Eagle," she said, "although I have chosen to bring you away from the party, I cannot be long gone. I would ask that you come to the point."

"Very well." He nodded. "Your journey northward—"

"You know of that?"

"Is it not common knowledge? Is it not the reason for this ball?"

"I suppose you are right. Yes, about my journey . . . Oh, look!" She pointed toward the sky. "Did you see it?"

He shook his head. "I did not. I fear my eyes see only you."

She smiled, her gaze skirting away from his. "'Twas a shooting star," she replied. "'Tis said that when a body sees a shooting star, he should make a wish, for it will certainly come true."

"And did you make a wish?"

"No, but let me do so now." She paused, then glanced back toward the evening sky.

"I wonder," he said, "what is the wish of someone as fair as you? She, who would seem to have most everything?"

"Oh, my wish 'twas not for myself, rather, 'twas for my friend, Sarah."

"For your friend. *Nyoh*, now I understand. As well as beauty, you are a woman of honor."

She shook her head at him. "I fear that you do me more justice than I might deserve. 'Tis no merit that I simply wish a good life for my friend and companion."

Black Eagle didn't respond. Instead, he leaned toward her, pointing to the night sky. "Do you see that group of stars? There in the north sky?"

"I do." She nodded. "We call that constellation the Big Dipper."

"*Nyoh*, I know. My people, the *Ka-nin-ke-a-ka*, call it the hunters and the Great Sky Bear."

"The hunters and the Great Sky Bear," she repeated. "Does it have a legend?"

He paused. Then, looking again toward the sky, he said, "*Nyoh*, it is a legend."

She smiled at him. "Will you tell it to me?"

"*Nyoh*, it would be my pleasure. It is told amongst my people that long ago a great bear terrorized us. The people were starving because none dared go out into the woods to hunt for food or to work the fields." He glanced back toward her, his look at her soft, yet passionate. "At that time, there were four hunters," he continued, "and they were the best hunters we have ever known. It is said that they would never give up a trail once they had set out upon it.

"They determined to kill this bear. But it could not be done easily. Each time the hunters tried to trap the bear, he escaped them, always climbing higher and higher into the white snows of the mountains. But the hunters were determined. With the help of their dog, Four-Eyes, they tracked the Great Sky Bear, heading always higher and higher into the mountains, until they finally found him and killed him. But once it was done, and they had feasted on his flesh, the bones of the animal reappeared and the great bear grew up again, and ran away, escaping them.

"Because the hunters could not afford to let the bear loose upon their people, they followed him. They continue to do so to this very day, so that he would not ever disturb our people again. Do you see the four stars there?"

She nodded.

"Your people say that is the bowl of the dipper, but to my people, that is the Great Sky Bear. And the handle is the hunters. If you look closely, you can barely see the small star, there. That is their dog. With each season, the constellation appears differently in the sky, showing my people the way of the chase. Now, because it is autumn, the great bear reappears in the sky and the hunters begin their chase all over again. Of course, they find him, and kill him. And so it is his blood, dripping down from the heavens, that colors the leaves of the maple trees at this time of year. And the fat that drips from his meat is what makes the grass white."

He glanced back up at the sky, and Marisa followed his gaze. Silence fell between them, until at last she said, "I believe that I like your story of how that constellation came into being better than the American version that originates from my own culture."

He nodded. "I, too."

As Black Eagle had related his tale, they had stopped at the side of a great oak tree. It was a large tree, and one she had always admired. Holding up the ends of her silken skirt, she stepped off the path, treading toward the tree, where, coming up close to it, she leaned back against it and turned toward him.

She bit her lip and exhaled. Moonlight, indeed, was this man's friend. As the silvery beams outlined the rises and falls of his face, she thought he was perhaps more hand- some than any man had a right to be. He was tall, proud, incredibly male, and, the good Lord help her, she had never felt more female.

Sadly, he was also the exact sort of person her step-uncle would forbid her from.

Perhaps it was this that triggered that latent spark of rebellion, and she asked, "Sir Eagle, tell me. Do Indians kiss?"

If he were startled by her question, he didn't show it. Instead, he stepped toward her. He answered calmly, "Of course."

"But I mean, do they kiss, lips to lips, like the English do?"

"I believe" he muttered, as he placed his arm against the tree, "that the English cannot claim complete ownership over something so common as a kiss. All human beings enjoy much the same thing."

As he spoke, his head had descended so closely to hers, that she realized she could read his thoughts; it was an unbelievably intimate feeling, as though he had become a part of her. He wanted to kiss her. She knew it as surely as the fact that she wanted to be kissed.

Yet, he didn't do it.

It was wrong of her, so very wrong, considering who she was and who he was, yet she found herself lifting her face up toward his, and she murmured, "I have never been kissed."

He didn't utter a word in response to her. Instead, he bent the fraction of an inch required, and gently touched his lips to hers.

Ah! At his touch, fire washed through her, the warmth of the sensation centering in on her lower abdomen. She swooned slightly, and her stomach lightened, then fell, as if butterflies had come to roost there.

The kiss deepened and she could feel her heartbeat race, not only within her chest, but high up in her throat as well. As the fresh scent of him filled her nostrils, her lips clung to his, and she thought she would never forget the clean and woodsy taste of him.

His embrace affected her strangely, causing her to feel as if she had come home; as if she had discovered a bit of heaven, and as every nerve within her clamored for more of something she could not put a name to, she realized she had never felt more alive than she did at this moment. She swayed forward against him, only to have him catch her in his arms.

Placing one of his hands against the small of her back, he urged her in even farther toward him, as close as her skirts would allow. And as his lips made a feast of her, he brought up his other hand to trail his fingers over her cheeks, her eyes and eyebrows, even around to each of her ears. Though his fingers were calloused, she realized that it didn't necessarily follow that his touch was any less gentle or that she objected.

Unexpectedly, his fingers trailed down over her exposed shoulders, and she moaned. She couldn't help it. It felt so good.

As if encouraged, his lips met hers again and again, and

as his tongue slid into the wet recesses of her mouth, she felt as though her body were ablaze. She sighed, the soft sound of her voice high-pitched against his lips. In response, he shuddered against her, and she wondered if she were having as great an effect on him as he was creating on her.

She wanted him closer, and although his body was pressed up against hers as tightly as possible, he still seemed too far away. In truth, had there been a way to crawl into his skin, she thought she would have gladly done so.

As though inspired by her response, he lifted her up, her feet leaving the ground, and he pressed her back against the tree. His tongue played with hers, foraging deeper into her mouth, then more shallowly. Deeper again, then withdrawing, over and over.

She moaned. She could barely help herself, and she murmured, "What are you doing to me?"

"I am kissing you," he answered, as he lowered her, allowing her feet to touch the ground again. "It is nothing more than a kiss."

"I think you understate the experience," she said. "Why has no one ever revealed to me that to kiss is to find . . . a little bit of happiness?"

He didn't answer at once, but her words seem to animate him, because his arms came around her, and he hugged her tightly. "Perhaps not everyone," he said, "finds paradise in each and every kiss."

However, as though to dispute his words, he touched his lips to hers again, and she found herself surrendering once more to his passion.

She whispered, "If you mean by that statement, that you do not feel the quickening of your heart the same as I do, pray do not tell me so."

"*Neh*, I was speaking of others, not of you and me. I feel plenty. Perhaps a little too much."

"Too much? Is there such a thing?"

He shrugged, and despite her most sincere hopes, he backed up slightly. He said, "It is hard to know. But one matter is certain: There is a delicate balance between desire and control, and when a man is with a woman, he must be in full possession of himself."

"Indeed? And are you in control now?"

"*Neh*. The truth is, I barely have any control left." He backed up a little farther.

She followed him, however, leaning forward and into his embrace. "Do not go away," she complained softly. "I fear you are not close enough to satisfy me."

He groaned. "I know," he said. He was holding her with one arm and massaging her cheeks and her face with his other hand. Yet, he kept a slight distance between them as he continued speaking, saying, "But since this is your first kiss, I fear to provide you with what it is that I know we both desire."

"Do not fear me," she said.

"It is not you that I fear, it is the possible harm I might do you if I give you what it is you seek."

"And do you know what it is that I seek?"

"Is it not obvious? You are a woman. I am a man, and though our paths are surely different in this life, I think that desire between two people, once it touches them, respects no boundaries."

"You speak of desire . . . ?"

He nodded. "It knows nothing of cultures or the problems that might be created because two people who should not want one another . . . do . . ."

She brought up her white-gloved hand to press it along his shoulder. "Then you admit that you want me?"

He nodded. "I do. But it is forbidden. We both know it. Therefore, one of us should think logically, and perhaps I am the best person to do so."

"Yes. Yes." She straightened. "Of course. I am certain you are right."

He inclined his head.

"Yet," her golden brown eyes sought out the dark brown of his, as she continued, "I ask for no more than one more kiss. Is it so very much to ask?"

For a moment, he appeared tormented, but the look was

quickly gone, replaced by a countenance that showed nothing as he said, "There is a danger in committing too many kisses. Perhaps you do not understand that danger, since this is your first experience. But I know what it is that may follow. Know that I am not immune to you. As you may remember, my admiration of you is great."

"But, pray, you have already kissed me. Surely one more . . ."

He moaned. He leaned forward. She closed her eyes.

"Miss Marisa!"

The call, though spoken no louder than the cry of an eagle, was still blaring enough to shock Marisa. She inhaled deeply. Why did the world have to intrude? And at such a time? Wrenching her glance away from Black Eagle's, she looked back toward the house.

It was Sarah, who was hurrying down the path toward them. With the dry leaves scurrying hither and thither, and her skirts flaring out behind her, she presented an odd image, as though Sarah were running away, instead of toward them.

Marisa took one more deep breath, and answered, "I am here, Sarah. By the large oak tree, the same one you and I have sat beneath on many a summer day."

Black Eagle stepped to Marisa's side.

"Ah, yes, I see you now." Sarah slowed her pace as she approached them. Briefly her glance took in Black Eagle's appearance, which she studied for a moment before she addressed Marisa. "I fear that your step-uncle is furious," Sarah said. "He has sent me here to seek you out and bid you to come back into the ballroom posthaste."

"I see."

When Marisa said nothing further, Sarah, still eyeing Black Eagle, went on to add, "However, if you would prefer to stay here, I can pretend I could not find you."

"And have you incur my step-uncle's wrath in my place?"

"It will not be the first time your uncle has shown me the edge of his tongue."

"Step-uncle," Marisa corrected.

"You are right, of course."

Marisa swallowed hard. "However, I suspect that it will do little harm if the three of us return to the party." Marisa took a tentative step toward Sarah. But Black Eagle didn't follow, and Marisa found herself gazing over her shoulder at him. "Sir Eagle," she said, "will you not escort us back into the hall?"

He didn't answer at once, and it took a few moments before he said, "*Neh*, no, I think not. Permit me to take my leave of you here."

Her eyes sought out his, clung to his, and she said, "I am afraid we did not discuss the matter that was most pressing to you."

"It will keep until we meet again."

"And do you suppose that we will meet again?"

"I believe that we shall."

She glanced down, then back up at him. "I am not certain that I agree with you, sir, on that regard. You see, I leave Albany in the morning."

"I know."

"Ah, yes. So you have said."

"It is about your journey that I—"

"If you will await me here," she interrupted, "I will try to determine what it is my step-uncle seeks, and then, since you had little time to tell me what is in your mind, I would return here and hear you out."

"Would that I could stay and await you," he said. "But I, too, must leave. There is much preparation I must attend to."

"Oh." It was all she said, for the significance of what he was saying became clear. She would never see him again.

Without willing it, emotion welled up within her. It choked her.

It was strange, she thought. The sensation of being let down was almost unbearable, and a part of her rebelled at the idea of never again being able to see or speak to this man.

Yet, what had she expected from him? An undying

exclamation of love? A willful agreement to put all else in his life, save her, aside?

They barely knew each other. It was unheard of.

Yet, the sense of rejection was strong. To her credit, however, well-ingrained manners came to her rescue, allowing her to rise above such negativity. She smiled as she presented Black Eagle with her gloved hand, and she said, "I . . . thank you for . . . I thank you."

He took her hand, held it a moment, and as his dark eyes stared deeply down into her own, he smiled at her. It was a crooked grin, yet so very endearing that it tugged at her heart. She wrenched her gaze away from his.

"Come Sarah," said Marisa as she spun around and presented Black Eagle with her back, "let us go and see if there is anything I can do to appease my step-uncle."

And Marisa had no sooner spoken the words, than she was gone.

Black Eagle watched her departing figure. Perhaps he should have insisted on telling her that he would, indeed, have the pleasure of her company in the very near future. But Black Eagle had been uncharacteristically tongue-tied; he was also very aroused.

Mayhap this was his defense. Had she stayed longer . . .

He sighed, while his gaze followed her progress away from him. He could almost hear the blue silk of her dress rustle as her steps carried her closer and closer to the ballroom. Tendrils of her auburn hair swept over her shoulders, while pearls and decorative ribbons of blue fell down her back. A gentle breeze blew those ribbons backward, their movement seeming to accentuate her motion away from him.

He turned his glance elsewhere, forcing himself to listen to the crickets and locusts, instead of to her footsteps. It would not do to become too besotted with her, he reminded himself, although, perhaps this was a dubious point at present. Though he feared to admit it, he might very well have already lost his heart to her.

# Six

*He was gone. She would never see him again.*

Except for a chance meeting here and there, which, given their two cultures, was nearly impossible, she would never again have the pleasure of his company. The feeling of loss that had settled in over her was an uncomfortable sensation at best.

Yet there was nothing to be done about it. She had known, even as she had flirted with the young man, that there was no impending happiness for them. For one thing, their cultures were too different; for another, he was what her step-uncle would call a savage. And whether or not she agreed, it was her step-uncle whom she was duty bound to appease.

At least parting now lost nothing more between them than a few kisses. What might be if they were to pursue their attraction further, she dared not consider.

As she and Sarah stepped toward the ballroom, Marisa silently thanked her friend for allowing her the time and space to compose herself, as well as to come to terms with the upset. But why was she upset?

She barely knew Black Eagle. Therefore, a few kisses should not a heartache make.

Yet she could little deny it. *And she would never see him again.*

She sighed. Such thoughts would never do. Indeed, she could almost hear the disapproving voices of tutors from her past, lecturing her on proper behavior. They would say, *"Your guardian might be a distant and stern man, but because he has provided for your upbringing, you owe him your loyalty. 'Tis your duty, nay, your obligation to submit yourself to his will."*

Marisa frowned as she stepped from the veranda into the candle-lit hall of the ballroom. However, the hum of the gaiety of the dance, the music and the violins, were all lost to her as she glanced forward, seeking out her guardian.

It took little effort to find the man, since most people in the room catered to him. Across the room, her survey caught onto the disapproving frown of John Rathburn, and the condemnation that she witnessed there, written so abundantly upon his countenance, sent yet another spark of defiance rushing through her.

But, as was expected of her, she quelled it. After all, she was not a common rebel.

She watched her guardian set down his wineglass, watched, too, as he made to cross the room toward her. He was enraged, that much was evident, and he was going to have words with her. Sighing, Marisa prepared herself for the coming battle.

While it was true that she did owe loyalty to her step-uncle, an inner voice would not be silenced. Troubled, she glanced away. Her thoughts seemed to be her enemy; she didn't want to revolt, yet . . .

As though Sarah were reading her thoughts, she murmured, "It is too bad that your step-uncle feels he must dominate and control you. One would think, from the way he acts, that you were as much an indentured servant as I am." Sarah paused, then, "The only difference is that in six years I will be free of him."

Free? As though suddenly jerked awake from slumber,

Marisa lifted her head, and her gaze came up to lock with that of her guardian's.

Freedom. It was an enticing concept. What would it be like to be free of her step-uncle's plots? To make her own choices? To act on her own decisions?

These were scandalous ideas, ideas that seemed to be afloat and alive in these American states of late. Perhaps it was the very air of this place that bred them. However, their cause little mattered.

"Sarah," Marisa muttered softly. "Forgive me. If I fail to return before the party is ended, I shall meet you at the stables at first light, and we shall leave this place, perhaps forever." And before Sarah could speak, Marisa had picked up her skirts, had spun around and had fled out through the open doors of the veranda.

The swish of a skirt and the delicate hammering of slippers over the hard-packed footpath had Black Eagle realizing that someone was hastening toward him. He turned swiftly and watched as the vision of loveliness fled toward him.

"Sir Eagle!" she called.

What was this? The beauty was deserting the party? Was there a reason?

Perhaps so, but he didn't think to contemplate what that reason might be. Instead he responded, and he turned and rushed toward her, closing the distance between them. He opened his arms, and she ran headlong into them. He took hold of her, and held her, simply held her.

"You have returned," he whispered, stating the obvious.

"Yes. Do not let me go," she said.

"It is not in my thoughts to do so."

"Take me somewhere else, somewhere private, and hurry. They may come after me."

"They?"

"I will tell you later. Please hurry."

"Then come!" He dropped his hands from around her to

take hold singly of her hand, and turning, he broke into a
fast walk. "Can you keep up with me if I run?"

"I will try," she said, "but my shoes have a high heel,
and this may slow us down."

"Then we must leave the path, and take to the ground,
where it will be harder for others to follow. Come!" He
broke into a run, but kept his pace slower than what he
would have done, were he alone.

"Where are we going?" she called after him.

"Into the woods. Our trail will be harder to find there."

"Yes."

Under normal circumstances, Black Eagle would never
have doubted his ability to outrun an opponent. However,
the lady's silken skirts were long, and he could hear the
material catching onto stickers and other brambles under
foot. Plus, her shoes were unfit for the tangles of the various
grasses and bushes. As he jumped a branch that was blocking his path, she tripped over it, and fell face forward.

Luckily, her skirts buffered her fall, and though he was
certain she was unhurt, he ran to her, and bending toward
her, said, "Forgive me. I thought the branch was low enough
to cross easily. Are you injured?"

"No, but I cannot run as fast as you."

"Then if you will permit me . . ." He reached his arms
around her, his embrace encircling her. "I will carry you."

She didn't object. Truth be told, when he stood up to his
feet, she wrapped her arms around his neck, and he found
himself delighting in their soft feel against him.

"Are we to camp here in the woods, then?" she asked.

"*Nyoh*. Yes."

"Have you considered that if they follow, they might
find us?"

"We will remain in the woods, but in a place that I doubt
they will see."

"Truly? There is such a place? Even if they look for us
far and wide?

"Even then."

"Yes. Oh, please do hurry there."

He didn't really need to be told. Though he little understood what drove her, he sensed her urgency.

What had happened? he wondered.

As he ran, he enfolded her more securely in his arms, and she was so close that he could sense the fear in her. Alas, every cell in her body communicated it.

Had someone threatened her? If so, whoever it was would have to deal with him.

As he hurried forward, his feet found their pace and his exertion practically lifted his feet off the earth. The wind against them, however, had her skirts flying up in his face, but she grasped hold of her petticoats and folded them in toward her. Then she turned her face in toward him, hiding her eyes against his chest.

What a feeling she created in him. It was as though she were saying with her body that she placed herself completely in his trust. It made him feel a little taller, a little bigger, a little stronger.

As he ran, his senses leapt into full play, and he could practically taste the odor of her cologne. He was also more than aware of the enticing scent of the delicate femininity of her; a heady seduction that her perfume could little hide. At first whiff, pure male desire soared within him, but he held it in check. He had one duty and only one duty at present: find them a safe spot.

His direction found him soon within the denser and deeper part of the forest, one that the white man seldom entered. And there, far ahead of him, loomed his destination. It was the tree. Perhaps the only one of its kind, it was an ancient and grand oak tree.

Measuring perhaps six to seven feet across, and with its main trunk standing about ten feet in height, it had at one point in its history been hit by lightning. And what had failed to kill the tree, had become its strength.

The hit had been to the center of the tree's main trunk; it had left an open scar in the center, a scar that over time had developed into a crater that was itself about four to five feet in diameter. The hole in the tree could be seen from above, if one were to climb high up onto the tree's branches. But it could be little detected from the ground.

He shot toward it, splashing through the shallow stream and carrying his prize to the tree, and without explaining why, he lifted the beauty up as high as he could hold her. But the lowest branch was still a little beyond what he could reach.

He said, "Can you scramble up and sit on one of the tree's low branches?"

"Yes," she answered, "I am certain that I can. But why? I'm afraid anyone coming into the woods would be able to see me there."

"Yes, that is true. But there is a reason for you to do so," he answered. "I will lift you up and push you while you grab hold of the branch."

Without further objections, she did so, and it turned out to be easier than he had suspected. Within minutes, she was seated on one of the tree's lowest branches. He climbed up to sit beside her.

"Do we make our way to the top, then?" she asked.

"*Neh*. No."

"But we can be very easily seen."

"It is true. But then, perhaps you should not look down."

She frowned. "Do not look down?"

He nodded. "Beside you. Do not look down."

She glanced all around, looking toward the ground, out into the distance, above her, then down again. But still, she didn't see what was most important to observe. She said, "I fear that I little know what it is I'm supposed to see."

"There." He pointed toward the gaping hole in the tree's trunk. When she still didn't see it, he rose up and maneuvered himself until he was standing beside the cavity, and when she chanced to look away from him, he jumped down.

It didn't take long before she missed him. "Sir Eagle?"

"I am here," he answered.

"Where?" She was scooting on the branch toward the

sound of his voice. "Oh," she murmured barely, before she fell, head first into the hole.

He caught her, although the motion of her fall pushed him back against the "wall" of the tree. But he held her fast, and gradually, he lowered her to the ground. "Can you stand?" he asked.

"I think so. Is the ground uneven?"

"A little."

"And is it filled with dirt and debris?"

"Perhaps. But weather, time and perhaps an animal or two has smoothed the ground a little." He lowered her, letting her feet touch the solidness of the tree's cavity.

She seemed to find her footing easily enough, and standing on her own, she asked, "However did you find this tree? I have lived on this estate all my life and I have never been aware of it."

"That is to be regretted. Perhaps because the white man is not as comfortable in the forest as the Mohawk, he seldom comes here. That might explain it, because it was not a task to discover it. There were signs pointing to it. They only needed to be followed."

"I am certainly glad that you were able to see those signs, then."

From somewhere close to her feet, an animal scurried past her, and startled, she shrieked. He immediately took advantage and pulled her into his arms.

"What was that?"

He chuckled. "I believe it was a squirrel." Then addressing the animal, he said, "You will have your home back tomorrow, friend squirrel."

"Are there other animals here besides squirrels?" she asked.

"There might have been once, but if there were, I think they are gone now."

"Good," she said. Her fear had abated, yet she made no move to leave his embrace. Indeed, she slipped her arms around his neck.

In response, he quietly rejoiced. After a time, he said,

"Tell me, what is this all about? To what do I owe the pleasure of your company?"

Only a sliver of moonlight filtered into their sanctum from above them. Yet it was enough light so that his eyes could see her as well as the space around them. There was not much to their temporary haven. It was crude, smelled musty and woodsy all at the same time, yet he thought he could have willingly stayed here with her in his arms for his entire life, were it not for the necessity to venture forth and eat occasionally.

She didn't answer him at once. Instead, she backed up slightly within his arms and turned her face up toward his. The moonlight caught and captured her features within its misty beams, accentuating the curves of her face. That she glowed with her exertions made her all the more desirable, and he thought he might quietly go out of his mind with the lovely picture she presented him.

Her reddish brown hair had come undone from its confines, and cascades of curls had fallen to her shoulders, presenting her for a moment with a little-girl appeal. As her gaze caught onto his, she said, "I have returned to you against my step-uncle's will because I cannot let you go away from me without letting you know that I . . ." She stopped.

"That you . . . ?" he asked, his tone of voice encouraging. One of his hands nudged her head back against his breast and he rested his chin against the top of her head, where the balmy fragrance of her hair teased at his nostrils. Desire, pure and carnal, washed through him, causing his blood to pool in the center of his body. But he ignored the stiffening of his member, since it was an inevitable result. When she didn't continue speaking, he said, "What I fail to understand is what it is that you fear."

"I little know myself," she said. "Something about my step-uncle is different tonight. Though he has always been a coldhearted man as concerns me, there was an aspect about him tonight that caused me to be uneasy." She hesitated. "I little understand it. But maybe the problem is of my own making. If I hadn't left the party to engage in conversation with you, his disapproval would be less, I think."

He nodded. "It is to be expected since our two cultures understand so little about each other."

"Yes. And yet I am glad that I defied his authority, and that I left to talk to you."

"I, too, am happy about this." As he spoke, his hands began an exploration of her back.

"If you must know, I came back to you to tell you that I will never see you again after this night, and before I go away—before you go away—I would like to know what . . . I would like to know . . ." Again she stopped.

Perhaps he could have taken this moment to ease her concern, since they would clearly be in one another's company in the future. But he was curious as to what was on her mind. And so he waited.

In due time, she continued, ". . . what it's like to . . . if you be willing, that is . . ."

He frowned, and backing away from her slightly, so that he might look down into her eyes, he asked, "Willing? To do what?"

"Can you not venture a guess at my meaning?"

Half teasing, he asked, "Have you returned so that we may engage in more kissing?"

"I have, indeed, done precisely that. Perhaps more, too."

He didn't comment. He couldn't. His heart seemed to be lodged in his throat.

She said, "Tonight is the first occasion where I have had the pleasure of being kissed. And I find that I like the experience very much. But there is more to be accomplished, I think."

"*Weh-yoh*, there is more."

"I suppose that if I were to put it to words, I would have to say that I would like to be loved."

Had he understood her correctly? Was she really admitting what he thought she might be? His body was already prepared for her, but perhaps not so his mind. Therefore, he would be certain, and he murmured, "I love you already, and I have probably done so since the first time my eyes beheld you. Never has a heart sung so gladly as mine did when I first looked upon you."

"No, I fear you do not understand me completely. This time tonight that we spend with one another is all that we will ever have—"

"I must correct you in that idea, because—"

"Please, let me finish," she interrupted. "Our time together is short, tonight only I fear, and I find myself unable to let you go without . . ."

He waited.

"Sir Eagle, I want you to not only love me, but to make love to me." She said it in a rush. "Perhaps I wish this as an act of defiance against my uncle. Pray, do not think that by admitting that I take away your influence upon me. In truth, I little know why I have chosen to do this. I can only say that it feels right, that I seem to be unable to leave you this night without coming to know what it might be like to love and to be loved. Perhaps I may never have this opportunity again. If I use you for this purpose, please forgive me."

"There is no need for me to forgive you. You do nothing wrong."

"In truth?" she asked. "Mayhap only time will tell. All I am certain of at this moment is that . . ."

"You wish to engage in a night of love . . ."

She was silent, but she fell in toward him. It was her unspoken consent.

He needed no further proof, and while his heartbeat hammered in his chest, he whispered, "A man would be foolish, indeed, if when presented with a gift as precious as what you offer me, he would question it too thoroughly."

She whimpered slightly.

"Then come," he said, "let us make ourselves as comfortable as possible."

As the night air took on an atmosphere of softness and security, he turned her round and pressed her back against the "wall" of the tree.

"Is it safe here?" she asked in a voice no louder than a murmur.

"I believe that it is, and though this is not the most comfortable, nor romantic setting, the white man seldom comes this far into the forest."

"Pray, I think you misunderstand me," she said, "I mean is the tree strong enough to hold us if we should be too . . . active . . . ?" She paused, while his heart quietly sang.

His voice, he feared, trembled with unspoken emotion, as he said, "There is none so sturdy as the mighty oak. Her roots grow deeply in the earth, for her will to survive is great. She is strong and will protect us."

He sensed more than he could see that her gaze at him was wistful, urgent and sensuous. It was this last that caused him much trouble with logical thinking, he feared. Now that they had arrived at a degree of some safety, and he knew with certainty what was demanded of him, his body reacted in the age-old language of love.

Pressing her up against the tree, he commenced to kiss her, his tongue darting in and out of her mouth. She swayed in his arms, and he went quietly out of his mind. He pulled up her dress and pushed her up a little higher, his arms holding her. He whispered, "Have you ever been loved by a man?"

"Never, but please do not let that stop you. I want . . . this."

He groaned. "I, too," he whispered. "I, too. Come, wrap your legs around me."

She obeyed as if only in this way could she ease the need within her. He kissed her lips, her face, her throat, all the while he held her above him.

"Oh, please," she urged, as she leaned her head back, opening herself up to his kisses. "Hurry. Please."

"Hold tightly to me," he said, "for this will hurt at first. I am sorry, but it cannot be helped this, your first time."

"Hurt? How can something so exciting hurt?"

"I fear it cannot be helped. And I would be less a human being if I did not warn you."

"I . . . thank you, I think."

He reached up under her skirts to discover that pure femininity awaited him: There was no barrier of clothing to bar his access of her. He kissed her urgently, his tongue playing with her as he trailed his lips down over her cheeks, her eyes, her ears. And as he kissed her, and she sighed, he gradually made himself a part of her, there at the junction of her legs.

But he could only go so far; he knew it hurt her. He stopped, he waited, and he said, "We will proceed only when you are ready. Know, however, that though it would be hard on me, I would tell you again that there is no need for you to go further into the deed if you have changed your mind."

"Sir Eagle," she said, "it is not in my nature to stop when I have committed myself to a course. Please, make love to me."

He swallowed hard, wondering what he had done so right of late that he should deserve this little bit of paradise. At her acquiescence, however, he became more fully a part of her, continuing to halt for a moment with each thrust. Then it happened, and he felt her protective sheath surrender to him.

Though his spirits soared, he was well aware of the hurt she was sustaining, and after another moment's pause, he breathed, "There is no going back now. But the worst is over. When you are able, try to move against me. After the first few attempts, it may yet feel good to you."

Dutifully, she obeyed and its effect on him was more than he would have thought it would ever be. Indeed, as her hips moved over him, he quietly went out of his mind.

Taking her lips into his own, he thrust his tongue into her mouth as urgently as if he would make love to her in this way alone. As he kissed her, he thrust his manhood into her sheath more urgently, then he retreated, repeating the motion over and over. And when she sighed, he sighed with her.

The rhythm began in earnest, thrust, withdraw, thrust, withdraw. She tightened her inner muscles against him, and it was all he could do to hold back his seed from her and allow her some measure of pleasure.

"Do you feel anything but pain?" he whispered urgently.

"Oh, yes." And she whimpered a little.

He sighed, "I am thankful."

Her breathing was erratic, and when she strained against him at the zenith of her exertion, he gave to her exactly what he knew she craved. His seed burst from him and her cries of exaltation were caught by his lips. Over and over the pleasure washed through him until at last he stood quietly against her, his arms, as well as this thighs holding her up.

He could barely move, was still very much joined with her, when the feeling of rightness swept over him. And as the scent of their lovemaking became heavy on the air, it alone seemed to act as an aphrodisiac. Indeed, instead of softening and becoming less, he found himself hardening, ready to continue.

He moved against her, and to his amazement, she was ready for him all over again. And so they danced and they swayed to the rhythm of love, until at last well exhausted, they fell against each other.

It felt so right, yet how could it be so? They were wrong for each other, and he knew it. Despite this, he had told her tonight that he had loved her. And strange though it was, he had meant it. However, if he had thought that he had loved her before making her his own, it paled in comparison to how he felt now.

Nonetheless, even as his body rejoiced in hers, a wiser part of him questioned how this had happened. How had he fallen in love with someone who, because of their differences, could prove to be antipathetic to him?

But with her body pressed up closely toward his, it was

difficult to continue along this line of thought. Ecstasy was simply too pleasurable a mistress for such negative thoughts.

Gradually he lowered her to the "floor" of their nook, and taking his blanket from around his shoulders, he made a bed for her, bending to place her gently upon it.

"I will never forget you," she whispered.

"Nor I, you," he uttered, as he took her in his arms. Perhaps now would have been the right time to tell her that he was to be her guide through the wilderness, and that they would be spending much more time together.

But alas, the words never found their way to his lips. Instead, as he laid down beside her, it wasn't long before he drifted off to sleep.


He awoke much later, alone. He knew his mistake at once. He should not have fallen victim to his lethargy; he should have told her.

It was strange that her preparation to leave had not awakened him. His exertions this night must have had more effect on him than he would have ever suspected.

As he sat up and glanced around their woodsy nook, he wondered if it had been no more than a dream. Yet as he rubbed his hands over his face, he realized it could not have been so. His spirit felt too exhilarated for it to have been less than real. Plus, her tantalizing scent was still upon him. Perhaps, he thought, he would never wash again.

He inhaled sharply, as the details of the previous few hours lingered in his memory. And he knew with certainty that he should have told her that their futures lay entwined. He cringed, for he suspected that she meant the experience to be one night, and one night, alone.

To himself, he justified that he had tried to tell her. But, he admitted, his attempts had been meager. Perhaps he had feared that with the truth she might change her mind.

There was no mistaking one detail, however. Her urgency had been such that there must have been some outside influence driving her to seek him out, since he was under no delusion that what she did, she did out of love.

Something had caused this. But what?

As he sat up, he thought that he would find out soon enough. Best to arise, bathe, and prepare to meet the day. After all, he was quite certain that as soon as she discovered her mistake, he would need his wits about him.

# Seven

As Marisa stepped nearer to the Rathburn mansion, she feared to look too closely behind the trees, afraid that she might find some agent of her step-uncle's there. Interestingly, she was not overly concerned over the enormous step into womanhood she had taken—there would be time to explore that later. Rather her mind was awash with reasons and excuses that she could forward to her guardian as a justification for her actions.

*Snap!*

What was that? Was it a twig cracking beneath someone's foot? Although her eyes were well adjusted to the night, she felt momentarily blinded by fright, and she stopped, glancing to the right and to the left. But when nothing materialized to attack her, she stepped forward again, and within moments, broke into a run, the sound of her slippers echoing like a phantom over the ground of the forest.

The hour was late. Perhaps John Rathburn would have retired. Was she being silly to hope that she might escape his wrath?

If only . . .

She, however, expected no mercy. Chances were that her guardian or one of his henchmen would be in attendance in the mansion's corridors, watching for her return like a hawk might anticipate a mouse.

As she ran farther, she at last burst out of the woods, and as soon as her footfalls fell upon the well-beaten path, her steps slowed. Her mind, however, raced. A consideration she hadn't ventured until this moment, came to the fore of her mind, and it was haunting her: Might her actions tonight endanger Sarah's chances of leaving?

Though Marisa had certainly obtained John Rathburn's agreement to release Sarah, might he not change his mind? It would certainly be in character for him to heap his wrath, not on the person responsible for his anger, but rather onto some other poor soul.

Marisa frowned, and was mentally preparing herself a defense for this newly assumed injustice when all at once, the Rathburn mansion loomed largely in front of her. Swallowing hard, she opened the doors of the ballroom's veranda and as quietly as possible, slipped into the house.

Expecting to be halted and upbraided at any moment, she was more than a little concerned when the opposite happened. No one accosted her.

Indeed, she even attained the third floor landing of her wing of the house, and let herself into her own quarters without being stopped or questioned. How strange it was, even eerie. Perhaps it was a symbol of good luck?

But she feared she was being overly optimistic, since it would be out of character for John Rathburn to ignore an opportunity to bring his step-niece to task. Perhaps he would await her at breakfast.

Marisa sighed, realizing that it did absolutely no good to ponder details that hadn't presented themselves. She would learn soon enough what her guardian intended.

Lighting a candle, she immediately set to work. There was much to be done if they were to leave at first light, which from all indications was only hours away.

Should she seek out Sarah's quarters and awaken her?

No. Sarah was the dependable one. She was probably ready to leave, and had been so for many days.

Dragging her trunk out to the middle of the floor, Marisa opened it only to find that it was already packed. Sarah's doing, of course.

Rummaging through the clothing, Marisa pulled out a clean chemise, as well as fresh petticoats. Her dress would need a change, and she opted for an ivory silk brocade with a patterned, floral design. It was cool to the touch, its silky texture sliding against her fingers.

Her body would require a wash, as well, but first, closing the lid, she sat down on the trunk, whereupon she allowed her thoughts to drift to other matters. For the first time since leaving Black Eagle's embrace, she took a moment to consider what she had done.

Was she sorry? No.

Would she commit the deed again, if the opportunity presented itself? Most likely.

Her actions had been, in effect, a declaration of her independence, though perhaps this had been accomplished with some naivety, since only now did she consider that there might be a price to pay—in the form of a child.

A child . . . The thought was extraordinarily pleasant, and she sighed. However, if a pregnancy did occur, she supposed her guardian would whisk her into a speedy marriage of convenience, one that would be, of course, financially prudent for him.

However, upon further thought, she doubted that a child had been formed from this union tonight. Due to Sarah's confidences, Marisa had taken to keeping track of the rhythm of her monthly cycle, and she was certain she had a fragment of protection.

No, all things considered, Marisa was not sorry for her actions. Indeed, it was likely the opposite: This night would be imprinted on her consciousness for the rest of her life.

She would never forget what had happened; she would never forget him. Perhaps now she could marry as her station in life, as well as her step-uncle, mandated was necessary.

A gentle knock came at her door, and she sighed. Time to come back to the world as she knew it.

"Come in," she called softly as Sarah opened the door.

Sarah entered tentatively. "Are you all right?"

"I am well," said Marisa. "I am very well, though tired." Looking up, Marisa started to smile, but the look quickly froze on her face. "Sarah," she said, rising, "what has happened to you?"

Sarah bit her lip, looked away from Marisa, then winced. Her lip was swollen and there was a jagged line of red running from her eye to her nose, as though she had been slapped, or perhaps hit. There were also tears in her eyes and, upon close inspection, there was a rip in her dress.

"Sarah?"

"I have been waiting for you, Miss Marisa. I've been hiding."

"Hiding?" Marisa gulped. "From what? Or from whom?"

Sarah didn't answer.

"Sarah, who did this to you?"

"I . . . I escaped," she said, taking a step forward only to collapse onto Marisa's trunk.

Marisa followed her and knelt down in front of her. "Was it my step-uncle who did this to you? Did he try to . . . ?"

Sarah shook her head. "'Twas not your guardian. 'Twas . . . someone else."

"Someone else? Someone close to my step-uncle? Who could it . . ." Marisa gasped. "Was it James?"

Sarah nodded. "It seems that James took it into his mind to punish me for what he thinks was a wrong that I committed against your . . ."

"Yes?" asked Marisa. "Against my . . . step-uncle?"

Sarah nodded.

Marisa reached up to run her fingers over the rip in Sarah's dress. "Did he . . . did he . . . I have always known that James was a bully, as well as a very bad butler, but . . . He didn't manage to . . . Sarah, did he defile you?"

Sarah shook her head. "He tried to. He did have a whip,

but no, I got away." For a brief moment, Sarah gave the semblance of a grin. "I'm afraid the whip scared me and I bit him."

"Oh, my dear, dear, Sarah!" Sitting up onto her knees, Marisa took Sarah into her arms, and despite the ten year difference in their ages, for an instant, Marisa felt the older of the two. "Has anyone tended to your bruises?"

Sarah shook her head. "No. I've been hiding, waiting for you to come home."

"I see. Can you rise? If so, let us get closer to the candle-light, so I can assess the damage to you. And do not fear. After I have settled you a little, and ensured your safety, I will go to my step-uncle and—"

"No! Please! I fear your guardian worse than I fear James."

"Oh. Yes, of course." Marisa shook her head frowning. "But James should be punished or he might be likely to do something like this again."

"True. However, are we not leaving soon?"

Marisa nodded. "Yes, we are. Perhaps we should go from here at once without any fanfare or 'well thee do.' Let's mend your wounds, change your clothes, and as soon as you've rested a little, we will leave here. I swear, Sarah, once we are away, you needn't ever return. I have obtained my guardian's signature on a document that effectively makes this so."

"You have? But when?"

"Days and days ago."

"But why did you not tell me?"

"I was hoping to make it a present to you, as well as a surprise."

Sarah attempted another smile, but the effort communicated itself more as a gasp. She murmured, "You are too good to me."

"No, 'tis you who have been good to me. You're the closest thing I've ever had to a mother, or perhaps an older sister. All the good of the world as I know it is because of

you. Now, come, I'll take you to your room where you can
rest, if only for an hour or so.

"No," said Sarah at once. "I don't need to rest. In truth,
I also fear going to my quarters for anything, whether it
would be to dress or to rest."

"Yes, of course. Then you shall stay here until we are
set and ready to go. Now, can you remain seated while I
bring the pitcher of water and bowl over here so that I can
dress your wounds?"

Sarah nodded, and Marisa, arising, stepped across the
room to her dresser, there to seize hold of pitcher and bowl.

What a strange night this was, she thought as she picked
up the items needed, which included a bit of muslin to use
in washing. First she had acted out of character, then James.
Even Sarah had reversed roles, going from being the strong,
outspoken nursemaid, to the one needing nursing.

Somehow Marisa couldn't help wondering, was anything else yet to happen tonight?

She hoped not. She sincerely hoped not.

There were already bruise marks forming over Sarah's
arms, and they were almost too numerous to count. Marisa
frowned. There were tears in Sarah's chemise and petticoats, and even a bruise already forming on her hip. Worse,
that particular marking had all the stampings of a whip.

How had that happened? As Marisa pressed the area
gently with a cloth, she noticed that Sarah flinched.

"Did James use a whip on you?" she asked Sarah, as she
touched the area more gently.

"A little. He tried to put me over his lap, as though to
spank me, but I resisted."

"Oh Sarah, 'tis like a nightmare, except that it is wretch-
edly real. Thank heaven we leave here at daybreak."

"Yes. Thank heaven." Sarah paused as she sighed. After
a moment, however, she asked, "And you, Marisa? With
all of my adventures tonight, we have not discussed what

has happened to you. Do you wish to tell me about your exploits tonight?"

Marisa exhaled slowly while she held a cloth to one of Sarah's wounds. Luckily, except for the red welt on Sarah's face, there had only been one place on her upper arm where the skin had been broken.

Slowly at first, Marisa said, "Yes, I do wish to tell you about it. But not now, I think. We have little time to finish the preparations for our journey, and I fear that the telling of it might take hours and hours." Setting down the cloth, Marisa placed her hand over the top of Sarah's and smiled at her friend. "There will be time enough on the trail. For now it is enough to hold the events close to my heart."

"To your heart? Do you love him then?"

"Not love, I think," answered Marisa. "I mean, would I not be a fool to give my love and devotion to a man I could never marry?"

Sarah nodded. "Perhaps. But one cannot always dictate matters of the heart."

Marisa paused. Was she in love? No, it could not be and she would not allow it to be. She understood her role in life, and it was certainly not to become the squaw of some Indian brave.

Glancing up at Sarah, she said gently, "Dear Sarah, now that your bruises are attended to, and you are properly dressed, I should like you to lie down while I set to work on the details of our leaving. Tell me," Marisa continued, arising, "what is left to do to allow us to depart?"

"There is little more that needs being done, I think, except for you to ensure that all the things you wish to bring are packed in the trunk. Then, after you change your dress—you may have forgotten that you need to do that—we have nothing more to do other than to pack our things onto the horses, have a bite of breakfast and be on our way."

"Good," said Marisa. "By the way, did my step-uncle have much to say after I left?"

"Strangely, he did not. He was furious. That much was obvious. But he said nothing to me, nor to anyone else. Instead he retired to his own quarters for the rest of the evening."

"How strange," said Marisa, frowning. "This has, indeed, been an evening of odd occurrences, wouldn't you agree? Do you suppose that my guardian will come down from his apartments early enough to wish me a farewell?"

"It would be strange if he did not, since it will be several months before he will see you again. But do not fret if he misses the opportunity. He might be sulking. As you are well aware, he has been known to do so in the past."

"Yes. So he has. Come Sarah, and let me help you to bed so that you can lie down," encouraged Marisa. "I will need to wash and dress quickly. Are your own things packed and in your room?"

"They are."

"Good. Then I will send for the servants to bring your things to the stables. They can return here later, to attend to my things."

"Yes," said Sarah, and taking Marisa's directions, she lay down on the bed. "Forgive me for saying this, but it will be a pleasure to leave the Rathburn estate."

"I believe you are right," Marisa said, nodding. "I do believe you are right."

The morning was waning, and still the Englishman's servants (three of them in total) were descending on the stables en masse, loaded down with food stuff and feminine articles. They each had dumped—and kept on dumping with each trip—their burdens next to the horses. Each domestic also seemed under the impression that it was his own special duty to instruct Black Eagle on the best manner in which to carry and pack these items.

Although Black Eagle listened to each attendant patiently, he did little more than nod and let the pile accumulate. Thompson could deal with the servants and the supplies. *He* had been hired to lead the English, not to do their bidding.

However, when the darkness before dawn descended upon the countryside, and still Thompson had made no appearance, Black Eagle decided it was prudent to take matters into his own hands. It was time for the constant procession of supplies to end.

How the Englishman thought to travel through the forest so burdened down was best considered by fools and simpletons. Didn't the English realize that these "things" were useless on a trip such as this? Didn't they know that, if overloaded, these "valuables" became more than a mere burden? That they were a means by which any enemy could detect and track them?

Perhaps the English didn't understand that only those men who were heavily armed, who could muster sheer numbers of manpower, dare travel so heavily weighted down. That this party had neither would cause them to be as easy to attack as a wounded deer.

Standing with his arms crossed over his chest, Black Eagle gazed out toward the manor house, where he beheld two more servants approaching the stables. This time they were weighted down with a trunk. Black Eagle shook his head, inhaled deeply and prepared for the verbal battle.


"He will not allow the clothes to be loaded onto the animals, Miss Marisa."

Marisa, who was seated in her room, sharing breakfast with Sarah, stared at the servant boy with dismay. Taking up a napkin, she patted her lips before commenting, "He would not allow . . . what was that again?"

"He told me that no more of your things can be loaded onto the horses."

"None of my things, you say? Who is this man?" asked Marisa.

"The scout, miss."

"The scout? Do you mean Thompson?"

"No, Miss Marisa."

Marisa frowned. "Is he a hired man, this scout?"

"Yes, Miss Marisa."

Marisa grimaced. The morning was indeed becoming surreal. To add to their already numerous troubles, John Rathburn had failed to respond to Marisa's appeal to see him this morning, and Thompson seemed nowhere to be found. Now this.

"I'll go and see to this man." It was Sarah speaking, who, though she was sitting up in bed, munching on a dry piece of toast, yet looked frail and weak.

"No, no, that is unnecessary, Sarah," said Marisa, then to the boy, "Now, let me ensure I understand this. What you are saying is that, late as it is, because of this scout, none of my things have been loaded onto the animals?"

"Yes, Miss Marisa."

"And this trailblazer, if you will, believes he has the authority to tell me what we can and can't take?"

Perhaps her voice was raised up too loudly or too high, she thought, because she witnessed the boy wince. Marisa shut her eyes on a sigh. What else was going to go wrong?

One thing was certain, however. It was useless to take out her frustration on the poor servant. *He* was not to blame. It was this scout, this man who was no more than a mere guide for them.

Marisa opened her eyes and glanced at the boy. "I'm sorry you are having this problem," she said. "Know, however, that it is not your doing. Please, if you would, point me in the direction where I might find this man, since it appears that I will need to see to this myself."

"He is at the stables, Miss Marisa."

"Thank you." Leaning over, she finished scribbling something onto a piece of paper. Done, she folded the note and sealed it, then said, "Please go and take this letter to Sir Rathburn, whom you should find in his rooms. Tell him that I require a word with him before we leave, if you please."

The boy nodded, though he yet looked nervous. He said, "Yes, Miss Marisa."

Marisa smiled at the lad. "Cease your worry," she said. "You've done as well as you could. Now that my breakfast is finished, I will find this scout myself and take the matter up with him personally."

"Yes, Miss Marisa," said the lad as he turned to leave her rooms and go in search of John Rathburn.

Marisa watched the lad's retreating back for a moment, before slapping down her napkin.

"Who can this man possibly be?"

"I little know," said Sarah, "but you should remain here while I go to the stables and resolve this matter for you."

"And have you run the risk of coming into contact with James?"

"I am not a baby, nor am I a rich woman to be waited on."

"Dear Sarah. All my life you have cared for me. You have been more than a governess to me. You are my best friend. It's my turn to serve you. My only concern is that you will be here in my rooms alone, and James could . . . Have you a pistol?"

"No."

Marisa walked to a desk where she opened a drawer and withdrew a weapon. "I know that you can use this," she said, "since we learned to shoot together. Now, if James comes here, use it." She shoved the pistol into Sarah's hands. "I should be gone but a moment."

And while Sarah was examining the pistol, Marisa let herself out of the room, and turned the key in the lock.

Who was this man, she wondered. Who was he, this mere servant, who seemed to believe that he could order their lives? Weren't scouts hired to do little more than lead and mark the way? They were not hired to become small tyrants, were they?

What a morning.

As she stepped away from the door, she picked up the folds of her petticoats, as well as the silk of her dress, and she trod down the corridor, then to the stairs, and finally out onto the grounds outside. She was headed toward the livery. Unfavorably for her, every step along the way served to increase her ire, which was already stirred up by the many peculiarities of the morning.

Thompson still had not arrived, but though the man might see the edge of her tongue, she thought she might forgive him more easily than the next person, if only because she knew he could not be trusted.

But there was no excuse for her guardian, who even now remained locked in his chamber. To date John Rathburn had refused entry to every servant she had sent to bring him greeting.

Marisa grimaced. She could understand that her stepuncle was upset with her, undoubtedly he was also disappointed in her, but his brooding nature this morning only served to indicate his utter lack of regard for her, since even a dressing down was better than nothing.

And then there was Sarah . . . and James to be considered. How could she leave without ensuring that James would be reprimanded?

She reminded herself to remain calm and in control of her mounting anger. After all, such behavior on her guardian's part was nothing new. However, miserably, he was the only family she had ever really known. Quite naturally she wanted to like him and be liked in return . . . an ideal she had long hoped for, but had never attained.

She sighed. Despite herself, it hurt.

# Eight

It was she.

At the mere thought of her approach, Black Eagle could feel his heartbeat lighten, then speed. Unfortunately for him, simply watching her caused his blood to pool in the region of his groin. And like a lad of sixteen, he was ready for her.

But he was a man, not a lad, and, as a man should when passion is uncalled for, he curbed his body's inclination. Truth be told, he fully expected her to be upset with him. After all, he had missed his opportunity to inform her of his role, and it took no genius to realize that she was going to be less than pleased when she discovered that he was her scout.

It did him little good now to proffer the justification that he had thought she would still be with him when he had awakened this morning. Unquestionably, he should have told her who he was and what part he was to play in her life as soon as passion had risen between them.

He sighed, watching her approach with an adoration that he could little suppress, prizing the way she moved, the manner in which she dressed, the motion of the wispy

hairs at the nape of her neck as her auburn tresses fluttered
back against the wind. Her dress was flattering to her skin,
as well, being the ivory color of the palest sunrise, with
the sides of the skirt flaring out in the style that the English seemed to favor. That it caused her waist to appear
as though he could span it with one hand was a fascinating illusion. However, haplessly for him, it brought back
to mind the delicate treasures that lay hidden beneath her
gown.

He stirred uneasily, wondering again what would she
say, what would she do, when she discovered who he really
was. Especially in light of the fact that she had clearly
thought to never see him again.

Though Black Eagle might be fierce in battle and coura-
geous against an enemy, he felt neither brave nor gallant
against what he predicted would be her negative reaction. As he stood in the shadows, watching her approach,
he decided that he would wait before announcing himself
openly. And though he appreciated every fluid movement
of her body, he braced himself for the coming skirmish.

"Scout! Where are you?"

Black Eagle frowned. Her tone of voice was harsh, and
she hadn't even seen him as yet. Was there some other
problem?

He didn't step out of the shadows. But he did respond,
saying, "I am here."

"Where? I do not see you."

"I am here by the horses."

She glanced in his direction, and so great was her
beauty, it was all he could do to keep himself from overly
staring at her.

"Oh, there you are. I see you now." She stepped toward
him.

"Scout," she began, "you have taken much upon yourself by denying mine and my maid's clothing and articles
to be packed on the horses. I insist that you allow my servants to load these things at once."

Ah, so that was her distress. Expecting this new problem to be an easier handling than what he had anticipated, he stated simply. "I cannot allow it."

"You! You cannot allow it? And who are you to dictate to me what I can and cannot do? What I can and cannot take on this journey?"

He frowned. "I am your scout. I am also the defender of this party. Your things will be in the way. Therefore they stay here. I have said so."

He watched as her eyes flashed. Watched as her color deepened.

She said, "*You* have said so? I beg your pardon. You have no authority to even have an opinion on this matter."

Unconsciously, he drew his brows together and said, "All creatures have a right to an opinion. The Creator has made it so, and not all the earthly authority of the English can make this different, since only He, the Creator, can take that right away."

She shook her head, took a deep breath, and said, "Do not lecture me. I am not talking about rights. I am discussing what is to be taken on this trip. What gives you the authority to dictate to me? Why, you know nothing about myself or my maid. You know not how long we intend being gone and why each and every item we choose to bring is important. Therefore, you will interfere in this no more, and you will cease harassing my servants in this regard, thank you very much." Picking up the ends of her dress, she turned to leave.

"I disagree."

She stopped and spun back around.

"You? You disagree."

"I do. I am your scout. As such I have the authority to do exactly as I am doing."

"You dare to speak to me in such a manner? To defy me and argue with me? You have been hired, scout, to lead us. No more. What we seek to bring is not within your realm to adjudicate. Indeed, you have no rights in this matter. Understand, please, that your duty on this journey is to obey me."

"I still disagree."

"You cannot disagree. You are a servant. Our servant."

He said, simply, "I am a servant to no man and no woman, and since you cannot find your way through the forest without me, what I say stands."

That he was frustrating her was evident, for she folded her arms over her chest, and frowned at the place where he still lingered, the shadows hiding his identity. She said, "Perhaps you are confused. Is it not you, then, who has been hired to lead us east to the New Hampshire settlements?"

"It is I."

"Do you not realize that by agreeing to do this, you have become my servant?"

"Have I? Did anyone say this to me? Did I openly assent to be your servant? No. Therefore, I disagree."

She sighed. "Understand me. It is a part of the agreement between servant and master that when you are hired, you are beholden to the one who hired you."

"I am beholden to none, and so long as I am scout for this party, I will continue to agree or disagree, and will say what I think at my leisure regardless of what you or any man says."

She bemoaned and glared in the direction where he stood. She said, "Who do you think you are?"

"I am your guide."

"Obviously, but I meant . . ." She paused without finishing her line of thought. Instead, she said, "Who hired you? Thompson?"

"It is so."

"Ah! That explains it. Perhaps you little understand that I hired Thompson; therefore, I could unhire you," she threatened.

He nodded, although he doubted that she could see the movement. He said, "You have that choice."

"And I shall exercise that choice as soon as Richard Thompson arrives. In the meanwhile, you will cease being a nuisance to my servants as they load my dresses and toiletries onto the animals."

"I cannot do that. I will not do that," he said. He took a step forward, coming for the first time into the soft, flickering light of the stables. "It is dangerous to take so many things on a journey such as this. Are you not aware of that?"

"No, and I—" She became suddenly cognizant of him, and as she stared at him, her lips were still parted from whatever else she had been about to say.

He well understood her plight, for she had not recognized him by his voice alone. Indeed, she was as shocked as he had feared she might be, and to reduce the edge of any surprise he had caused, he proffered, "I told you that we would meet each other again. Perhaps I should have spoken more plainly on this matter before . . ."

At first nothing happened; she merely gaped at him. Then her eyes widened, and her expression became set. "You!" she said at last, then, "You!" she stated again, as though she could not believe what her eyes were telling her was so. She took a step away from him. "You are to be our guide?"

"I am."

"And you knew this when you and I . . . when . . ."

"I fear that I did."

"Of course," she said, "you said as much to me. I remember it now. It is only that I didn't realize . . ." She took a few more steps backward, away from him. "Why did you not tell me plainly so that I understood?"

"It was wrong of me not to do so."

"Indeed, it was." She turned so that her back was toward him, and she paced several more steps away from him. "This changes things."

"It should change very little."

"No, I am sorry, but it changes much. You cannot possibly lead us . . ." She paused as an emotion he could little interpret shook her body. Then, almost to herself, she muttered, "And yet you must lead us, since there is no time to hire another." She turned her face to the side, looking at him from over her shoulder. And he was struck by the beauty of her simple profile. So captivating was she that he could think of nothing to say. But it was unnecessary, for she continued, "Had I known that you . . . that we . . . that . . ." She sighed. "Had I known that it was you who had been hired to lead us, I would never have come to you. I would never have . . ."

He paused, as if awaiting her next words, when she said, "As soon as Richard Thompson arrives, I will tell him that you cannot possibly lead our party. Indeed, he will have to take us on this route alone."

"Why?"

"I should think that would be obvious."

"It is unwise to trust your safety to only Thompson. If you do that, then you will only have one man to defend you on your journey, and this at a time when there is a war waging over this land. It's unwise. Besides, there are few white men who know of the safe paths that run through the eastern woods."

"I am certain that he knows them well enough."

"To lead you through enemy country, in such a way that you might arrive with your life still intact?"

"Yes. I'm certain he's more than qualified."

"Qualifications mean nothing to a war party."

"I beg your pardon?"

"What you need is manpower. If you take only Thompson, it could kill you because there is only one to defend you."

She seemed not to hear him. Instead, she began to pace forward, then as though she were unaware of making the movement, she paced back; then forward again, back, which was repeated over and over. He watched her, fascinated.

"Dear Lord," she mumbled after a time, "this is a terrible turn for what has already been an agonizing morning."

"Has something else happened?"

"Yes. I was missed last night, and I'm afraid my guardian, my step-uncle, is set to dismiss me and my maid out of hand, without so much as a kind word in farewell."

"I am sorry."

"Are you?"

"I am, truly," he said. He took a step forward, into the line of her pacing.

But she skirted around him, and passing by him, she said, "I find that hard to believe."

"Why?"

"Because you should have told me about yourself. To not do so is a matter of dishonesty, isn't it? You should have given me the opportunity to think clearly with all the facts available to me."

"I was going to tell you afterward, but you left." He hesitated. "Why did you leave?"

"Because I had other matters to attend to," she said, her pacing growing faster. "And because I never intended to . . ."

He arched a brow at her. "To see me again?"

She stopped suddenly in her tracks, and she turned, presenting him with her back. She said, as though to herself, "What am I to do? I must leave, and yet now I cannot."

"Why must you leave? If you are having trouble with your family, stay and settle whatever is wrong between you before you depart. When you are ready to go, I will be here."

"No, you don't understand. I have to go. Something else has happened that makes this imperative."

He pulled a face. "What else has happened?"

"I cannot speak of it. Know only that we, my maid and I, must leave, and as soon as possible. What a predicament," she continued. "We need a scout and yet I cannot possibly travel with you after . . . after . . ." Her voice broke.

"Is it that you feel I will admire you too greatly?"

She turned her profile away from him, presenting him with the back of her head. She didn't answer.

"Or do you think I might seduce you?"

"No, it is that . . . well, maybe." She bent her head.

He took a few more steps, coming up behind her, and, despite their cross words to each other, it was all he could do to keep his hands to himself. "And if I promise not to?"

"Promise not to what? Not to seduce me?"

"I admit, it will be nearly impossible for me to stay away from you." As if to give emphasis to this fact, he stretched out a hand to press his fingers over the nape of her neck. Nor did it bode well for him that she practically melted beneath his touch. He swallowed hard, then said, "We should marry. You realize this, do you not?"

She sighed. "Do not change the subject. Besides, why should I realize this?"

"Because of the way we are with each other."

"No, I can never marry you. You must see that."

"I do not see that," he said. "What I understand is that when two people share the kind of passion that we have, they should marry, and if bad things are to come at them, then they should face these things together."

"No, what you suggest is quite out of the question."

"And yet, even now you cannot ignore what happens between us; it is rare. Not always is it this way between two people, and where this kind of passion is found, it should be nurtured, for many good things can grow from it. To ignore this natural force, is to disregard the pulling nature of attraction. Always you might wonder about what could have been; I would feel much the same, also. It could destroy our future happiness."

"We will both have to take that chance, I fear, for what you suggest is impossible."

"It is not impossible. What are your objections?"

She blew out a breath. "My objections? Are they not plain?"

"Plain? What is it that you speak of? That we are so different? If so, then perhaps that is all the more reason to make a union."

She scoffed. "Are you mad? Surely you must realize that no one from my culture would recognize such a marriage. They would laugh at it; they would laugh at me. And if we were to have children, they would be born out of wedlock because no one would admit that there could even be such a union."

"Then come and live with me in my village." As if to convince her, he bent and pressed his lips against her shoulder. He noted well that she shivered. "My people would love you."

She moaned and took a step forward, away from him. He followed her, and she said, from over her shoulder. "No. It is entirely out of the question. I am sorry if I have misled you to think that a union between us might be possible. What you ask could never be. Not in *this* world. Besides, we leave the point."

"The point? About your things?"

"No, about your leading us."

He shook his head. "If you must go today, then there is no one else to take you but me. I could ask my people if there is another who could do it. But, know this, it is already the end of the Harvest Moon. Soon the Falling Moon and the Hunting Moon will be upon this land, and no Mohawk will wish to be away from his people when he should be hunting food for the coming winter."

She hunched her shoulders, and he went on to say, "Besides, I would be close to you, if possible. If you would know, it was not my desire to take this job until I discovered that it was you whom I was to lead. Only then did I agree."

Still she remained silent, her head bowed and her shoulders rounded forward.

He proffered, "If you wish me to take an oath to remain distant from you, I will."

"No, you still don't understand. It is not you I fear. It is myself."

He was amazed that she would admit the fact, since it showed a weakness; he loved her all the more because of it.

He said, "If that be the case, then it is important that I do come with you, and if you want me to swear an oath to remain apart from you—"

"No, an oath is not necessary, although it is true that if we were to travel together, I would like you to keep your distance."

He nodded.

"And were we to journey together, I would also like to bring more of my things than what you are allowing."

He shook his head. "Nature will provide all that you will ever need. To take more than this could prove to be a disaster. As it is, I am not in favor of bringing the horses—they are too easy to track. Take only what you alone can carry."

"You would have me walk, then?"

"It is the safest way to travel through the woods. Perhaps we will be able to go by canoe from time to time. But to do otherwise is to court trouble. I would have you safe."

She sighed, and he took the few necessary steps to come up behind her and press his body against hers. "Come, let us forget our disagreements," he placed a hand around her waist and drew her close. "Come share my life with me. Marry me."

"This is madness," she said and she stepped out of his embrace. "I cannot marry you. I will not. Last night was meant to be no more than a sweet indulgence . . . something to remember when I do eventually marry a man of my guardian's choosing, as I am bound to do."

He turned her round then and took her in his arms, and when she provided no resistance, his heart sang. Her words might reject him, her body did not. In truth, her head came down to nestle upon his shoulder as though his strength was there to give no other service than to fit her head perfectly. And he held her; he simply held her.

He sighed. It felt so right, what was between them. Perhaps in time, he might yet persuade her into his life. It was certainly not in his nature to give up.

Bringing his lips to her ear, he first kissed her, then whispered, "Go get your things. Bring only what you can easily carry. Though one might hope that it will never be, there may yet come a time when you will be glad to have brought so little. Go, get your things and let us leave here at once."

She sighed. "You are certainly a unique man. Perhaps the most unusual man I have ever known."

"I am not unusual."

"I beg to disagree. Here I have come to you to either persuade you into doing my bidding or to fire you, and instead, I find myself persuaded."

"Persuaded to marry me or to let me lead you?"

She shook her head. "I can never marry you. This will not change. But I will let you lead our party. Especially since I feel you are right about Thompson. He might only get us thoroughly lost."

"Indeed. It has long been an observation amongst my people that without a Mohawk by their side, the English are as lost in the forest as a child. However, what you say about change is not true. All things change. It is the one thing a man can always depend on. Nothing stays the same." He kissed her, and though she might object to many things about him, she did not reject his kiss. In truth, it was several minutes later before he set her from him, and he said, "Go now, *Ahweyoh*. Get your things. I am prepared to leave here at once."

*"Ahweyoh?"*

"It is what I have decided to call you. It is a good name, and someday, I will tell you a story about *Ahweyoh*, for the two of you have much in common, I think."

*"Ahweyoh*," she repeated. "What does it mean?"

"Water Lily."

As her light-brown eyes sought out his own, she smiled. And it was, indeed, endearing, especially when she proceeded to do the unexpected. She did exactly as he said.

# Nine

As the events of the morning unfolded, Marisa at last managed to influence Black Eagle into readying one of the horses to carry her and Sarah's trunks. Except for food, their trunks were, from her viewpoint, the only articles worth taking. Indeed, once she had narrowed her choices to them alone, all that had been required to win Black Eagle to her cause had been a smile.

Their party, which consisted of herself, Sarah, Richard Thompson and Black Eagle, had left the Rathburn estate much later than originally anticipated. In truth, it was almost noon before they were away.

Much of the delay, she admitted, was due to her own desire to speak to her guardian. However, it had been to no avail. John Rathburn had not, would not, leave his apartments . . . not even when Marisa had sent him a written note asking to see him.

True, he was brooding, but his indifference stung. Alas, it had brought her to tears. But in the end, outside of storming his room and forcing him to talk to her, there was little she or anyone else could do. As Sarah had once observed, one couldn't force another to love them, since, if it were so, all the dreaded tyrants of the world would be beloved instead of loathed.

Thank goodness for Sarah's presence in her life. As Marisa glanced toward her friend, her heart stirred. The cuts on Sarah's face were clean, but they served to strengthen Marisa's determination to see Sarah safely settled. After all, for so many years, Sarah had been forced to endure living within the house of the man who had caused her much grief. And now James was added to that list. Sarah deserved better.

When Black Eagle had first seen Sarah, he had stared at her bruises openly. But then he had looked away and had not said a word. It left Marisa wondering if he were fitting the pieces of the puzzle together.

Marisa took a deep breath and leaned sideways in her saddle. She was tired, having received no sleep the previous night. But the notion of dozing while on the trail was lost to her, due she supposed to the magnificence of the land that surrounded the trail, as well as to Black Eagle, himself, whose unusual way of dressing was having an effect over her pulse rate.

Gone was the black tunic and black leggings from last night and early this morning. In its place, Black Eagle wore a dark blue tunic, belted at the waist. The tips of a buckskin breechcloth, which fell between his legs, were barely visible beneath his tunic, while tight-fitting leggings came up high on his thigh to tie to a belt under his shirt. Red beaded garters were tied around those leggings, just under the knee. That this style of dress left an occasional glimpse of his upper thigh and buttocks was heart-stopping from the feminine perspective, and Marisa found herself gazing at him more often than she thought she ought.

A beaded red blanket laid draped over his left shoulder; it was brought in close to his body and held there by his belt. Also, worn crisscross over his chest were straps that held attached to them pouches for ammunition, as well as a powder horn. There was a tomahawk tucked in securely to his belt and he carried a musket cradled in his arm. Around his neck was a silver gorget as well as a knife case, and there were silver arm bands encircling each arm.

She sighed. His was a slender figure, yet if memory served her correctly, there was solid muscle beneath his clothing, and as her gaze caught again onto the red blanket draped over his shoulder, a vision of that same blanket, which had been laid out beneath her own body last night, came vividly to mind. Despite herself, she felt the blood rush to her face, and to avert her attention away from him and the memories this man invoked, she gazed out into the woodland environment.

The trail was flanked on both sides by deep growth and tall trees so numerous, that at times, they seemed to overpower the sun. At present, both Marisa and Sarah were riding sidesaddle, while the third horse carried their supplies. But it was not visible to her at the moment, since Thompson led the animal, and he was pulling up their rear.

Sarah was lagging behind, Marisa noticed, and reining in her mount, she sent a glance back over her shoulder. She called out, "Sarah, are you all right?"

"Yes," Sarah answered, and brought her horse toward Marisa. "I fear I have been taking too much time admiring the woods. It's beautiful country, yet, it is quite frightening, as well. I keep imagining unknown Indians behind every tree."

"I, too." As Marisa waited, she gazed upward, her vision taking in the cloudless blue sky. To her right and to her left were trees of maple, elm, birch and more, and they seemed to go on forever.

None of this territory was entirely new to Marisa, however, since she had grown up in the woodlands of upper New York State. However, the forest was so beautiful at this time of year, that its charm quite outweighed its terror, at least in her view of it.

When at length Sarah caught up with her, Marisa said, "I think that you should not lag too far behind, Sarah. Perhaps we should make a pact to stay close to one another. Then if something happens, we will each one be there for the other."

"Yes," agreed Sarah. "I'm certain you are right. And I wish I could enjoy it without fear, for it holds much charm."

"Yes, I agree." Marisa smiled. "The woods are beautiful. Perhaps the longer we are on the trail, the more you might come to admire it without fear. Look there, the reds of the maple trees, the oranges of the oaks, the yellows and the greens, they are so vibrant at this time of year. And there are so many of them, that it seems as if the whole forest is afire with color. And overhead"—she gestured upward—"is the bluest of skies."

Sarah nodded. "It almost seems as if the hills themselves are alive."

"Exactly."

By mutual consent, the two women nudged their mounts forward, following after Black Eagle. Within a moment, however, Marisa was contented to continue in the same line of thought, and she said, "Even the air is different from Albany. It has a slight fragrance of pine. Have you noticed?"

"I have. It is, indeed, most invigorating."

At present a westerly wind brushed against Marisa's backside, imparting with it a sense of security, and off to the eastern side of the trail, the sound of a rushing brook lent the air an ongoing sort of music. Moisture from the stream cooled the atmosphere, and made the air sit more easily on the lungs.

Black Eagle, who was in the lead, was by now far ahead of them. In fact, Richard Thompson, who normally lagged far behind, was almost upon the two women.

"Come, Sarah, let us catch up to Sir Eagle. It wouldn't do to have him outdistance our horses."

Sarah nodded, and as they set their mounts into a faster walk, the two women fell silent.

The path they were following was well traveled, and since it took little attention to steer the animal, Marisa let her attention slip back in time, to a few hours previous.

After Marisa had left Black Eagle in the livery, she had discovered that Richard Thompson was awaiting her at the

Rathburn mansion. She, however, had spared the man little regard, not even to admonish him for the lateness of his arrival.

Instead she had gone straight to James. It had been a difficult thing to do, particularly so since the only communication she desired with the man was one that was best done with a firearm. However, she'd had no choice, since he had stood between herself and her guardian.

After admonishing James for his behavior with Sarah, and threatening him with the Albany authorities, Marisa had demanded to speak to her guardian. Now she wished she hadn't even done that. There had been no visible result because of it, and it had required her to speak to a man that she now abhorred.

She had finally written Rathburn a note. Putting her feelings into words had been most agonizing, her shame deepening when her guardian had refused to acknowledge her.

In her note, she had offered her step-uncle an olive branch, had apologized for her "crime" of upsetting him, had even gone on to explain why she had felt it necessary to assert her independence. She had also assured him that he need not worry, for she had every intention of doing her duty by him and, upon her return, would consider marriage.

The last part of her letter, however, caused her to cringe in remembrance; she now wished she could take back the words:

Step-uncle, I beg you to come down and see me off on this journey. Let us put the last few days behind us and renew our liking for one another. I beseech you not to let me go without so much as a fare thee well.

But her pleading had been for nothing. John Rathburn had remained adamant in his condemnation of her. She supposed that to his way of thinking, her independence had wronged him, and there was nothing she could do to repair the damage done.

Marisa sighed, and turning her attention to the spectacular sights of the beauty surrounding her, she tried to set her mind to other things. But like a dark cloud that followed and vexed her, her step-uncle's rejection was not to be put so lightly aside.

The sign read:

### WILTON'S TAVERN
### Last Chance for Rum in the Adirondacks
### Established 1679

The hut was situated about twenty-five miles north of Albany, on the eastern side of the trail. Built of crude logs, the tavern seemed to be an oasis, and Marisa thought that it might very well be the last trace of civilization to be found, at least until they at last arrived on the eastern seaboard in New Hampshire. Positioned on the far right side of the trail, with its front facing out toward the road, it was an unusual place in that its back was built downward, extending out toward a fast flowing stream. Even from a distance, Marisa could see that there were logs cut out for stools, as well as crude tables, which were scattered out back of the tavern. Plus, because the inn was situated on slightly higher ground than the stream, there was a swinging footbridge that extended over the water.

At present, no one was taking enjoyment of the picnic area, and Marisa wondered if the fault were that of the establishment itself, or if the men who might frequent the place felt more at home inside. Whatever the reason, it didn't matter to her. After several hours on the road, it looked to be a little bit of heaven.

Black Eagle, who was at the lead of their party, had paused here, awaiting the women and Thompson, the latter very far to their rear. When Sarah and Marisa drew rein in front of the tavern, they found Black Eagle deep in conversation with the man who might be the tavern keeper.

Upon seeing the women arrive, Black Eagle finished his exchange with the man, and both men turned to walk toward the women. Taking hold of their horses' reins, Black Eagle led the animals to a wooden post erected in front of the tavern, while the innkeeper followed.

As Black Eagle tied the reins to the post, he said, "The innkeeper says there is a room that you could rent for the night, and venison stew for supper. It might be wise to take advantage of the room and the food, rather than exhaust our own supply."

"I think you are right," said Marisa, who accepted the innkeeper's helping hand down.

"Injuns," commented the man under his breath. "Don't rightly know why they feel it beneath them to help a lady down from her mount. Just tain't in their manners, I guess. Welcome, ladies."

Marisa smiled at the man. "Thank you. Am I right in assuming that you might be Mr. Wilton?"

"No, ma'am. Mr. Wilton was my grandpappy. My name's Stiler. Matt Stiler."

"Well, hello, Mr. Stiler. I am Marisa Jameson, and this is my companion and friend, Sarah Strong. We are en route to Portsmouth, New Hampshire, to visit the Appletons, who own property there and who are good friends of my family."

"The Appletons, eh?" Mr. Stiler rubbed his stubbled chin. "Don't think I know of 'em, Miss Jameson, but don't make no difference. You and your maid are welcome to stay here for the night. No charge. Tain't often we have a lady such as yourself stay with us." Stiler paced toward Sarah's mount, whereupon he helped Sarah down from her seating.

"I wouldn't hear of imposing on your hospitality without paying sufficient coin," Marisa said, opening her purse and offering the man two gold coins. "Both Sarah and I understand the inconvenience of guests, though I can assure you that we appreciate your offer."

"Thank you, miss." Stiler pocketed the coins. "Now if you'll both come this way, I'll introduce you to my missus."

Marisa nodded, and taking hold of Sarah's arm, they followed the innkeeper, leaving Black Eagle to await Thompson.

Thompson was drunk. No doubt, that was his slurred voice, along with a few others, that was raised in singing a ditty or two, with one song following right after the other. But the good Lord be praised, Thompson was at least keeping himself holed up inside the tavern and hadn't ventured out into the back, where both Marisa and Sarah were seated.

At present, both the young women were surrounded by log stools and carved tables, which were scattered out back of the tavern. About ten feet away ran a shallow, quick-rushing stream, its splashing against the rocks and the shoreline a welcome backdrop to the rustling of the wind through the trees. Crickets and other nightly creatures were beginning their serenade, while within her line of vision Marisa could discern the figure of Black Eagle, who stood sentry off in the distance.

He was leaning on his musket, and though Marisa was still feeling less than kindly toward him, there was one aspect about the man that she could not deny: He cut a handsome figure. Though she could barely make out the blue of his tunic, the remembrance of how the style of his leggings allowed for a clear view of masculine thigh and buttocks remained etched upon her mind.

Evening was falling over the land, the last rays of the sun coloring the golds, reds and oranges of the leaves with the pinks and corals of sunset. Even the brown bark of the trees, and the dry grass mirrored the sky, allowing a pinkish glow to settle over the landscape. It was an extraordinary sight.

Above her, the clouds were set afire with the same fiery color, while closer to hand, their crude-cut tables and stools mirrored the evening sky. There were trees everywhere, pine, oak, elm, maple and white birch; they surrounded this place, and they sheltered and hid the two women. The scent of smoke, of barbecued venison and of stewing meat permeated the air, and combined with the fragrance of the last vestiges of fall, it induced a feeling of well-being within Marisa.

Odd that such a feeling should come over her in this rough and untamed place. Yet she couldn't deny that something here moved her; it was as though she were awakening from a slumber of mind and soul, as though something within her were being coaxed to life.

She inhaled deeply, recognizing the scent of pine mixed within the other fragrances pervading the air.

"Are you tired?" asked Sarah.

"No," answered Marisa, as she gave Sarah a critical look. Sarah's color was good, however, Marisa feared that only time would heal the cut to her lip, as well as the gash that extended from her eye to her nose. "Are you?"

"Yes. I'm afraid I am very tired," said Sarah. "Indeed, I am looking forward to that bed in the inn. In fact, I think I might enjoy it all the more since it may be the last true bed that we'll be seeing for many a night."

"I believe you are right. Are you thinking of retiring, then?"

Sarah yawned. "The thought has crossed my mind." She smiled. "What of you? Are you ready to go to bed?"

"Not yet I think. But please, don't stand on ceremony. I beg you to seek your bed and rest. It has been an unusual as well as a long day."

"But are you not tired? You have had little to no sleep."

"No, perhaps I should be tired, but I am not. For the moment, my mind is racing and I fear that I would find little sleep if I sought my bed so soon."

Sarah nodded, although she could barely stifle another yawn. She said, "Perhaps it is the food that makes me so sleepy. It was delicious."

"Yes, it was." Marisa's glance at Sarah was again studious. "Should I take you to the inn and tuck you in?"

Sarah grinned. "No, but the idea has some merit. Still, I'm not accustomed to going to bed before you do."

"That very well may be, yet I see no harm, and a great deal of good, in your retiring now. Sarah, I think you need the rest."

"No, I'll be fine."

"Are you afraid I'll be assaulted if you leave?"

"The thought has occurred to me. We are, after all, surrounded by men, many of whom appear to be intoxicated."

"True, but if the men in the tavern get too rowdy, I can appeal to Sir Eagle, who seems to be standing guard over there." Marisa nodded toward him.

"Mayhap that is the reason I should stay." There was a twinkle in Sarah's eye.

"I wouldn't hear of it, Sarah. I'll be fine."

Sarah leaned forward to place her arms on the table. "Marisa, tell me. Do you think you are in love with him?"

"Who?"

"Sir Eagle."

Marisa could feel a muscle twitch briefly in her cheek; she also took her time in answering. But at last, she said, "Were there no one else to worry about—no one to scold me or reprimand me, I might be inclined to consider that question more deeply, since I do find the man fascinating. But as it is impossible to live in a world where there are no other people, I would have to say that I am wise enough not to fall in love with him."

"And if people's attitudes were different?"

"But that is an impossible question: Their attitude is not different. 'Tis bad enough that the one time I decide to rebel, I am unable to hide the occurrence from one and all. 'Twas my fault, I admit, but . . ."

"Ah, I see. When taken as a whole, it would be easier had no one known?"

"Indeed. But I had little time to consider such matters at the time. As you might recall, it all happened quickly. Looking back on it now, I can hardly credit what came over me. There I was at the dance, glancing over to see my guardian's disapproval of me, and the look on his face, and all simply because I was talking to someone he believed was beneath me."

"'Tis too bad that one man feels superior to another simply because of differences in culture."

"It angered me, because it was done despite the fact that the young man has done nothing but flatter me and make me smile."

Sarah shook her head.

"But there was more. For whatever reason, while there at the ball, I had recalled that time long ago, when my step-uncle had called me to his study and had made his plans for my future well known to me. I had forgotten."

"So had I," said Sarah.

"And then there was James. I swear that man has no leave to think badly of me, yet he, too, scowled at me for simply associating with someone that he considered beneath me, and he made a move toward me, as if to stop me. Had I not done what I did . . ."

"You would have been made over into a slave to your step-uncle's whims," said Sarah. "I see it now. If you were to be true to yourself, you literally had no choice but to rebel against your step-uncle."

Marisa frowned, but said nothing.

"And so here you are," continued Sarah, "on a journey with a man upon whom you conferred your favor, thinking to never have the pleasure of his company again."

"Yes. And I fear that each time I see him, I am not only reminded of my folly, but I fear I recall again the satisfaction of his embrace. And Sarah, I cannot do it again. Not ever. You do understand that, don't you?"

Sarah frowned.

"'Tis one thing to do it once in an act of rebellion." Marisa continued, "To then try to put your fall from grace behind you, and to settle down and endeavor to become respectable. It is quite another to continually commit the act that should be confined to only those who are married, or to those who make their living by it."

"And of course you can never marry him, thus to continue the affair would put you in the class of the latter."

"Exactly." Marisa paused. Then wistfully, she murmured, "He most definitely should have told me who he was."

Sarah sat silently for some time, then clearing her throat, she said, "Did you and he talk of what might happen if there were to be a child?"

"No," Marisa answered at once. "But I should have thought of it. It was sheer madness on my part. A pleasant madness, I confess. But madness, nonetheless."

Sarah looked hesitant, but after a time, she said, "Well, since this is to be your only induction into a real romance, I should hope that he showered you with love."

Marisa smiled. "He did."

"And did you return it?"

"At the time, I think I did."

"You could simply refuse to return to Albany," suggested Sarah. "Once we are in New Hampshire, you could find a new life for yourself there."

"You know that is not an option for me. Whatever else my step-uncle might be, he also ensured my upbringing, and for that I owe him at least my loyalty."

Sarah sighed. "Was Sir Eagle's loving enough, do you think, for the memory to last you a lifetime? I ask because you do realize that if you return to Albany, your step-uncle will marry you off to someone else, and certainly to someone of fortune, be the man old and decrepit or young and ugly."

"Yes, I understand," Marisa said, "but have you considered that the man he chooses might be young and handsome?"

"Do you really think so? With your step-uncle doing the selecting?"

Marisa stirred uneasily. "How right you are. And yet I

cannot do anything other than give my step-uncle my loyalty. I do owe him that."

"Do you?"

"You know that I do."

"Yes, I suppose I can understand why you would think so. And yet, I can hardly keep from observing that if a man does not have your best interest at heart, do you truly owe him your allegiance? If a man raised you, yet wished to kill you, would you let him do so?"

"I hardly think he wishes to kill me."

"No," said Sarah, "of course he doesn't. However, the point still remains."

"And it is a point I cannot consider. John Rathburn may be all kinds of vile things. But he took me in and raised me. And I would hardly be worthy of being human if I didn't wish to contribute back to him, would I?"

Sarah touched Marisa's hand. "You are one of the sweetest people I have ever known. Perhaps too good for the likes of John Rathburn."

"If I am so, then it is your making," observed Marisa. She sighed and, extracting her hand from beneath Sarah's, she placed her hands in her lap.

Sarah said, "'Tis too bad that cultures are what they are. Your Sir Eagle is a fine figure of a man, and very devoted to you, I think."

"Yes, and I will take the memory of our night to the grave. But I am who I am."

Sarah nodded. "Do you think he will understand?"

"He will have to."

"Perhaps," said Sarah, "he has a different idea about that than you do."

"Yes," agreed Marisa, "I think he might. Sarah"—Marisa reached out to take Sarah's hand in her own—"you will do your best to shelter me from him, won't you?"

"Of course I will, but I understand now why you did what you did. After all, a little bit of John Rathburn goes a long way. He has kept a stern and unemotional eye on you, ensuring that you have had little contact with anyone else, except of course for me. And this is especially so with regards to the opposite sex. I believe he has overprotected you, and it seems to me that he has done his best to mold you into the image of what he believes you should be, little knowing that sooner or later, you would become your own person."

"Yes."

"He also withheld love from you. And this, when love is so very important."

Marisa nodded, not understanding why there was a knot in her throat.

"I fear that the Iroquois Indians are right in one regard."

"Oh?" said Marisa. "And what is that?"

"A person should be sovereign," said Sarah. "Perhaps because God in Heaven created human beings in his own image, a person, then, was made to rule his own life."

Marisa frowned. "Is that what the Indians believe?"

"Yes, I do believe they do," said Sarah. "Though I know little of them, of course. But as a governess, I have studied them a little, and I am aware that they have a form of government that owes its allegiance not to itself, but to the people."

"Truly?"

"Yes. 'Tis a far cry from England, I must say, where the people are expected to support and give allegiance to the king regardless of what he does, right or wrong."

"Are the Indians a little like the Greeks, then?" asked Marisa. "Have they managed to carve out a republic here in the wilderness?"

Sarah shook her head. "I truly don't know. All I am aware of is that, in their view of it, no one can own another person. And I should say that the more I hear of it, the more I agree. Men and women were meant to run their own lives, not allow a monarch or anyone else, who little knows them personally, to make decisions for them."

"Indeed."

"So perhaps 'tis not so unusual that you would rebel

against the ironclad hand of your guardian. Such sentiments seem to be caught upon wind of late."

"Yes," said Marisa. "Thank you for trying to make sense of it. I'm glad that at least one person on the face of the earth understands."

" 'Tis very easy to understand. Know also that I will do my best to protect you from a man who seems to admire you greatly."

Marisa looked away. She said, "That would all be very good, indeed." She sat in silence for a moment, then said, "I wish my step-uncle had come to see us off."

" 'Twas very ill of him not to do so, and were we still at the house, I would take the matter up with him."

"To your further detriment, I fear."

"Perhaps. But his behavior was reprehensible and someone needs to tell him so."

"I did try to see him before we left. Unfortunately, that required my confronting James, as well."

"Oh?" Sarah glanced down into her lap.

"James was long ago bought and paid for, Sarah. What possessed him to do what he did is beyond me, but I told him to his face that when I returned, if he had not brought himself up before the authorities of our church, and if he had not sought forgiveness from our Lord, I would go immediately and inform the deacon of our church as to what he did to you."

Sarah nodded, and the two women fell silent.

"Well, Sarah," said Marisa in due time, "I think that you can safely seek your bed. I shall join you shortly. But I fear I'm still too overwrought to come to bed yet."

"Yes, I understand. Yet, it is my duty to stay here, not do things to suit myself."

"It is also your duty to take care of yourself. My darling, Sarah, you look exhausted. Now go! I'll be fine. It won't be long before I, too, will seek my bed."

Sarah stifled another yawn. "If you are certain."

"Please," Marisa shooed her off with the flick of her hand. "Go! I promise you that I will be fine."

Sarah nodded, and rising slightly, she placed her hand atop Marisa's shoulder, and said, "The making of one more memory should not scandalize you overly much, but if you are certain you must return to Albany, it should be only one more memory."

Marisa frowned. "I have no intention of seeking Sir Eagle out in order to make one more memory."

"Perhaps not. But I think he does." Sarah smiled. "After tonight, I will guard you well. Good night."

"Good night, Sarah," said Marisa, and glancing in Black Eagle's direction, she wondered if perhaps she should follow Sarah's example and go to her bed this very minute.

It might be safer. However, for the moment, her bed would remain cold.

# Ten

The evening was turning cool, and though Marisa longed for a wrap, she stoutheartedly endured the crisp breeze. From her position on the inn's porch, she could see that the evening star was becoming evident in the night sky. The moon was also rising, and it was extraordinary, being a large, orange orb just above the horizon.

Marisa smiled in fascination of its beauty, and inhaled deeply. This was going to be an exceptional journey, she thought. Indeed, she felt privileged to simply be alive and to witness the panorama of nature, as it spread out its magnificence before her.

Sarah had left, to go to their shared room, but Marisa had been quite truthful when she'd said that despite having no sleep the night before, she was far from tired. Indeed not.

Arising from the stool, where she had been positioned for the past few hours, Marisa stepped toward the flying bridge. At present, the orange moon was reflected on the fast-running water, making the stream appear as if tiny orange jewels were bobbing to and fro within its waves.

How she would love to step onto the bridge. To look

down into the water and admire its sparkling grace. But was the bridge safe?

It rocked slightly in the wind, but then wasn't that the way of bridges that were simply tied down and moored to each side of the water? Surely it was safe enough.

Besides, if it fell, all she would receive was a short dunking, since the bridge was not more than three feet above the water. Plus the stream itself was not deep.

Why not do it? Especially because she might never have another chance.

Stepping her foot onto the bridge, it took a moment to attain her balance, due to the bridge rocking back and forth. But within moments, she had conquered her fear, as well as having attained her balance, and she stepped farther out onto the swinging structure, about midway across.

A warmer and kindlier breeze blew against her, pressing back the tendrils of her hair. It billowed at her dress, as well, causing the silky material to flutter back, accentuating her figure.

The pure scent of the babbling stream beneath her and the pine-scented air caused her to inhale deeply.

Ah, what a feeling. A part of her reached out to the environment, as a peace settled over her. She felt less confined here, freer, as if the woods themselves had coaxed her very thoughts to gain space and move away from her.

It was a good feeling.

A deeply masculine voice said, "How my heart sings to see you. You appear as though you belong in the heavens above us instead of stepping here on the face of this earth."

She looked over her right shoulder to observe that it was, indeed, Sir Eagle, who had joined her, and who was standing on the shoreline of the creek. He was gazing at her with that look of admiration that she was beginning to appreciate greatly.

She said, smiling at him, "Thank you, Sir Eagle. But I assure you that I belong here on this earth, same as you. At least until He decides to bring me home again."

Black Eagle nodded. "Then you do believe that there is a Creator of this earth and sky, a Maker of human beings?"

"Most definitely," she said. "Did you think otherwise?"

"No, but an Indian mind cannot be certain how the English may view life. In many ways, the Mohawk and the English are alike, but often I find differences I cannot explain or understand."

"Differences? What differences are these?"

"Differences of the heart. The heart of the people, for He has created all people."

She sighed and carefully made her way back across the bridge to the shoreline. As soon as she had attained her footing on solid ground, she asked, "And what has caused this desire to delve into the Englishman's heart, Sir Eagle?"

He paused slightly, then said, "I seek to understand you."

"Me? That is not so difficult a task, I fear."

"I disagree. But perhaps I should not try. Maybe these differences are between man and woman and not Mohawk and Englishman." He turned to walk away.

She started to follow him, but hesitated. Was that it? Was the man going to explain himself further or not?

Apparently not. Watching his retreating figure, she knew a desire to call him back, but stopped herself short. It would be better to let the man go, better to not foster any attraction between them, even though she found she had more to say on the matter.

Yet, she wondered about him. What did he mean? Differences between men and women? Eventually, she called out, "Wait." When he didn't respond or comply at once, she raised her voice slightly and commanded, "Sir Eagle, I have more to say on the matter. I order you to wait."

He turned halfway around, a slight grin pulling at his lips. He said, "There it is again. Your ordering me to do your will."

"I simply asked you to wait for me. Besides, I am accustomed to command, since I have that privilege."

"Privilege?"

"Yes, I am at liberty to command others. After all, 'tis natural. Certain people have special privilege and a right to expect others to do their will." She swept forward, pacing toward one of the crude, wooden tables. "Such is the way of things," she continued as she walked. "I did not make the rules. I simply follow them."

He stepped back toward her. "And who," he asked, "gives these people special rights that others do not have?"

"Why the king of course."

"The king of England?"

"Naturally."

"Not the Creator, who made all men?"

She frowned. "Say what you mean."

"Did not the Creator make the king, as well as all human beings? Are we not all here in His image? And if this is so, then all people should have the same privileges, not simply a king."

She frowned. "Sir, what you are saying strikes at rebellion, and I cannot consider it. For, if all of us have the same privileges in the eye of the Creator, then the king would have no authority at all."

"But think, do your own Black Robes not teach that He favors no one man over another?"

She paused. Frowning, she said, "You have taken the concept too far, sir. If what you say were true, then we would all of us have the same intelligence, the same talents, the same beauty. This is easily disproved. Therefore, the Creator must favor some over others. Besides, most people are happy to have no responsibility, to do no more than to serve another."

Black Eagle shook his head. "I have not observed what you say. All people want the same things. They want to eat and be well, to marry and have a family, to watch their family grow and to help them along the way. Where are these people who are happy to have no life of their own, but live only to apply themselves to the will of another?"

"Sir, you confuse me. There are those who command and those who serve. It has always been so."

"It has not always been so. Not with my people. A man is not quite a man unless he is free to determine his own destiny."

She smirked. "This is easily contradicted, sir. If what you say is so, there would be no leaders. Are you telling me that you have no leaders?"

"We have leaders, but a sachem amongst my people would never presume to tell another man how to live, or expect him to do no more with his life than serve the sachem. In my village, a man or a woman is free to make up his or her own mind about all matters concerning their own needs." He stepped forward toward her. "Our chiefs meet in council, not to force people to do their will or command them, but rather to straighten out problems and determine how to serve the people better."

"How to serve? A leader, a mere servant? I find that hard to believe. How can a man be in charge of a group of people and not only *not* tell them what to do, but act toward them in no more capacity than a servant? How is anything to be done?"

"We do much. Do you not have ample proof?"

"What proof?"

"We have fed the English and the Dutch when they were starving. Even the German was welcomed into our homes when his children were crying. We tend our fields, we protect our boundaries and our enemies fear us, for we are unequalled in war."

Marisa wasn't certain what to say. Such thoughts were ideas she had never considered, and she wished to have more time to mull them over. However, when she didn't respond, he went on to add, "All men are and ought to be free to determine what is best for themselves and their families."

She shook her head. "Yes, but sir, consider. If this were so, who then would cook the dinners? Who then would do the many menial jobs that need being done for any society to exist? It sounds like chaos to me."

"It is not chaos. You come to my village and see for yourself."

"I may do that one day. But not now. For now, it is my intention to reach Portsmouth, New Hampshire. That is quite enough for me. All I know is that there are those who rule and those who serve. And I am quite happy with the arrangement."

"Perhaps that is because you command. Tell me, do you consider yourself superior to me? Or perhaps to Miss Sarah because she is your maid? Do you think Miss Sarah would be happier waiting on others, or devoting her energies to making her own life?"

"I . . ." Marisa was aware that she hesitated. She didn't know how to respond to such radical thoughts, and she stammered, "I . . . I . . ."

Picking up his musket, Black Eagle stepped toward her, and he said, "Although I realize that you may have been taught that some men exist to be subservient to another, and not to follow the path of their own lives, I do not agree. There are some things that cannot be taken from a man that make this impossible."

"Oh?" She scowled at him. "And what things are you speaking of, sir?"

He paused directly in front of her. He said, "All men, regardless of who rules over who, will think his own thoughts, he will have his own opinions, and he will speak those opinions even if someone tries to keep him from doing so. These things cannot be taken from an individual. They are as much a part of who he is as the color of his skin, the blood that runs through his body. And there is one other thing that cannot be taken from a man," he added, reaching out to run his fingers over the few wisps of hair that had escaped her coiffure, "and that is that he will love whomever he loves, regardless of what others might try to enforce on him."

"Perhaps. But these things you speak of are attributes of a king or a nobleman, not attributes of a simple man."

"Then perhaps we are all of us kings. Kings of our own lives."

Again, she snorted, "What sort of a land is this, where everyone in it is a king?"

"It is the land of the Mohawk, the land of the Iroquois," he said, as his fingers came down to run over the bare skin at her neckline.

She sighed, then whispered, "I fear I still disagree, for I have seen that what I say is true. There are some men who have more intelligence than others, more ability. They were made to take command over others. It is natural."

"It is not natural." He spoke slowly, softly, as though his words were pure seduction. "It is the symptom of a man who has been in too close a contact with the darker side of his character, and has weakened himself because of it."

She opened her mouth to disagree, but he held up his hand and leaned down to whisper in her ear, "A man might have more ability than another, but if he should give in to the impulse to command or enslave another because of that, he is doomed."

It was becoming apparent to her that they were speaking of one thing yet doing another, and to counteract the urge to throw herself into his arms, she took a step backward away from him. She said, "Did you say doomed, sir?"

"I did."

"At risk of repeating myself, I dare to disagree."

Again, Black Eagle shook his head at her. He said, "Being able to foresee events and problems that others cannot envision gives a man only the right to help others to see. As our elders have taught us, he who would stoop to enslave, always becomes himself enslaved in the end. His destiny is forever damned."

She blew out her breath, perhaps to show him that she still disagreed, but instead, the motion came out as a sigh, and she swooned in toward him.

He continued, "Perhaps the Creator made it so as a test of a man's nature. But as our elders have often counseled, he who abuses his power over another is ruined, and from that moment on, is forever cursed. He might amass material things, but that is all he can, all he will ever have. His future, his soul is forever destroyed."

She gasped. Whether she liked it or not, Black Eagle had struck a chord with her; he might have been discussing her step-uncle . . . Her step-uncle had amassed material wealth, he commanded others, he destroyed others for profit. Was he forever doomed? Was she, since she had been raised under his roof, thinking much the same as he?

Stunned momentarily, she became silent. Turning away from Black Eagle, she paced back to the bridge, and placed a dainty foot upon its edge. She noticed without really taking note that the moon was now higher in the sky, and that it had changed color. Now, instead of the water reflecting orange-colored jewels, it looked to be a cascade of shimmering diamonds, floating aimlessly toward an unknown source. She was tired, however. She wanted time to consider these matters in her leisure, and so she said, "Let us not argue about this. Can we not agree to disagree?"

"Yes," he said, and his voice was close behind her. "Perhaps we can do that for now."

She stepped out farther onto the bridge, and silence fell over the two of them, until she asked, "Won't you join me on the bridge?"

"No," he said. "I can better protect you from here."

"Protect me?" She turned too suddenly, and the bridge swung out from underneath her. Quickly, she took hold of the railing and, gaining her footing, righted herself. "I was about to say that I felt we were in a safe place, but perhaps I had better state such things once I reach firmer ground."

She smiled, and had barely uttered the words, when a shot rang out beside her. As though in slow motion, she realized that she could feel the air of that passing musket ball as it sailed much too close to her head. Was it intended for her?

"Get down!" shouted Black Eagle.

But the bridge was already swinging to and fro, and she was slow to action, and as another shot rang out, again, she could feel the wind of the passing bullet. This time the reality of what was happening became a horror, and she screamed.

Meanwhile, Black Eagle had leapt toward her, and tackling her, he pushed her down onto the bridge. But their motion only served to set the bridge, which was already swinging, into further motion, and within moments, one of the ends of the bridge came loose. It shot downward, then stopped.

"Stay with me," Black Eagle coaxed. "We will slowly crawl back to solid ground."

But it was useless. No sooner had they started a crawl toward the shoreline, than another shot rang out, but this time, it hit the knots holding the bridge secure. At once, the rope unraveled, came loose from its ends and the bridge collapsed.

Marisa screamed, and Black Eagle yelled, "It's going down, hold tight to me!"

And then they were plummeting feet first into the cold, liquid depths of the stream. The water wasn't deep, perhaps no more than six feet in depth, and they hadn't far to fall. Although it was a given that they would most likely survive the dive, the mere shock of the cold water might have caused Marisa to panic and drown herself, were it not for Black Eagle, who kept a firm arm around her.

A wooden log from the bridge came down fast and hit her in the shoulder as it went sailing down the stream. She screamed under the impact.

And then the undertow of the water took hold of them, washing them downstream.

"Do not fight the water," Black Eagle shouted at her, as she kicked out against him.

"But we'll drown!"

"We will not drown. I will not let you. Hold tight." A strong current momentarily tugged them below the surface of the water. But he quickly emerged, bringing her with him.

And then they were riding out what seemed to her to

be a watery highway. There were sharp rocks and shoals waiting, however—she remembered seeing them from her former perch on the bridge.

But soon, she realized that her feet could touch the bottom of the stream, and that she could stand up against the flow of the stream, though the water came up to her chin. But she couldn't move, the impact of the water was that strong.

A muscular arm still held her round the waist and she looked up to see that Black Eagle was forcing his way to the shore, bringing her with him. Only a few feet stood between them and safety.

But it might have been a hundred feet if only because the force of the water barely allowed for movement. *This man must be made of pure determination*, she thought, for it wasn't easily done. He forced his way to shore, even though the current kept tugging them farther and farther downstream.

Never had Marisa swum in water that swirled and dipped and coaxed a person under its surface so furiously. Yet the shore became ever closer and closer until all at once Black Eagle picked her up in his arms, and carried her out of the water, up the stream's steep banks.

They were wet. They were both breathing heavily, but as Black Eagle set her down, not even the mud and the sharp rocks on the shoreline could daunt her from the urge to kiss both him and the ground at the same time.

Throwing herself in his arms, she did exactly that. Had she been on her own, she thought, she might have given up, she might have drowned.

Luckily for her, Black Eagle had been there for her.

He set her on the rocky shoreline, brought himself up over her and bending, kissed her firmly on the lips. And she kissed him right back, and with fervor. The kiss was long, however, and he seemed to suck the breath right out of her, and when she squirmed beneath him, unable to breathe, he must have realized what effect he was having, for he blew breath right back into her, then he drew away.

She gasped. But the good Lord be praised, oxygen filled her lungs.

"Are you all right?" he asked, his own breath coming in spurts.

"Yes, I believe I am," she panted between sobs.

"Come, I am sorry, but we cannot stay here. There is no time to relax."

"Who's relaxing?"

He didn't answer, instead he said, "We must hurry. I cannot leave you here, because if I did, whoever it was that shot at you could find you. But I cannot stay here while there are fresh footprints to find. Whoever fired that shot will try to cover his tracks. Can you walk?"

"Yes."

He pulled her up, and letting her lean in against him, they began their trek back toward the inn.

"Someone took a shot at me," she stated the obvious, even as she struggled to keep her pace the same as his.

"Yes, I intend to find out who that was." He fell into silence. "Have you any enemies?"

"No."

"No one who would wish to see your demise?"

"No, certainly not."

He didn't answer, but rather remained a rock-solid pillar for her as she struggled to merely put one foot in front of the other.

At last the inn came into view. There were voices, all loud and raised, and as she and Black Eagle came within sight, the first person who came rushing toward them was Sarah.

"Marisa! Marisa!"

"I am here, Sarah!"

There were tears flowing down Sarah's face. She took hold of Marisa and squeezed. "I swear I will never leave you again. Thank you, Sir Eagle, for your assistance, and for saving her." Sarah placed her arms around Marisa, and

Marisa shifted her weight from Black Eagle's embrace to Sarah's.

"Are you all right, miss?" It was Stiler, the innkeeper, who was followed by his wife. " 'Twas Jacob, miss. He was drunk. He said he thought you was a deer."

"A deer?" It was Mrs. Stiler speaking. "Why I never heard of such a thing. Come here, child. I've got a nice fire ready to warm ye and some soup to give ye back yer strength." Coming up on Marisa's other side, both Mrs. Stiler and Sarah helped Marisa to walk back to the inn.

Mr. Stiler followed. "We's sobered ole Jake up, ma'am, if'n you want to come and speak to him. Yer man, Thompson, was beside himself with worry. 'Twas he who found Jake. I's a heap sorry for the trouble, and I'll give ye back yer gold pieces, as well."

Marisa was beyond words as to how to respond to the innkeeper. She was simply happy to still be alive, and apparently well loved.

And so it was that, after a good hot meal, and the affectionate nursing of Sarah and Mrs. Stiler, Marisa met Jacob, who had approached her with hat in hand. It was easy to forgive the man, especially being surrounded as she was by such friendly and concerned friends.

The only detail that marred her happiness was that Black Eagle hadn't stepped foot into the inn to participate in the luxury of the hot fire and taste the delicious soup. And she couldn't help but consider that he had to be as tired as she was.

It was odd, because, the Lord help her, she missed his friendly, and his sometimes not-so-friendly, presence.

# Eleven

The imprints left in the earth clearly showed two men's tracks, not one. One of the men's prints was, indeed, Jacob's. The other, however, was that of Thompson.

Black Eagle frowned, and rose up from the ground. Looking forward, toward where the footbridge had once been, he could see that Jacob would have had a clean shot. Most likely the man had missed due to the swinging of the bridge, rather than intoxication, as both he, and the others had indicated. Had it truly been an accident?

If not a mishap, however, the incident could only indicate that the action had been deliberately meant. Though it seemed unlikely, he wondered if someone were trying to kill Marisa? And if so, why?

Drunkenness aside, who could have possibly mistaken *Ahweyoh* for a deer? Could it have happened the way the other's explained it?

Perhaps. After all, Marisa had been wearing an ivory-colored dress, a similar color as the underside of a deer.

The only fact that bothered Black Eagle was that both shots had come dangerously close to her, since Marisa had explained that she'd felt the passing whiz of the shots. This

alone, because of the swinging motion of the bridge, insin-
uated that the shots had been carefully aimed, and not the
result of a drunken escapade.

But there was no proof of ill doing, outside of specu-
lation.

Black Eagle's frown grew strained. First the cinches,
now this. Was this incident, like the other, simply a case of
neglect, or was there something about both incidents that
had been carefully orchestrated?

Planned or coincidence, it little mattered. The point was
that he would be well-advised to be on his guard. Events
concerning this party might not be as they seem.


The morning dawned dark and rainy, cold and dismal. Not
the sort of weather one treasured when traveling. It hadn't
started out well, either, not from the very beginning. Upon
stepping from the inn, Sarah had been struck from above
by a heavy branch, which had been precariously perched
on the roof of the establishment.

Luckily, outside of a bruise to her arm, no damage had
been done. But the accident had delayed their start. And in
truth, Marisa felt more than a little happy to remain where
she was for the time being. After her wet escapade the previous night, she was in no mood to travel in the rain.

But Black Eagle was insistent, it apparently being his
opinion that a day consumed in rain-weary travel was a day
well spent.

"We must leave as soon as your maid is ready to proceed," Black Eagle had told Marisa only moments ago. She
had been huddled in a corner of the tavern, where she had
been looking out one of the hut's small windows, awaiting
a change in the weather.

"But why?" Marisa had asked, turning her attention to
him.

"Because it is usually a safer time to travel. If a war
party is about, unless it is pressed, it will seldom move its
position when the weather is bad."

Marisa had sighed. "But it is wet, it is cold, and after last night . . ."

"You should prepare yourself well. If you have a heavy coat, wear it." And with those final words, he had turned to leave, perhaps to make ready for the journey ahead.

After last night, Marisa realized she wanted no further arguments with the man, and so she had capitulated, and had retired to the room that she'd shared with Sarah the previous night. Both women had readied themselves as though they expected a blizzard. Luckily both she and Sarah had brought along umbrellas, as well as heavy, woolen capes for traveling. This, in conjunction with their riding habits, might serve as adequate protection. Marisa hoped it would be so.

However, because of all the delays, their party had once again secured a late start. It was noon, and both the innkeeper and Black Eagle had been working nonstop, equipping the horses for travel.

Marisa, upon stepping foot from the inn, glanced back at the establishment. In reality, she was more than a little apprehensive about leaving. Perhaps it was because their departure today signified a farewell from the civilized world, even more so than their exit from Albany, which had seemed a relief.

Perhaps the feeling might also be due to the fact that now that she had been on the road, the truth of how much her own and Sarah's life depended on the skills of Black Eagle and Richard Thompson became a full actuality. In truth, since her escapade the previous night, she was beginning to wonder if she had really done well in arranging this journey. What had seemed a good idea at the time, was fast becoming an ordeal.

However, whether it was a mistake or not was a moot point at present. The deed was done. There was nothing for it but to press on forward and hope for the best.

Sheets of rain had drenched them all day long. with seldom a letup, and Marisa was cold, wet, ready to stop, set up

camp and recover. However, it appeared that this was not to
be an option. Rather than sleep under a rainy canopy, Black
Eagle had decided to keep moving, even though night had
long ago fallen over the land.

Somewhere in the middle of the evening, Marisa had
decided that traveling in the darkness was eerie. Trees that
during the day were already thick and full, seemed to take
on an additional facade in this unlit realm, giving them a
ghostly appearance. Their branches hung in a phantomlike
manner, as though shadowy arms and fingers were reaching out to capture. Even the hooting of an owl added to the
gloom.

In addition, Black Eagle no longer led their procession
so far in advance. Rather he stayed close beside both herself and Sarah, as if he would protect them from any danger, be that of a human or animal influence . . . or perhaps
that of wandering spirits. Even Thompson, who guarded
them from the rear, and who usually hung so far back as to
be undetectable, was staying close by.

"Do you intend to travel the night through?" Marisa
asked Black Eagle when he had ventured so close by her as
to be within hearing range.

"*Nyoh*, yes," he answered without looking up at her.

"But why?"

"It is safer."

"And yet we are wet and bone weary, and deserve to
stop."

He shrugged. "But at least we are alive and safe. Besides,
there is some adventure to be had in traveling through the
night." He slanted her a glance.

"Oh? And what would those adventures consist of?"

"The exploits of storytelling, of course."

"While we are traveling, and in the rain?"

"*Nyoh*," he said. "Although the Iroquois ofttimes believe
that one should not tell stories in the woods for fear the
animals will hear and become alert to the ways of humans,
I think the rain makes it safe. I cannot participate, but you
and your friend could relate stories to each other, as long as

you keep your voices low. When it stops raining, we will make camp."

"And if it continues to pour all through this night, as well as tomorrow?"

"Then we will carry on and make good time through Adirondack country, I think."

She sighed, and Black Eagle hurried forward, placing himself out of hearing range. But as he had suggested, Marisa and Sarah began to relate various fairy tales to one another. Unfortunately for the both of them, it seemed to cause them to become uncommonly sleepy.

But their drowsiness was destined to be fleeting. So far the weather had produced nothing but rain. That was about to change soon.

*Crash! Boom!*

As Marisa's horse shimmied, she came wide awake. Beside her, Sarah's mount was neighing. Both women reached down to calm their animals.

Another crack darted through the sky, followed by an even louder blast that appeared to set the night on fire. Again the horses protested. Above them, the heavens rolled with white light, hurling swiftly across the sky, and the rumbling of thunder overhead pressed down on the two women ominously.

Looking up, Marisa was struck by the observation that were the lightning not quite so close or its rumbling so frightening, the sky might have provided a beautiful show. But with the crashing of the thunder, the trembling of the ground in reaction, and the fear of a lightning strike seeking them out personally, it was hard to appreciate what might have been a natural fascination.

*Crash! Boom!*

All at once Black Eagle appeared close beside them, and placing himself between the two horses, he took hold of the animals' reins, leading their mounts, himself.

*Crack!* A streak of light slanted through the sky, striking the earth much too close, perhaps only a mile away. An almost instantaneous roar followed, and the ground reverberated under Nature's assault.

Her horse reared.

"Whoa!" Black Eagle sang out to the animals, and Marisa watched as the muscles of his arms strained to keep hold of the two animals, keeping them both grounded. She was doing little more than admiring the sight, when it came.

A flash of light! *Bang! Boom! Crack!*

A tree directly in front of them teetered.

Her horse again reared, but this time it jerked its reins partially out of Black Eagle's grasp, and before Black Eagle could grab back complete control, the animal jumped forward, pulling its reins completely out of Black Eagle's hands.

Instinctively, Marisa screamed, which frightened the animal all the more, and with nothing to hold it back, her mount shrieked away, shooting through the trees and brambles at an alarming and dangerous rate. Instantly, Marisa's world changed, centering on her struggle to keep from falling. Her screams faded, and since the night was black as sin, she realized her only option, if she wished to remain alive, was to lean down over the animal, to pray that its feet were true, that it would not fall, and to hold on for dear life.

She tried to calm the horse with soft words, but it was impossible; over the rain she could not be heard. Besides, she, also, was panicked, and she was afraid that her voice might communicate her own fear to the animal.

How long her mount leapt through the forest, inflicting danger to both their lives, she could never be certain. It felt like a lifetime, however, and as pictures of her life flashed by her mental eye, she wondered if this was to be her last day upon this earth.

She heard the pounding of another horse approaching her from the rear. Was it Sarah come to save her? Or Black Eagle? Or was she imagining it?

Suddenly her nag splashed into water, showering her with a curtain of water, but it hardly mattered. She was already soaked from head to foot.

It did do one thing, however. It slowed the animal down.

"Whoa!"

She recognized Black Eagle's voice.

"Whoa!"

And then he was there beside her, riding Sarah's mount, and he was reaching out for the reins of her steed. He shouted at her, "Fall!"

"Fall?" she yelled back at him. Was he crazy?

"The water will cushion you. I can only hold back your horse for a moment. Fall!"

Only later, in a brief moment of safety, did she realize that she must instinctively trust Black Eagle, for she did exactly as he instructed. She threw herself off her mount, spiraling down into the rushing brook, which, because it was shallow, instantly carried her downstream.

The water was perhaps only two feet deep. But that was enough to cushion her plunge and when at last she was able to find her footing, she came up onto her knees, coughing and spitting up water.

Looking around, she noted that Black Eagle had hurled himself off his mount, and that he was stamping through the water, leaping over it in an effort to get to her as fast as possible.

"Are you hurt?" he asked as soon as he caught up with her, and coming down onto his knees, he ran his hands over her face, her neck, her arms and chest, on down to her waist.

"I am fine, I think," she said between coughs. "Merely frightened."

He let out his breath, and seemingly satisfied, he sank back on his heels. He was kneeling directly in front of her, when he said, "I beg you to never do that again."

"But I didn't—"

"Come here," he said, opening his arms wide to receive her. She didn't even think. She threw herself at him.

It was an infusion of body against body. They were both of them cold, and she was shivering, but as the water gurgled around them where they sat, knee to knee and thigh to thigh, heat began to fill her, and her head came down to rest in the crook of his shoulder. The water, which was at thigh level, pushed against them, and his arms pressed her in so tightly against him, that she thought he must be afraid that the water would sweep her away.

And then he was kissing her as though he might never stop. At first his lips were rough over hers, but then, as passion took hold of them both, his lips became gentler, his tongue delving into and out of her mouth, exploring her as though his most important mission in life was to know her every nook and cranny, not only of her mouth, but of her being, as well.

The kisses never stopped, but the fingers of one of his hands became free and began to explore her, and his palms lingered over her breasts; she groaned and pushed herself in closer to him, wiggling against him, as though she were struggling toward an inevitable result, one that she recalled all too well from the previous evening. His response was to moan deep in his throat, and without preamble, he lifted her skirts up to her waist.

Petticoats and chemise became a cushion, welcoming him to her. And when his fingers came down to explore the warmth and inner sanctum of her femininity, she swooned against him. Again he groaned, again the sound urged her further into passion, and she mirrored him with a higher-pitched moan.

Her response seemed to drive him mad, and placing his arms around her buttocks, he lifted her up over him. It was inevitable. They had already once partaken of the delight that was flaming between them even now, and pushing his breechcloth out of the way, he pressed her up and down over his rock-solid manhood.

She caught her breath. Dear Lord, this felt so right. It was right, and as he became more and more a part of her, she moved against him, savoring each precious moment that he was within her and a part of her.

The rain had turned soft, as though it, too, conspired to bring them together. She moved sensuously against him, and he thrust into her, out, into her again, over and over, the strength of his arms holding her up so that she could fidget in a most feminine way.

Perhaps it was because of her near escape from death. Or maybe there was simply something about this man that excited her. Whatever it was, she wondered if she had ever experienced anything more powerful, yet more precious? It could not be.

An excitement was building down there at the apex of her legs, and, having once experienced love's finale, she recognized the sensation for what it was. It was a moment of wonder, of pure sexuality, and as she pushed toward its peak, her breathing was strained, rapid and, most delightfully, it appeared that what she was experiencing was mirrored in him.

She pressed herself upward, her head back, giving herself up to him, as he accepted, thrusting upward and inward within her. And then it happened; she, who was precariously perched on a precipice, tripped over the edge of that elevation, spiraling into that blur of fulfillment.

She strained against him, that she might expand on the feeling, begging him without words for that firmness she craved, and he gave her exactly what she desired, pressing up hard within her. Faster and faster they strained against each other, and then he released within her; she followed him almost simultaneously. As the rain gently fell over her, she cried out into the silence of the rain-soaked forest, and he groaned, the sound pure male sexuality.

It was perfect bliss, it was sensual beauty, and it was love. Defiantly, as the pleasure of sexual satisfaction filled her body, the truth of her feelings rose up to confront her forthwith, so that she could no longer deny what was so obviously true.

She loved this man. It was an inescapable truth; it was also an enormous, terrible thing to realize, for it was all wrong.

But she was not so foolish as to deny it. Not this time. She loved him. And she need no longer wonder why it felt so right to be in his arms.

But dear Lord, she reflected, what was she to do?

She was given little chance to ponder the possibilities, however, for Black Eagle was still hard and full within her. Once again, he was stirring against her and within her, and the marvel of his lovemaking was beginning all over again.

Once more he brought her to that precipice; once again she tripped over its edge, once again she was ascending upward, as though their love were so great, her spiritual being expanded.

Afterward, he picked her up and carried her to shore, where he set her down on the stream's white, rocky shoreline, its pristine pureness a contrast with the dark, cloudy sky overhead. He came down beside her, instantly wrapped her in his arms, and there they sat, each one quiet, each one content it would seem, to be at peace with their own thoughts.

Sweetly, yet seductively, he leaned down to spread kisses over her cheek, downward and over toward her ear, then anew to her lips, and he said, between each and every kiss, "I love you."

She inhaled deeply, once, then twice, and lifting her chin, so as to give him easy access to her neck, she whispered, "I know."

For the moment, it was all she would confess, but she reckoned that he understood. There was no going back for her or for him. They were in love with one another. What they were to do about this newfound love, remained unknown, for to live their lives with one another could never, never be.


It took them little time to find the horses, since the animals had not strayed a great distance from the stream. Nor did they ride the nags back to where Sarah and Thompson were waiting. Instead, they walked, hand in hand, and like lovers everywhere, they couldn't seem to find a position that was close enough. Every now and again, he would stop, take her in his arms and steal a kiss. Not that there was much stealing about it. She was a willing recipient.

On a certain level Marisa realized she should confess that there could never be a future for them. But somehow the words would not find their way to her lips. Instead, she found herself saying, "What would I do without you? You, who have recused me twice, and in so many days?"

His response was an odd one, for he said, "So long as I live, breathe and walk upon this earth, you will not have to do without me. In truth, I fear it will be difficult for you to get rid of me."

She should have told him then and there. It was important that he be reminded that their lives could never be entwined. But she didn't tell him. It simply wasn't in her to do so.

Instead, she savored every moment with him, for she realized that this might be all she would ever have. There could not be a repeat. And with her hand grasped neatly within his, she pulled on him, bringing him closer to her, and placing her arms around his neck, she said, "I fear to think what would have become of me if I'd had my way and left you behind. I do hope, however, that these accidents are not to become a pattern."

"I, too," he said. "I, too."

# Twelve

After a week on the trail, Black Eagle was more than aware that their days were becoming strewn with too many mishaps. At present, they had stopped and set up camp for the night. Thompson was with the horses. The women were by the stream, rinsing their dishes after the evening meal.

Black Eagle was sitting atop a log, with knife and stick in hand. He was apparently whittling, apparently focused on the shape that was forming on the stick. The truth, however, was that his thoughts were far away.

What was the cause of the accidents? At first Black Eagle had wondered if the women were naturally clumsy. Or perhaps the fault was the weather, since they'd had almost a solid week of rain. But lately he was beginning to speculate that something more sinister might be at work.

That these misfortunes had resulted in only minor injury was hardly the point. That they were happening and that they were sometimes of a fatal nature was the real worry.

One of the mishaps had been related to a fire that the wind had carried into the midst of the women. The result had been that Sarah's dress had caught fire. What had made the incident extreme was that it had happened at a time when they hadn't camped close enough to water to put the fire out.

Luckily, there had been dirt, and much of it close at hand. Black Eagle, Marisa and Thompson had rolled Sarah round and round in the dirt, and though Sarah had required a bath later, it was a small price to pay. At least she had come away with her life, and outside of the shock and a few scratches, there had been little damage.

There was more. There had been the morning three days ago, when Black Eagle had awakened much earlier than the others; he had been away from their camp, hunting. Halfway through the morning, screams from the women had made his heart stand still, and he had rushed back to camp dreading what he would find.

It had been worse than even he could have imagined. A rattlesnake had taken up residence within the women's midst; it had been coiled and ready to strike.

To add to the horror, Thompson had been carelessly aiming at the snake, and had he fired, the shot would have maimed *Ahweyoh*, who was in his line of fire.

Only the utmost presence of mind had enabled Black Eagle to throw a knife fast enough to prevent Thompson from firing that shot. An arrow then sent directly into the head of the snake had ensured that no danger had come to his precious *Ahweyoh*, who had been closest to it.

That this had happened on top of another accident the day previous when one of the horses had kicked out at Sarah, barely missing her head, was stranger yet, since something had fallen onto the horse from above it. A close inspection afterward had found a fallen tree branch; he had also discovered curiously that Thompson had climbed that tree at some time during their stay.

Was it a coincidence?

Or perhaps a wiser question was, were these incidents intended or not?

The problem was, though he was highly suspicious, Black Eagle could prove nothing. Nonetheless, he was finding himself awakening each day, worrying what new misadventure might lie in wait for the women. An even further concern was that he might not always be near to ensure their continued safety.

Noting lazily that *Ahweyoh* had finished her chore and was stepping toward him, as soon as she came into range, he voiced, "There have been many accidents on the trail."

"Yes," she said as she sauntered in closer to him.

Not looking up from his work, he said, "Is it your and Miss Sarah's custom to have so many ills befall you?"

"No," she answered, "I admit it is not." She sat down beside him and placed her legs out in front of her, appearing to be stretching her calf and thigh muscles. "'Tis strange. Have you been considering some theory as to what is happening to cause this?"

He shrugged. "A little. But I have nothing to report except to tell you that you were in Thompson's line of fire the day when you awoke to find a snake as a bedfellow. Had Thompson fired, you might have been killed."

She nodded. "That's why you stopped him from shooting?"

"It is."

"Do you think Thompson was being careless?"

"It is either that or he aimed to do you harm."

"To do me harm? Surely not. Is that what you think?"

Black Eagle didn't answer the question, nor did he defend himself or his theory, rather he said, "I've also discovered that Thompson had climbed one of the trees that hovered over the horse that day when it kicked out at Miss Sarah. I believe a branch had fallen on the horse, which caused its reaction."

Marisa met this news with silence. After a time, however, she said, "Do you suspect Thompson is trying to do us harm?"

"It is either that or these accidents are the subject of misfortune."

Again, Marisa was silent.

He proffered, "You can decide for yourself which is it.

I'm merely speaking to you to inform you of what I have found."

"But if it were intended, why would he do it?"

Again, Black Eagle shrugged. "Have you insulted the man?"

"No."

"Have you done his family any harm?"

"Of course not. In truth, I don't believe he has a family."

"Then perhaps it is coincidence," said Black Eagle. "I have no proof of wrongdoing, and it is well that if a man is going to accuse another, he should be certain of his facts."

"I see. What do you suggest we do?"

"Stay alert. Check over your supplies daily, prepare yourself for anything and be surprised at nothing. But stay alert."

She nodded. "How many more days do you think we have on this trail before we find ourselves in Abenaki country?"

"Not many, perhaps two or three."

"And will we change the manner in which we travel once we are in Abenaki territory?"

"*Nyoh*, yes, since it will be dangerous to travel during the day, we will sleep when the sun is up and travel by moonlight. The Abenaki hate the English almost as much as they do the Mohawk. So, yes, we will change the time in which we travel."

"Will that cause the danger of these accidents to become even more . . . dangerous?"

He paused, then said, "It is so."

She rocked back on the log where they sat and she swallowed hard. "A gunshot, a scream, any loud noise could prove disastrous?"

"It is so."

She sat up and placing her hand over his thigh, she said, "Tell me what else to do."

"I little know since I cannot predict these accidents. All I can advise is to stay alert, and once we reach Abenaki country, to remain quiet, no matter what happens."

"I fear it will be difficult," she said, rubbing her hand over his thigh muscle. "However, I am glad that you're here. Thank you."

He nodded, and ceased his whittling long enough to squeeze her hand. They sat, looking deeply into one another's eyes, before he set back to work with knife and stick. Marisa rose and swung around, and in doing so came face-to-face with Thompson, who was looking at her as though she had taken leave of her senses, as if she were a breed apart.

But he said not a word to her. Quietly, he turned and walked away.

Marisa swung back toward Black Eagle. "Thompson was standing behind us. Do you think he heard us?"

"He might have done so. Therefore, beware," he said. "Trust nothing, and keep your eyes open."

"Yes," she said. "I will."


"Thank you, Sir Eagle," said Marisa, as she stepped up to her horse, where Black Eagle was checking the gear on her mount. He nodded toward her, petted the animal and offered Marisa a hand up.

Marisa accepted his assistance, and as she found her seating, she smiled down at him. How he had changed in regard to English custom, she thought. When they had first started their trek, he'd not lent her any assistance on either mounting or dismounting from her horse. Now, however, he didn't miss an opportunity to help her. However, whether this was due to an inclination toward English manners, or from a desire to touch her was in question.

Of course, she had changed, too. Over and over her thoughts turned to Black Eagle's observations about king, country and servitude . . . and her step-uncle, John Rathburn. Ungraciously, perhaps, John Rathburn was becoming the loser in her musings. Was it wrong to believe that some people were beneath you? That some men and women were born to toil for another? That being cunning and accumulating wealth was more important than life?

Or were all people born with innate freedoms? Details so intrinsic that they could not be detached from one?

Marisa didn't know. Once she had thought she had known. Now she wasn't so sure.

But Black Eagle was speaking to her now, and he said, "Was it you who saddled your pony for me this morning?"

"No," she replied. "Why?"

He frowned. "No reason. But it was already done. Perhaps Thompson completed the task."

Marisa gave Black Eagle a knowing look. "Thompson? When has Richard Thompson done anything on this trip without being asked first? More likely," she added, "it was Sarah."

"*Nyoh*, I'm sure you are right, but perhaps I should ask her, if only to settle my mind."

"Mohawk!" It was Thompson bellowing, and Marisa couldn't help wondering why the man couldn't seem to address Black Eagle by his rightful name. "I need help over here, Injun," Thompson continued. "Damn nag won't stand still."

And Black Eagle, slanting her a look, said, "Stay alert," under his breath and went to do as bid.


"Sarah, look there! Did you see it?"

Sarah drew her horse to the side of the path. "No, what was it?"

Both women, who were sitting sidesaddle, leaned forward, to stare into the forest glen. Marisa said, "I believe it was a bear."

Sarah shivered, and straightened. "If so, then 'tis the first we have seen on this trip. And here I was, hoping we would not come across any a'tall. What kind of bear?"

"I little know," said Marisa, as she too straightened up in her seating. "I hardly had a glimpse of it. 'Twas standing over there," she pointed, "in the dell. But when it saw me looking at it, it turned and sauntered away."

"Good. Let us hope that you frightened it."

"Yes," she said, though personally she thought that was unlikely.

It was still early morning. Gone was the rain that had plagued them last week, and in its place was the most glorious sunshine a person could hope for, the kind that made a person glad to be alive. It was as if Nature were making amends for what might have been her anger this past week or so.

On this day, the fragrance of pure oxygen was in the air, and sunlight was bouncing off droplets of moisture, which still clung to the leaves and the bark of the trees. The ground was muddy and slick, but the clouds overhead were fluffy and light, and the land looked as if it had been washed anew. Black Eagle had once again taken the lead, and was at present so far ahead, that Marisa could no longer see him.

For a moment, she panicked. If something else should befall them, was he close enough to avert a disaster? But then, common sense prevailed, and she assured herself that her worries, and his, were unfounded. Her step-uncle had hired Thompson personally, and while he might be many things, her guardian was not a killer, nor would he hire a killer. Although there was that Pennsylvania town . . .

That they were still traveling during the day seemed to indicate that they were still within safety. For this, she was glad. Riding through enemy territory was likely to be more of a trial than she had ever anticipated. It was odd how, in Albany, the reality of the trail had seemed so much easier.

Albany. Thus far, with the track before them and the beauty of the landscape to take her attention, the journey was serving to put Albany and the problems there behind her. Indeed, it seemed to her as if the more distance that intervened between herself and the town, the less Marisa thought of her step-uncle's displeasure with her. Perhaps when she returned to Albany, John Rathburn, too, would have had the space and the time to shake off his animosity.

At least Marisa hoped so.

Looking forward again, she found that she could still

not see Black Eagle, and she discovered that she missed watching his figure. On that thought, she sighed. What was to be done about him? About them?

Nothing, she answered her own question forthwith. Nothing was to be done about the two of them. Love him, she did. There was no denying it. But as regards any future with him, there was none. On this fact, she would remain firm.

Suddenly she slipped backward in her seating. "Oh! Sarah!"

"Marisa! What is it?"

Marisa's saddle gave, and as she slipped farther backward, she reached out for Sarah when it appeared she could not keep her seat. She screamed. As though from far away from herself, she heard Sarah echo her scream, watched as Sarah rode toward her, as Sarah reached out to her. But it was too late.

Her mount shimmied, neighing, and then it reared. Marisa held tightly to the reins, using all her strength to pull herself up. Sarah, meanwhile, had come up beside her and was reaching out to grab the reins.

Sarah was trying to help, attempting to settle the animal down. However, her actions only served to pull the reins out of Marisa's hands.

Thrown off balance, Marisa grasped for her mount's neck, but she missed and in a split second realized there was no preventing it. She was going to fall. No sooner had the thought manifested itself than she plummeted off the animal, landing between the two horses. Reaction made her scream once, then again, until she hit the ground with a loud *ump*, her left hip and elbow taking the majority of the impact.

Her position, however, put her squarely between her own and Sarah's horse, a very dangerous place, and it took no genius to realize that all that stood between life and a trampling was Sarah's ability to calm both horses.

Sarah might be, and was, the most wonderful person of Marisa's acquaintance, but Marisa knew her friend was not an expert horsewoman. She simply lacked the experience.

"Whoa! Whoa! Stay down!"

As though in slow motion, Marisa listened to Sarah's voice, knowing that her attempts to keep the animals calm wasn't working. There was panic in Sarah's intonation, and the animals sensed it. Marisa's horse reared yet again, barely missing Marisa as its hoofs hit the solid ground. The action also tugged the reins out of Sarah's hands.

What was bad had suddenly turned worse. Marisa's horse was now fully out of control. Bringing her arms up instinctively to protect herself, Marisa hugged the ground, expecting the worst to happen at any moment. But the worst never came.

"Whoa! Whoa! Down, boy! Down, boy!"

It was Black Eagle. It was strange how split-second thinking had her wondering if Black Eagle and his name-sake shared more than a title in common. How had Black Eagle sprinted back to them so quickly? He had been so far in the lead, that it seemed impossible that he should be here now.

Though she expected to be tramped at any moment, Marisa yet looked up to witness that Black Eagle had gained control of her mount's reins, that he had jumped onto her horse's back, and that he was exerting every ounce of his strength to settle the animal.

It was impossible. Marisa thought it was so. Yet it worked. Though his strength was surely tested, Black Eagle's voice remained calm, soothing. Under Black Eagle's guidance, the animal settled down, and what had started as a near tragedy turned melodramatic. Almost at once, and con-trarily, as though nothing untoward had ever happened, her horse quieted and commenced munching on the grass at its feet.

But Black Eagle wasted no time. No sooner had the horse settled down, than he jumped off the animal, turned the reins over to Sarah, and rushed back to Marisa.

He knelt down next to her, and though he said not a word to her, he ran his hands over her everywhere. It was nothing personal, he was merely checking for injuries, and Marisa understood this, yet she found herself basking beneath his touch, wishing for more.

When he was satisfied there was no outward injury, he asked, "Are you hurt?"

"A little," she answered, noting that her voice shook. Still, using her one good arm, she brought herself up off the ground, situating herself into a seated position. "I fell on my hip and my elbow."

"Can you move them?"

"I'm not certain." She raised her arm. It was sore and it hurt, but it seemed she could move it. "My arm appears to be all right," she said. "Can you help me to stand?"

"Not yet," he said. "When you are ready, we will get up. For the moment, collect your breath."

She nodded. "I little understand what happened. One minute I was sitting safely astride my horse, the next I was falling. I hadn't moved or done anything to cause it."

Black Eagle shook his head, but he was looking elsewhere, and when she followed his line of vision, she saw that he was staring at her saddle, frowning at it.

"Lass, are ye well?" It was Thompson, big, sweaty and surly Thompson, who was trudging toward them. He was leading the pack horse behind him, but as soon as he saw her on the ground, he dropped its reins to rush toward her. "What has happened to ye?"

He was the last person she wanted to see, yet she kept her voice civil, when she said, "My saddle would not hold me and I fell."

"Yer saddle would not hold ye?"

Marisa watched as Thompson glanced around the clearing. His gaze alit onto something, and he strode toward the object, which was lying about thirty feet away from Marisa. "Is that the one?" he asked, pointing.

Marisa looked up to see what he was referring to.

"Yes," she said, "that's my saddle."

Thompson squatted down next to it, appearing to study it. At length, he picked up the two leather straps that were used to buckle the saddle into place. They were clearly severed.

"This be the problem, lass," said Thompson. "'Tis the fault of the leather cinches. They be old and insecure. This saddle should never have been used. Did ye check it, lass?"

"Well, no." *But Black Eagle had done so this morning*, she added to herself. Or had he? Hadn't her nag already been saddled?

Marisa turned her attention toward Black Eagle, who had come up to his feet during this exchange. There was a look about him that appeared to be stoic, and as though to further the impression, he said nothing.

"Ye, Mohawk, come here," demanded Thompson.

But Black Eagle remained where he was.

Thompson ignored that fact. "Did ye check over the cinches?"

Black Eagle nodded.

Thompson stood to his feet, and he was frowning as he took in Black Eagle's measure. He said, "This be yer fault, Mohawk, since it was yer duty to ensure the safety of these animals, as well as the quality of their equipment. Did I not hire ye to do this? Did I not make it plain to ye?"

Black Eagle didn't answer. Instead he glared at Thompson.

"Do ye see this?" Thompson held the ends of the leather in his hand. "It be an accident waitin' to happen. They be old and withered. By God, man. The lass could have been kilt dead. Why, I've a mind to give ye a sound whipping."

Still Black Eagle said not a word. Nor did he flinch. Instead, he leaned calmly against his musket, which he had positioned on the ground next to him. His look at Thompson, however, was not pleasant.

"Sir Eagle?" Marisa said, as she came up to her feet without assistance, though she did notice that she couldn't put her full weight on her hip. She said, "Sir Eagle, you did check them, didn't you?"

Black Eagle nodded.

"Then ye are clearly to blame," spat Thompson. "Why, I ought to whip ye where ye stand—"

"There will be no whipping of anyone on this trip. Not now, not ever," said Marisa. "After all, little harm was done. I've had another adventure, but I am on my feet and ready to continue traveling, if it is possible to do so without a saddle."

"Ye, Mohawk! Gimme yer blanket for the lady!"

Black Eagle didn't move. Instead, he faced Thompson and the two men stood off against each other, staring at one another as though a battle waged between them.

Marisa, gazing alternately between the two men, said brightly, "Why, that's a good idea. Sir Eagle, may I use your blanket for a saddle? The one that you are wearing draped against your shoulder?"

But Black Eagle didn't answer. Nor did he argue. He said, "You will not need it."

Marisa opened her mouth to speak, possibly to refute him, but it was unnecessary. Black Eagle went on to elaborate, "We will go no farther this day. Prepare to make camp." And without awaiting a reply, he took up his musket, turned around and strode away.

"Damn!" muttered Thompson. "It be the middle of the mornin'! Damn Mohawks! This be no place to make a camp!" As he leaned over to the side of the path, he spit on the ground.

But gross as the action was, as was the man, himself, Marisa hardly noticed. As she watched Black Eagle's retreating back, she realized she hardly knew what to think. Old cinches could be dangerous, and Black Eagle was in charge of the horses and their equipment, but it didn't ring true that he could be negligent; he, who seemed to be always aware and in command of himself and the world around him.

Besides, hadn't he said himself that he hadn't saddled the horses this morning? Who had?

Thompson? Sarah? But did that even matter if the cinches, themselves, were old and worn?

It felt wrong to doubt Black Eagle's competence. He was the man she loved, the man who had come to her defense three times already.

But then, look at who was accusing who. Something about this was wrong, but what that was, she didn't know.

# Thirteen

It was obvious to Black Eagle what had happened, and it was almost certain that it had occurred this morning. Someone had saddled Miss Marisa's mount, not out of a sense of duty or assistance, but rather with the hope of diverting his attention away from a problem.

Certainly, he had performed a routine check of the equipment. But with the saddle already in place, he had missed this.

In the confusion of handling Thompson's mare this morning, Black Eagle had overlooked asking Sarah if she had saddled the animal. Clearly, this had been a mistake, for had he done so, he would have realized that she hadn't accomplished it, and that something else was afoot.

Of course, Black Eagle hadn't expected to have to give the saddles undo attention. Hadn't he observed their ill repair at the beginning of their trip? Hadn't he demanded and received new saddles? There shouldn't have been a problem.

But there was.

Briefly Black Eagle looked up from his work to take note of his surroundings. He had positioned himself on

a large, flat rock that was situated next to the Lake-that-
turns-to-rapids, a body of water that skirted their camp.
As he looked westward, across the cool, clear water, he
reminded himself of the lake's deceptive nature.

The lake was aptly named. Farther to the west the pool
made a sharp turn and began to flow downstream. From
that moment on, the character of the water changed from
one of calm negligence, to one of sharp rocks, waterfalls
with white-crested waves, deep currents and eddies. It was
known to his people as a watery grave, and thus it was a
place to avoid, especially since here, a little farther to the
east, was a calmer water. A place made for easy crossings.

Across the water, his attention centered on the deep,
dark forest that characterized that part of the country. It was
a territory that bordered between Mohawk and Abenaki
land, and since it was fused between the two warring
tribes, the forest was not frequently used by either Mohawk
or Abenaki hunting parties. Thus there would be weeds
and undergrowth that would make their travel difficult.

But it was still the best route to take, if they continued
onward. He had hoped to discourage the women from
leading their horses through such a place. But seeing their
dependency on their trunks, which contained their dishes
and clothing, he had abandoned that hope.

Glancing back toward his work, he examined the cut
leather. At least the damage was repairable, he thought,
and he set himself to work. Gradually, the familiarity of
the chore, as well as the calming sound of the water hitting
the shoreline, allowed his mind to wander.

Marisa's screams from earlier in the day echoed in his
memory. The sound had been heart-stopping, and taken as
a whole, amidst the neighing and commotion of the horses,
he had thought the women were under attack.

And so they had been, but not from a wandering war
party. No, the assault today was something more sinister;
at least with a war party, one knew and could understand
what he faced. Not so this enemy.

The scene that had met Black Eagle, had been a vision

he didn't want to relive, yet the memory kept replaying in his mind. There Marisa had been, huddled on the ground between two horses, one of them with its hooves raised high in the air, ready to trample her.

Even now, he didn't like to consider what might have been, had he been a trifle late. But one thing was certain. What had happened here this day was no accident. Though the leather had been cut to appear jagged and to give the impression that wear alone had severed it, it was evident to Black Eagle that these straps had been deliberately slashed.

It had been for this reason, and this reason alone, that he had issued the decision to make camp early. Not only did he require the daylight to inspect the damage done and to ponder over the probable cause, it would also be easier to mend the saddle in the light of day.

As he continued his work, he noticed that the women had come to sit close by to him, and he listened to them at their work; they were at present engaged in preparing the midday meal. Their feminine chatter was a familiar sound, and the background noise of their voices served to quiet his thoughts, at least a little. For a moment, he let his mind drift from what was really plaguing him, to the women. What would they say, what would they do, if he suggested that they return to Albany?

At present it seemed the only safe alternative for them, and he would put his concerns to them as soon as possible. To continue onward would be insane: This had been no accident.

It was also evident to him that the culprit was Thompson. Who else could it be?

What Black Eagle didn't understand was why. Why was Thompson sabotaging their trip? As its master, wasn't it his duty to ensure their safety? And if Thompson were guilty—and he had to be—was he not then capable of anything?

Out of the corner of his eye, Black Eagle noted that the two women ceased their work. Arising, Marisa took off in the direction of the horses, opposite him, perhaps to check their food supply, while the other woman, Miss Sarah, approached near to him, her direction headed toward the water. As she came in closer, however, she hesitated, then stepped toward him. She said, "Sir Eagle, is the saddle able to be repaired?"

"It is," he replied without looking up at her.

"May I see it, please?"

He nodded, and she strode toward him. Reaching out, she fingered the leather where it had split apart, then she set the pieces back on the ground. "Thank you," she muttered, turning to leave.

But Black Eagle needed some hard questions answered, and this woman might have knowledge of a few facts that were not evident to him. Setting back to work, and without looking up at her, he asked, "Has Thompson a reason to seek vengeance on *Ahweyoh*?"

*"Ahweyoh?"*

"Miss Marisa," he explained. "Has Thompson any reason to want her death?"

"Thompson? Miss Marisa? Why no," answered Sarah. "Why do you ask?"

Instead of answering her question, he asked another. "Are you certain there is no quarrel between her family and his?"

"No, none."

"Has any blood been spilled between them?"

"Of course not. Miss Marisa has led a sheltered life. In all her existence at the Rathburn estate, I am certain that she has rarely, if ever, spoken to the man."

Black Eagle nodded.

"Sir, have you a reason to ask?"

"I do."

"And that reason is?"

Briefly, he glanced up toward the woman. "This"—he raised the leather—"was no accident."

Sarah frowned. "Are you certain? It seems clearly evident to me that the leather is worn."

"So it would appear to the casual eye. But *Ahweyoh*'s and your saddle are almost new. Before we left, I ensured this, myself."

Sarah paused, shifting her weight from one foot to the other. "What you're suggesting, sir, is that t'was done deliberately?"

He didn't answer immediately. In keeping with Mohawk tradition, Black Eagle took his time in replying, choosing his words with caution. Thus, when he spoke, he didn't answer Sarah's question, but went on to say, "In trying to understand a matter that is incomprehensible, it is ofttimes necessary to ask questions. It is not my intention to alarm you, but rather to obtain facts."

"But they barely know one another," Sarah uttered. "Richard Thompson is a business acquaintance of John Rathburn, and John Rathburn is Miss Marisa's guardian, as well as her step-uncle."

Black Eagle nodded. "Then *Ahweyoh* did not hire Thompson?"

"I should say not. Such arrangements are carried on by the men of the family, and that man would be John Rathburn."

Black Eagle nodded, and believing their conversation was at an end, Black Eagle mentally dismissed the woman and set back to work.

However, it appeared that Sarah had further questions, for she went on to say, "Sir, since Miss Marisa's guardian is not here to put some pointed questions to you, I feel it my duty to inquire after a matter of importance."

Black Eagle nodded, but did not look up. He said, "I am listening."

"Sir, what are your intentions as regards Miss Marisa?"

Black Eagle raised his head, and looking up at the woman who was *Ahweyoh*'s companion, he stared openly at her. Then he again dropped his gaze, looking back toward his work. He said, "It is my intention to make her my woman, if she will have me."

"And by 'make her your woman,' do you mean that you intend to marry her?"

"I do."

Sarah paused briefly before saying, "Then allow me to warn you, sir, that such a union can never be. Miss Marisa was but four years of age when her parents died and she was taken into the care of John Rathburn. Since that time, Miss Marisa has been carefully groomed to marry a man of position within Colonial society, a man who will be chosen by John Rathburn when the time comes for Miss Marisa to marry, which will be soon. Therefore, it would do well for you to realize that though Miss Marisa may be fond of you, there is no future in courting her. For her sake, and for your own, I would ask you to refrain from actions that could steal her heart. I, for one, would not see her heartbroken."

Black Eagle inclined his head, hesitating a moment in consideration. In due time, however, he said, "Then she has promised herself to another?"

"Not yet. But she is of age to marry, and soon her guardian will settle her with a man of his choice."

"Of his choice? She is not free to choose a husband of her own accord?"

"No."

Black Eagle's pause was stretched out a little longer this time, and he said, "The English have many customs that baffle the Indian heart. How does this man, her guardian, expect *Ahweyoh* to be happy under such an arrangement?"

"He does not expect her to be happy. Marriages are seldom a matter of the heart. Surely you know this. They are made to settle estates, to join families of prominent people and to promote the general wealth of the two families."

"And happiness is not a consideration?"

"No, although it sometimes happens that couples become happy with one another in time."

"And the children from such a union, are they cheerful?"

Sarah sighed. "I wouldn't know."

"Do you come from such a family?"

"Indeed, I do not. My mother and father were in love, but they were simple folk, of Dutch descent and not English."

Black Eagle nodded. "I appreciate what you say," he uttered, "and you are a good woman to protect the one who is in your care. But what sort of man would I be if I didn't endeavor to make myself known to the woman who holds my heart?"

"A very good man, I should think" said Sarah at once, "since I fear that your actions might hurt her, and yourself, too. Please try to understand that what you suggest can never take place. The English will not permit it."

Looking up fleetingly from his work, he said, "Why would the English not permit it?"

Sarah glanced this way and that, looking anywhere but at him. At length, however, she said, "If you must know, though the English might make treaties with your people and hold to a covenant chain with them, the truth is that they consider the Indian, all Indians, beneath them."

Black Eagle might have been insulted, but he wasn't. Instead he nodded, and said, "Ah, now I understand. On occasion my people also think the same way about the English. All I can promise you now is that I will consider all that you have said, and I thank you for bringing this to my attention."

Sarah might have gone on to explain more, but Marisa had returned and outside of exhaling a heartfelt sigh, Sarah remained silent. However, before she left, she added, "Please consider it well." And turning on her heel, she was gone.

It was all very illuminating, thought Black Eagle. Apparently attaining *Ahweyoh*'s favor as a husband might be a harder task than even he had appreciated. Perhaps it was, as Miss Sarah said, impossible, but that didn't mean he wouldn't try.

As Black Eagle returned his attention to the leather cinches, he realized that, outside of Sarah's warnings about the Englishman's strange rules for marriage, there was one very important detail in their conversation: Thompson had no blood vengeance to account for his actions.

If *Ahweyoh* had done him some wrong, then it would be easier to understand why Thompson might be attempting to kill her.

But to seek to murder a person without some justifiable reason was insane, unless there was more here to be understood. To his way of thinking, there were few reasons to excuse murder. Blood revenge was one. But according to Sarah, and to Marisa, herself, there was no such reason. Defending oneself or one's family against an enemy was another. But *Ahweyoh* was hardly Thompson's enemy.

Bringing war to a man or to a tribe that had done you an injustice was another reason that might excuse murder, although the injustice had to be great, since the action of taking another man's life was akin to entombing oneself in an eternal conflict with another's soul.

*But a white man could be bought with the Englishman's gold nuggets.*

Black Eagle frowned. The concept was one that was foreign to an Indian mind. However, Black Eagle had often heard William Johnson talk of this sort of arrangement.

*Had another person enlisted Thompson to kill Marisa?*

It would explain much if this were so; the lack of driving cause, the underhanded manner in which the deeds were being attempted, the method by which Thompson sought to blame another, thus bringing doubt upon Black Eagle's character.

Yet, if this were so, if someone had hired Thompson to do his dirty work, who was this unknown person?

Black Eagle shook his head. It was unlikely that he would know such a person's identification, since he did not have knowledge of *Ahweyoh*'s acquaintances. However, one thing was certain: If someone had lured Thompson into committing murder, that person would likely be situated in Albany. And if this were so, then that city was not a safe place for his *Ahweyoh*.

*Wah-ah!* This made the dilemma even more complex.

To push ahead without solving the matter of the cinches was to put *Ahweyoh* into constant contact with a killer. But conversely, to return to Albany would be as to put her in contact with the real killer.

What to do?

To Black Eagle's mind, such matters should be handled in a straightforward manner. Therefore, in his consideration, there was only one thing to be done: confront Thompson. Confront him and send him away, back to Albany. And do it as soon as possible.

Glancing toward the women now, he made up his mind to tell them his plans as soon as the chance provided itself.

# Fourteen

"Miss Marisa, mightn't I have a moment of yer time?"

With his three-cornered hat in his hand, Thompson approached Marisa as she stood off to the side of the horses. She was placing their silver dishes, which she had recently dried, into their trunk.

Looking up, Marisa glanced right and left. Where was everybody? Where was Sarah and Black Eagle?

Ah, there they were; she caught sight of them out the corner of her eye. They were close to the water, too far away to provide an excuse to avoid Thompson.

She sighed. She realized that traveling as they were afforded them all with little opportunity to appreciate the finer qualities of life. But Thompson's clothes were greasy and smelled sour, his face was unshaven, his hair was uncombed and his breath would have stopped a rattlesnake's bite.

Indeed, the furthest thing from her mind was to speak to Richard Thompson. Lucklessly, she could think of no valid reason to deny him a chance to present his cause, whatever that cause may be. Closing the trunk that carried their dishes, she sat down upon its lid and said, "Yes? What is it Mr. Thompson?"

"It's about our Indian scout, Miss Marisa."

"Yes?"

"I seen ye two together."

Marisa hesitated. "Yes, I know. Have you an objection?"

"No, miss, exceptin' for this. If'n yer thinkin' of marriage to him, it'll never be."

"Mr. Thompson, I—"

"I know them kind of Indians," he interrupted, "and they don't rightly have real marriages. Two people get together to have children, but afterward, the man can go about his business and have all the women he wants."

"Mr. Thompson." Marisa stood up to her feet. "I think I must remind you that this sort of talk is out of line."

"But if'n I don't tell ye that them Indians don't rightly hold to the same kinda morals as us English, then who's to tell ye?"

"Who, indeed? I thank you for your concern, Mr. Thompson. Your advice is kindly taken, but that will be all for now."

"But Miss Marisa, ye're judging a savage as though he was all civilized, and he ain't. Now, I can see this scout's weaved his spell over ye, but he canna be trusted. These Indians are pagans, savages. Have ye considered that maybe he deliberately let those cinches turn to dust?"

Marisa exhaled on a snort. "Hardly. Sir Eagle has proved himself to be quite competent. Besides, what possible reason would he have to do so?"

"So as he could save ye to get yer favor."

Marisa sneered. "Letting them turn to dust would hardly buy my favor, I assure you. This is nonsense, Mr. Thompson. He risked his life to save me. That alone has won my regard."

"But that's exactly what I be sayin'. He cuts the cinches, keeps himself close by to ye, and then when they give, he rushes back to save ye."

"'Tis utter nonsense," said Marisa. "And what about the other times Sir Eagle has come to my aid?"

"Same thing, miss."

Marisa sighed before she said, "Again I thank you very much for your concern, Mr. Thompson. But I think you have missed the mark on this. Good day."

Thompson's face screwed up into a frown. "Do ye not see? It's workin' on ye."

"Thank you, Mr. Thompson." Then sternly, "That will be all."

Thompson slammed on his hat and turned away, but as he left, he muttered under his breath, "Yep, I'd say he has yer favor." And he left.

Marisa watched Thompson's retreating back; she also fanned the air around her in an attempt to rid herself of the stench of bad breath and unwashed flesh. Perhaps she would lend the man her perfume.

However, Marisa was also frowning. It couldn't possibly be true.

After all, look at who was telling it. It simply was not possible.


The Lake-that-turns-to-rapids appeared to be a calm body of water from Marisa's view of it. It wasn't terribly wide at this section of it, although Marisa could see that farther east it became wider and perhaps deeper. But from her position, the lake appeared to be utterly calm—and teeming with fish.

Their supper had consisted of fish, a welcome surprise from the steady diet of corn cakes and jerky that they'd been subsisting on for the past few days. However, with what had been a pleasure also came a responsibility—there were dishes to be washed.

The sun was still fairly high in the sky, though it was starting its descent toward the western horizon. At present, she and Sarah were huddled next to the water, washing up their sterling silver dishes. Marisa sighed, then sat up and stretched. Both her elbow and her hip were still sore.

"Are you feeling well enough to be doing this?" asked Sarah, her brows pulled together in a frown.

"I am fine."

"You're certain? Because if you need to rest, 'tis not necessary that you help with the cleanup. I can do this by myself."

"I promise you, Sarah, that I am well enough. I've fallen from a horse before and little fuss was made over me then. 'Tis nothing to be concerned with now." Marisa stretched again, then lowered her arms and massaged her elbow. "Sarah, what is your opinion on the events of the day? As you know, Richard Thompson has made the point that Black Eagle should be blamed for the accident. He also spoke to me earlier, and he said quite plainly that he suspected that Black Eagle had let the leather rot quite deliberately—so that he could rescue me.

"Of course it's ridiculous," Marisa continued. "But still, if I might, I'd like your opinion."

Sarah hesitated before she commented. And then, as if choosing her words carefully, she spoke slowly, saying, "I engaged Black Eagle in conversation a little earlier this afternoon, and I saw and touched the cinches that broke. He is at present repairing them. In truth, Black Eagle believes that the cinches were deliberately cut."

"What?"

"'Tis true. He said our saddles were almost new when we started out, that it isn't possible that they would wear so quickly. Of course he could be saying that to cover up his own negligence, but . . ."

"Deliberately cut? But that would mean . . . I find that hard to believe." Marisa drew her brows together.

"I, too," said Sarah. "While I hardly trust Thompson, I did see the severed leather, and it appeared to me that it was old and much used. Not the sort of saddle that one would trust. Yet, I see no point in denying that Black Eagle might have a more discerning eye than I do."

Marisa remained silent, although after a moment, she said, "This is rather disconcerting."

Sarah laid her hand over Marisa's. "So it is. If true, it would mean that the action was consciously done."

"Yes. But it can't possibly be true. Richard Thompson has no reason to have done it; I barely know the man."

"I know." Sarah shook her head. "It is possible that Black Eagle is in error about the leather straps. These Mohawk Indians are not as acquainted with horses as we are, the horse having been in their possession for only a few years. Perhaps Black Eagle overlooked the weathering of the straps, and is trying to place the deed at Thompson's feet."

"But why would he do that?"

"To gain your favor, perhaps."

"Richard Thompson said much the same thing." At first Marisa became very still, then she looked down and murmured, "But he would have no need to do it. He knows he already has my favor."

"Does he? And yet today I warned him away from you."

"But you did so after the accident, didn't you?"

"True. Still, since Richard Thompson has accused him of negligence, Black Eagle might try to soften the blow, for I believe he plans to ask for your hand in marriage."

"In marriage? Did he say that to you?"

Sarah nodded. "Indeed, he did."

Marisa sighed, and looking down, she couldn't help but smile.

Sarah, however, witnessed Marisa's reaction, and she reached out to touch Marisa's arm. "Marisa, think," she said. "I fear it is not wise to encourage Black Eagle overly much. He is besotted with you, and although his embrace might be pleasant to you now, you must think of the future. Where would you live? How would you live?" Sarah paused, then added, "After your upbringing, I doubt that you would be pleased to set up house in a log cabin for the rest of your life, and if you were to take Black

Eagle as your husband, I fear that a log cabin would be your fate."

Marisa didn't respond. And when it appeared that she would add nothing to the conversation, Sarah went on to say, "If you wish to continue to live in the style to which you have been raised, I feel it fair to warn you not to associate with Sir Eagle too closely. There is danger in doing so, since you might fall in love with him. Have you considered that possibility?"

Marisa sighed. "Sarah, your warning is too late. I already am in love with him."

"Marisa!"

"But fear not. I have no intention of marrying him, though I must admit that the idea of doing so is pleasurable, indeed. However, as obstinate as my guardian is, I am and will always be loyal to him. And truly, I believe he would be most displeased to have Black Eagle as a nephew."

Sarah nodded. "Yes. As much as I dislike and fear John Rathbun, I am aware that you are devoted to him. And since this be the case, please, try to keep your distance from Sir Eagle. The man is a handsome man, after all, and he admires you, which is appealing in its own right. There is a strength about him, as well, an independence, if you will, that is alluring, I must admit."

Marisa smiled at her friend. "If you are attempting to dissuade me from my affection for him, you are not aiding your cause."

"Yes, I suppose you're right. 'Tis too bad that you are who you are and he is who he is. But I also know that your sense of duty to your step-uncle would not allow you peace of mind if you were to rebel against him permanently."

"Yes."

"I will do my duty, then, and protect you against Sir Eagle," continued Sarah, "or any other man who might take it into his head to ravish you with praise."

Marisa squeezed Sarah's hand. "Yes, but do not do your duty too well. I am in love with him."

This said, the two women fell into silence, until Sarah suggested, "Perhaps we should return to Albany. Neither of us knew of the exact hardships we would face on the trail. I know 'tis not what you have planned, but . . ."

"Return to Albany?" Marisa repeated. "That would, indeed, be wise, if Richard Thompson is to be trusted. But if he is not, and Sir Eagle is innocent, then the only motive I can fathom for Mr. Thompson's behavior is that of . . . of murder . . . In that case, I am not safe here, and certainly not in Albany."

Both women fell into silence.

"Do you think I may have angered someone in Albany, perhaps some suitor? I have not always been particularly kind to them."

Sarah nodded. "I doubt that a rebuff, alone, could account for attempted murder. But I fear I have come to the same conclusion as you have, although I hardly wish to think of its truth."

The lake was calm, the air was calm, which made the war whoop, off in the distance all the more chilling.

Both Sarah and Marisa looked up. Both looked eastward. Marisa barely suppressed a scream. There, in the distance were two canoes full of what appeared to be Frenchmen and native warriors.

Then came Black Eagle's voice. "*Ahweyoh*! Miss Sarah! Fall down! Stay low!"

They both obeyed at once, and looking up, Marisa saw Black Eagle sprinting down the shoreline, darting toward them, though he was stooped over as he ran. As soon as he reached them, he fell to the ground.

"You must be so quiet that even a mouse would not hear you—we are going to seek cover. Perhaps they didn't see you or hear you. Using only your elbows we are going to crawl to the bushes. Do you understand? Can you do that?"

"Yes." Both women nodded.

He led the procession, scooting inch by inch toward the

shelter of the trees that lined the shore. Immediately, the scent of the earth and the feel of the sharp rocks as they scrapped at her hands and at her skirts became as real as the danger they were facing.

At last the bushes and trees of the shoreline beckoned. Only a few scant inches remained.

Black Eagle was the first to reach the cover of the trees, and as he hid himself behind the bushes, he reached out to pull the women to safety, pushing them down into the grass and weeds.

"Do not arise," he said. "Lie quietly. It is to be hoped that they will go on by without seeing us."

Neither woman said a word back to him. But it seemed to be too much to hope for. From the shoreline, they all watched as both Frenchmen and Indians came canoeing softly into view, paddling on by them. "Ottawa!" whispered Black Eagle.

How Black Eagle could tell the tribe of those Indians from his vantage point, Marisa might never know, but she wasn't about to contradict him. All things considered, they might have managed to avoid detection, had it not been for a silver dish left indiscriminately next to the river.

It glittered and sparkled in the sunlight.

"They have seen it," murmured Black Eagle.

"What?" whispered Marisa.

"The dish. It is only a matter of time before they come to the shore and discover it, and with it, us. Go to the horses, mount them and get away from here. Ride away as fast as you can. Ride toward Albany. That will be safest."

"And leave you?"

"Yes, leave me, and at once. I will hold them off for as long as I can." He was already loading his musket full of powder and lead.

Marisa placed her hand on Black Eagle's arm. "I cannot leave you."

"You must," he said, pausing only briefly in loading. "If you stay, you might be killed accidently. Now go! Both of you!"

Sarah was already scooting away. But Marisa lingered. She placed her hand over his, if only briefly.

"Go!"

"I will, but before I go, I want you to know that I love you."

He squeezed her hand. "I know," he said. "Now go!"

And Marisa quietly backed away.

# Fifteen

There were eight of them, two French, six Ottawa. All were armed heavily: muskets, tomahawks, hatchets and knives, some carrying two muskets. Black Eagle had only the one musket, his hatchet, tomahawk and several knives.

He waited, trying to conceive of what possible advantage he might have over his enemy. He could think of none, not even the element of surprise. Perhaps the enemy would paddle on by without investigating.

It was too much to hope for. One of the canoes, the one carrying the two Frenchmen, carried on forward, the other canoe turned to shore. Black Eagle watched, preparing himself mentally and physically for what was to come.

In the distance and behind him, he heard the women saddling the horses; he listened for the sound of their leaving. There was jostling, the neighing of the animals, scampering feet, then came the welcome clamor of the horses being set to a run. Without looking behind him, Black Eagle drew a deep breath. At least the women would survive.

Perhaps, if he were lucky, the Ottawa would examine

the dish that lay next to the shore and do no more than be happy with the treasure. But even as he thought it, Black Eagle knew it would not be so. The warriors would see that the tracks on the shoreline were fresh; they would know that the imprints were made by the English and that he, their enemy, was among them.

Black Eagle checked his weapons, and clutching his knife in his hand, he waited.

"Sir Eagle!"

What was this? The whispered voice of *Ahweyoh*?

Briefly he swung his head around to look. It was, indeed, *Ahweyoh*. "Why are you not gone?" he asked. "I told you to leave."

"I'm sorry, sir, but we cannot do so," she muttered as quietly as possible. "I fear that Mr. Thompson overpowered us and before we had even attained our seat on the horses, he shooed them off."

This was not good. "Where is Thompson now?"

"He rode away on one of the horses. But before he left, I was able to secure this." She held up a musket.

"Do you know how to use it?" he asked her.

She nodded. "Sarah does, too."

His glance took in the fact that within Sarah's grasp was a pistol. "Both of you," he ordered beneath his breath, "move back behind me," he commanded. "Stay down. Fire only if you have a good shot; otherwise, do no more than watch. If I go down, do not fight the enemy. Yield to them. It is doubtful that they will kill you. Do you understand? Do nothing."

Nodding, the women backed away.

Meanwhile, the canoe slid silently to shore. Black Eagle watched as the warriors disembarked cautiously, keeping themselves low. Slowly, quietly, they brought their canoe inland, anchoring it on the rocks that lined the shore.

Stepping onto the ground, one of the warriors bent down, examining the tracks over the rocks. Another warrior crept forward toward the bushes, where Black Eagle and the women were hiding. The two other warriors were sneaking toward the item that had gained their attention: the silver dish.

Black Eagle waited until the warrior who was stealing toward the bushes was almost upon him. He waited. Then crying out, he jumped up, the savage attack and the element of surprise in his favor. The ploy worked, but only for a fraction of a second. Still it was enough: Black Eagle thrust his tomahawk into the warrior's neck.

However, with the first war cry, the three other warriors went instantly into action. Black Eagle had known that they would, and he was ready for them. With musket in his left hand, he fired a shot toward one of them. An almost instant scream, and another warrior, hit the ground.

Without thought, Black Eagle shot forward toward the other two. They, however, were prepared with muskets ready.

What they didn't know was that women were hiding in the bushes. One of the women fired. It was a good shot, carefully aimed, and another one of the warriors fell.

However, Black Eagle didn't wait to see if the shot had made its mark, instead, he hurled himself toward the remaining warrior. The Ottawa was ready for him, and thrust out at him with his tomahawk. It was a deadly joust, but Black Eagle had expected it and he threw himself down, turning a somersault underneath the man's arm. Coming up on the other side of the man, and with a back hand, Black Eagle rammed his tomahawk into the back of his opponent. The warrior was thrown off balance. Gaining his feet, Black Eagle finished the job, and slammed his hatchet into the warrior's arm, disabling the man.

But still the Ottawa was standing, and taking hold of his tomahawk, Black Eagle dealt the man a clean blow to his chest. The Ottawa went down.

Not wasting an instant, Black Eagle shouted to the women, "Come!" He pointed toward the lake. "Their friends have come back to investigate. Hurry to the canoe. We'll take our chances on the water."

Both women came instantly to their feet, and shooting out of the bushes, they made a line to the canoe. Black Eagle had already set the canoe out into the lake and the women hurriedly splashed toward it.

Once he was waist deep in the water, he shouted, "Get in. Pick up a paddle."

Already, shots from the oncoming canoe were hitting the water around them, their barrage a deadly reminder of what was to be if they didn't escape. The women had attained their seat in the boat, and were picking up paddles, when Thompson suddenly splashed into the water, and pulling himself up alongside of the canoe, he plopped himself into it. He picked up a paddle.

"Let's get out of here!" he yelled and Black Eagle didn't argue. Hoisting himself up into the boat, and settling his paddle into the water, Black Eagle guided the boat out into the deepest part of the lake, heading west, toward the rapids.

It was their only possible advantage. They were already outnumbered, the two men, against the four of the enemy, two French and two Ottawa warriors. Worse, Thompson was an obvious traitor, whose actions could not be trusted. Still, it was Thompson's neck as well as their own.

His plan was a risk. Black Eagle was counting on the fact that the French might not follow them into the rapids, it being well-known that only a fool, or one with no other choice, would deliberately seek out mountain-high waterfalls, which, with its deadly rocks awaiting, spoke of an untimely end.

"Faster!"

Arrows, aimed at them, hit the water beside them. Seeing them, Black Eagle wondered if this spoke of a possible advantage. Was their powder wet? Was that why they were using arrows and not firing on them?

"Faster!" he yelled again.

They had almost gained the passage to the rapids. Meanwhile the other canoe was speeding up on them, and it was a test to see which would come first: the watery death on the rapids, or death at the sure hand of the Ottawas.

And then there was no going back. The current took hold of them, pushing them on at an ever faster and faster rate toward what had to be a waterfall.

It was a double-edged sword: What was taking them away from their enemy held a certain death, as well.

Black Eagle chanced a look over his shoulder. The French and Ottawa were turning back, paddling toward the southern shore. It was surely a truth that if the falls didn't kill them, the Ottawa, tracking them, would.

Their only likelihood of survival was to paddle to the opposite shoreline and then run. Run for their lives.

Black Eagle set the canoe toward the northern shoreline, but the currents pulled him back.

"Damn!" he muttered, using the English cussword. With all his strength, he set his paddle in the water, and headed again toward the northern shoreline. But he had no more than set his course, when an unseen eddy took hold of their canoe and swung them round.

Suddenly another unforeseen force made itself felt upon them: The canoe rocked back and forth unnaturally, and Black Eagle, looking back over his shoulder, beheld Thompson, who had come up onto his knees, had taken hold of *Ahweyoh* and was struggling with her, attempting to throw her out of the boat and into the lethal undercurrents of the eddy.

Marisa was screaming and fighting, Sarah was yelling and beating on Thompson, but it was all for naught. Thompson was too strong.

Black Eagle faced around, and keeping low, surged back toward the struggle to confront Thompson.

*Let the traitor do battle with someone not quite so weak*, thought Black Eagle.

Thompson was big. He was strong. But Black Eagle was more determined. He was also in the right.

The two men wrestled. Thompson raised a knife, Black Eagle blocked his hand, raising Thompson's arm high in the air. Both came up to their feet, even though the canoe lurched precariously against the currents.

Their struggle pitched the canoe out of the eddy, but only into the rushing stream of the currents, washing them steadily toward an even deadlier end. Mountain-high falls awaited.

But the two men didn't notice. Thompson launched out at Black Eagle, socking him in the jaw. Black Eagle was sent backward, but he recovered; he shot forward and caught hold of Thompson's arm, raising it again high in the air.

Both men fell down into the canoe, Thompson looked up, and Black Eagle glimpsed the horror on Thompson's face. Without further pretense at the fight, Thompson let go of Black Eagle and dived over the edge of the canoe, disappearing into the water.

Black Eagle, still in the throes of battle, felt urged to do the same, and take their battle into the water's fatal depths, but with a quick look about him, sanity returned. There were women here to protect.

Glancing forward, he, too, experienced Thompson's terror. Their boat was on a one-way path to the falls.

This was it. They were doomed.

Black Eagle gazed at Marisa with all the love and admiration in his heart. If this were to be his last moment on this earth, by looks alone, he would shower her with adoration. As her look mirrored his, he knew a fraction of a second of happiness. How fleeting it was.

Ripping his glance away from hers, and scanning forward, however, he saw a thing that both he and Thompson had missed previously. It gave them a chance . . .

"Take Sarah's arm!" he yelled. "Don't let go!"

Marisa instantly took hold of Sarah.

With his left hand, Black Eagle grasped hold of Marisa's arm. "Hold tight to me!" he ordered. "Use all your strength. Use everything in you, but don't let go!"

Marisa nodded.

And then their boat, caught in the currents, tipped over the edge of the falls. But there was a branch—a sturdy oak branch—that was extending out over the falls. It was a risk, but if he could grasp hold of it with his arm . . .

Using his right arm, he grabbed hold of the branch as their canoe carried them past it. It worked, he held on with the crook of his arm. The force of the movement swung both Marisa and Sarah up and out, but Black Eagle held on tight. However, there they hung, delicately balanced, he holding *Ahweyoh*, and *Ahweyoh* clutching at Sarah.

Glancing toward shore, Black Eagle used the momentum of the natural force of their swing to aim them back toward the shore. It wasn't that far away.

"Hold on! I'm going to swing you both to shore!"

"I can't keep hold! It's too slippery!" It was Sarah yelling, crying.

"*Nyoh*, you can! You must!"

"I'm trying to, but—"

"She's slipping away from me!"

"I've got you!" He yelled at her. "Keep hold! Keep hold!"

But Sarah's hand was loosening. And though he was swinging them with all his might, Sarah's grip was failing. He could see it happening.

But Marisa wouldn't let go.

"Sarah!"

With a deafening scream, Sarah fell, and Marisa, casting a fated look up at Black Eagle, let her grip on Black Eagle's arm slacken but maintained her hold of Sarah. Black Eagle reached down to tighten his hold over Marisa. But it was too late. She had already let go of him, her screams echoing in his ears.

They were gone. Gone, into the sheet of water that was the falls. Not willing to assign them to their fate without his possible aid, Black Eagle let go of the tree limb. Whatever their destiny might be, so, too, would it be his own.

Somewhere between plummeting down the length of the falls and into the water, Sarah's hand became separated from Marisa's own. Had they not become dislodged dur-

ing the fall, however, the force of the impact into the water
would have accomplished it.

"Sarah!"

"Marisa!"

They hit the water and sank down, down, down. Under-
water, Marisa watched helplessly as Sarah became caught
up in an undercurrent, and before she could reach out to
save her, Sarah was swept away. The tow, however, didn't
take hold of Marisa, and she struggled to rise to the water's
surface. There was one good thing, and perhaps only the
one: Due to the recent rain, there had been deep, deep
water between them and any sharp rocks awaiting them
beneath the falls, thank the good Lord. But the undertow of
the current was another thing altogether.

She fought it, afraid that if she let it take her, there would
be no hope for her at all. Her lungs were aching and her head
was pounding as she struggled to rise to the surface. She
was almost there, and she reached upward, at last emerging.
She gulped in air as though it were a feast. But she had no
more than caught her breath when the water again took her
in its strength and swept her away, forcing her under. Briefly
she rose up again, then back down, over and over.

Had she been able, she would have cried out. But she
couldn't. She could only go with the tow and catch her
breath when possible. It seemed a hopeless struggle.

Still, she hung on, if only in the belief that, somehow,
somewhere, she might find and save Sarah. It was all that
kept her alive.


Black Eagle plunged down deep into the water. The
undertow tried to take hold of him, but he defied it with
raw strength and determination, and fighting to the surface
with all the power of his physique, he surfaced, immediately reaching out to find a grip on something solid, be that
a shoreline or a rock.

Within moments, he'd knocked up against a round rock,
but it was too slippery to cling to, and he washed on by it.

The next obstacle was again a rock, but it was too big and too sharp to grasp onto. Looking ahead, he saw a flat surface within his range—if he could but steer himself toward it. Perhaps he could push himself up onto it.

He kicked his legs, his arms stretching forward, and he fought, and he pushed his way stubbornly toward it. At last, his effort paid off and he grabbed hold of the rock's surface.

The rapids defied him, as if its power were trying to sweep him back into its watery grave, but he withstood its force. Utilizing every muscle fiber in his arms, he pulled himself up onto the rock's wet surface, struggling to pull himself up, until at last it was done. Lying down full face, he allowed himself a moment to catch his breath, and then he struggled to his feet. There was no time to rest. Not only did he have to find Marisa, he must avoid the enemy, who would even now be searching for them.

Looking back over the raging water, he examined its surface for a sign of her. Nothing. He jumped to another rock that was situated farther along the water's path, his eyes scanning, exploring over the water's surface.

What was that? Was it something coral? Could it be the color of her dress? There it was again. Was it the auburn color of her tresses?

A closer look revealed *Ahweyoh*'s body, as it twisted and plunged along with the current. He'd found her.

Never taking his eyes off her, he sprinted over the rocks, jumping from one to another, testing his speed against the force of the rapids. If he could outdistance the current and land on one of the rocks that lay farther out, into the force of the water, he could catch her as she swept by him.

Mustering all his strength, he jumped forward, flying toward another rock. He landed, slipped, caught himself, got his foothold, and turning back, he leaned down into the rapids. A fraction of a second later and he would have missed her. As it was, he had no more than spread out his arms into the water than it tossed her toward him. Reaching out, stretching, he grabbed hold of her with both of his hands and kept hold of her, despite the force of the water pounding against him, urging him to let go.

"*Ahweyoh*! Grab hold of me!"

But there was no response from her.

With one gigantic pull, he hauled her up onto the rock, quickly turning her over to check for a pulse rate or evidence of her breathing. He could find none.

He turned her over, and pummeled on her back to rid her of any water in her lungs. But she still wasn't breathing. Desperately, he turned her over, cleared her mouth of any particles and blew into it. He waited, then repeated the entire thing, blowing life-giving breath into her.

It took longer than he liked to consider, but all at once, she coughed up water, and struggling upward, she drew air into her lungs. He sat back, watching as she labored to find her breath. But finally, the worst was over; her chest began to rise and fall rhythmically and easily.

Only then did he sit back on his heels; only then did he realize that tears were streaking down his face.

*She is alive. She is alive.*

Reaching out for her, he pulled her into his arms, and with his lips, he paid tribute to her. He kissed her everywhere, from the top of her head, down to her forehead, to her eyes, her nose, her cheeks.

"You're alive!"

She laughed. Better yet, she was able to speak, and she said, "Yes! I seem to be!"

"Come." He picked her up in his arms, and carried her away from the rapids, and onto the solidity of the rocky shoreline. Seemingly content to let him do the work, she wound her arms around his shoulders and he thought he might never feel anything quite so wonderful as the feel of her body against his.

He set her down beneath a large maple tree. There was no grass here, only rock, mud and sand, but after their disaster in the water, it seemed as pristine as a sanctuary.

"I think I died a little," he said, as he knelt in front of her, "when you let go of my hand."

"I think I died a little, too. Did you find Sarah?"

He shook his head.

"Please, will you go and find her?"

He nodded. "But we are not safe here, you are not safe here. Even now the enemy looks for us. The enemy has only to go to a place where the crossing is easier and backtrack to find us."

"But surely they'll think we died. And it could have been true. We almost did."

He shook his head. "They will look for our bodies, and when they do not find them, they will come after us. Be assured, I have killed their friends, and they will not rest until they find me and exact their revenge."

"Then I'll come with you. I must find Sarah."

"And can you walk?"

"I will make myself do so."

"No," he said after a moment. "It will be faster if I search for her while you stay here and catch your breath. I will return."

On this point she didn't argue, and he thought that this all by itself was quite telling. She simply nodded. "Please find her," she said.

He agreed, and proffering her a knife, he instructed, "Use it if you have to."

"I will," she said, and with one final look at her, he rose and sprinted away, following the direction of the rapids. With any luck, he would find Sarah.

# Sixteen

The sun was a low, pinkish orange orb in the sky, announcing its departure from the day in glorious streaks of multicolored sunlight. Shafts of light, streaming from the clouds, beamed down to the earth, looking as though heaven itself smiled kindly upon the land. And what a magnificent land it was. The birch trees were yellow, the maples red, and the oaks announced their descent into a long, winter sleep with oranges and golds. The hills were alive with autumn color, while the air was filled with the rich, musky scent of falling leaves.

Into this world of beauty came the delicate and pale figure of a woman, looking as though she had been plopped down on a large, flat rock. To a casual eye, it might have appeared as though she were engaged in nothing as untoward as taking in the sun. However, closer inspection would have shown that she had only recently been washed to shore.

Soon, the lone figure of a man emerged from the forest. Buckskin clad, he was tall and brown skinned, with long, black hair that hung well down past his shoulders. He'd been hunting this day, very far from his home, and from deep within the forest, he'd felt the breeze, and heard the rustle of the water. It had called to him.

Stepping quietly toward the water, he looked up, his gaze one of admiration for all this, the splendor of the woodlands. Squatting down, and setting his musket onto his lap, he bent over to partake of a drink from the water's cool depths.

However, instantly he sat up, alert. From out the corner of his eye, he'd caught the movement of something, and glancing toward it, he recognized the image of a piece of clothing; it was a woman's skirt. Raising up, he stepped toward it to get a better look, if only to satisfy his curiosity.

That's when he saw her. She was a white woman, blond haired and slim.

Was she alive?

Hauling himself up onto the rock where she lay, he stepped toward her and bent over her. He placed his fingers against her neck, feeling for a pulse. Her body was cold, so very, very cold and he was more than a little surprised when he felt the sure sign of life within her.

The pulse was weak, but it was still there.

Turning her over, he was surprised at her pale beauty. Of course, being Seneca and from the Ohio Valley, he'd had opportunity to witness the unusual skin color of the white people. But it wasn't as familiar a sight to him as one might reckon.

Who was she? How had she gotten here? And what had happened to her?

Glancing in all directions, he took in the spectacular sights of the forest. Where did she belong? Who did she belong to?

But there was nothing to be seen, no other human presence to be felt within the immediate environment. There was nothing here but the ever expansive rhythm of nature.

Using his right hand to brush her hair back from her face, he noted again how cold she was, but he couldn't help but be aware of how soft her skin was, as well. Putting his fingers under her nostrils, he could feel the weak intake and outflow of breath. She was alive, but only just. If she were to live through the night, he had best get her to a place where he could nurse her.

Taking her up in his arms, he stepped off the rock and headed back into the forest. If he hurried, he could make it to a good spot before darkness fell.

Then hopefully, he could find out who she was . . . if she lived . . .

"Did you find her?"

He didn't answer all at once. Instead, kneeling down in front of Marisa, Black Eagle gathered her into his arms, and brought her up to her knees, where he drew her body in toward his. He wrapped his arms around her, and commenced kissing her face, her neck, her hair.

Though he was worried and rushed, for he was aware that the enemy would be looking for them, he first had a duty toward this woman. He dreaded telling her what he must, but there was no use hiding the facts from her.

"*Neh*, no, I did not find her," said Black Eagle at last, holding Marisa tightly against him. "There is no sign of Miss Sarah. I fear she has washed away to her death."

"No!" Marisa grabbed hold of him, and held onto him tightly. "No! I refuse to believe it!"

He nodded. "I understand."

"I know she is alive. I know it!"

Again he nodded. "If you desire, we can stay in this place a little longer and I will continue searching for her."

"Yes, please. You would do that?"

He nodded.

"Perhaps I can help."

"Perhaps."

He took note that *Ahweyoh* was cold, that she was shivering, and in order to restore some warmth to her body, he rubbed her arms up and down. She, however, responded to him in an unusual manner. At first, she remained mute, simply receiving his attention as her due, but then slowly she came alive, and her lips began an intimate exploration of him, there against his throat. Her fingers wound into his hair and rubbed against his scalp, and he thought that if possible, he might likely choose to remain here like this for the rest of his life.

At the very least, after the nightmare of Thompson's betrayal, as well as the ordeal of the rapids and falls, her attention toward him was a little like stepping into a bit of paradise. Mayhap the Creator, in His wisdom, was tempering the horrors of this day with some semblance of pleasure, after all.

Black Eagle groaned, and she, hearing it, whispered, "I thank the dear Lord that you are alive, and I thank you for following me into the falls. You could have easily left me to my fate."

"Not possible."

"I fear to disagree," she murmured. "It would have been more than possible."

He shook his head. "Not and remain honorable. Besides, when two people are bound together, not only with passion, but with love, the other person's fate becomes your own."

She gulped, then whispered, "I have been wrong, Black Eagle. I have been very wrong."

"Shhhh," he uttered. "Do not try to talk."

"No, I must. You have been right. It is not true that one person is another person's 'better' because of birth. The English think of the Indian as beneath them, not worthy or smart enough to have rights. Yet look at you. Look at me. I would not be here but for you. How can I ever thank you properly?"

He nuzzled his head into her neck, and he said, "I think that you are going about it in a very good way right now."

"Truly?" As if his words gave her courage, she ventured outward in her exploration of him, her kisses seeking out his cheeks, his eyes and nose, his lips. Her hands had twined themselves irreparably in his hair, and she confided, "I thought to never see you again, and were that to have been so, my feeling of loss would have been beyond endurance. How happy I am that you are here, and that I am here, and we are together."

"I, too," he said. "I, too."

And he began to return her embrace, kissing her, deeply, lovingly, sacredly.

*It is said by the elders*, he thought, *that if you save another from a certain death, their life belongs thereafter to you.* But, wise though this philosophy was, he felt the opposite was true for him.

He belonged to her. Now. Forever.

In his adoration of her, his tongue ranged into her mouth, withdrew from it, then reached in again, exploring the depths of her, thrilling to the clean taste of her. Again, he groaned. Again, she surged forward against him.

And she whispered, "Black Eagle, I little understand how it is possible after all that we have been through today, but I fear that I want . . . love."

When she added, "Do you object?" he thought he might likely go out of his head.

"Object?" he said. "What sane man would object to an act of love?"

"I am glad to hear that you're willing," she said. Her touch was broadening out in her survey of him, her palms extending lower and lower, down to his chest, which at present, was bare. Sometime today, somehow, he'd lost his shirt. He hadn't really taken note of the fact until this very moment. But he was glad of it. There was nothing there to stand between his skin and hers.

"There is a tattoo here on your chest and the same on your arms, as well."

"So there are."

"They are wolves."

"It is my clan."

She nodded. Farther and farther down, her touch ranged, her fingers coming to linger over his very erect, very male nipples. He shuddered with delight. And when her lips followed where her fingers led, he growled, deep in his throat.

"I want you to love me," she murmured, as she rose up to run her tongue over his lips. "I want to know in a very elemental way that you are, indeed, real."

"I already love you," he said. "But I will make love to you, if only to demonstrate how very real we are to each other."

"Yes," she said. "Please."

Her fingers fell down over him, to sweep away his breechcloth, hesitating there, over his stiff and erect manhood. She groaned, and, if possible, his hardening expanded. He might have brought her up over him, but she had already taken charge, and she moved into position so that she was straddling him. Bringing up her skirts, she settled herself down over him, joining their bodies in a most rudimentary way.

She sighed, and he moaned. And then she began to move against him sensuously, and bending toward him, she kissed his lips while her tongue delved deeply into his mouth, exploring his taste as thoroughly as he had many times done to her.

He was, indeed, a willing and active recipient of all she had to give and he let her take the lead, until, soon, he felt her begin that inevitable spiral toward release. It was an exquisite plateau she sought, and as her need for his strength consumed her, he took over command of their lovemaking, surging up within her. All the while his tongue swept the inner sanctum of her mouth, mirroring the active admiration of their bodies.

Her hands grabbed hold of his shoulders and her squirming took on a sensuality that had him spiraling out of control. He felt her plunging from that precipice, felt her release, and almost instantaneously he was bursting within her.

But it wasn't over. As their bodies opened up to each other, they became as one, together soaring upward above their physical being. Never, he thought, had he ever felt so close to another human being. Nor had he ever experienced being so close to eternity, as though by the act of love, some secret that bound them to this earth, was revealed.

With her, worlds opened to him. With her, he felt capable of anything. He loved her.

And when she whispered, "I love you. I will love you always," it felt as if the whole world had shifted.

He smiled, and bringing her head down to his, he kissed her long and hard. Words escaped him. And in the end, all he said was, "I, too. I, too."

They must have dozed, for he awakened suddenly. Alert, he listened, but he could hear little but the rush of the rapids. He said, "We must leave here at once and seek shelter." He kissed her gently, then pushed her up, disengaging himself from her.

"Yes," she said, as she came up onto her knees and flopped down beside him. "I do have a question I forgot to ask. Did you find any sign of Thompson?"

Black Eagle grimaced. "I found nothing of him. No trail, no clue, not even a remnant of his clothing."

As she straightened up, she said, "At least I now understand why there were so many accidents on the trail."

"Yes, I fear he was the cause. But come, we must move along. We are not yet in a safe place. Can you walk?"

She nodded. "Where will we go?"

"Not far," he answered. "But because our enemies will look for us, we will have to discover a place that will be so well hidden that it will disappear into the landscape. The Ottawa will not give up our trail easily, I think, and they will send their scouts out, looking for us, so I must build us a shelter very well. Know this, it is one thing to try to fool the white man into not seeing what is there before him, it is another to try to trick an Indian scout."

She sighed. "I suppose you are right, but won't they think we're dead? Why are they so persistent?"

"Because we killed four of their own. They will not forget easily. By now they will have discovered that there are no bodies, except perhaps that of Miss Sarah."

Marisa caught her breath.

"They may, even now, be searching the ground for clues as to what has happened to us. If we remain here, they will certainly find us, and our fate will be sure and exact. We must go." Arising, he helped her to her feet. "We must go quickly. Can you run?"

"I think so."

"Then come, we had best find a good place to erect a shelter. It may take some time."

And with this said, Black Eagle headed into the woods. "Lift your skirts," he said to her before he broke into a run. "The material you wear tears easily and could leave a trail."

She nodded, and then they were away.


They had literally run through the forest, sweeping over paths that weren't really paths, jumping over logs and branches, looking for what, Marisa could only conjecture. They climbed up a steep hill, ran down into the surrounding valley. And still they didn't stop.

And with each footfall, Marisa became more and more concerned over Sarah's fate. It seemed to her that they were traveling far away. Were they leaving her behind?

At last she had to know, and she called out to Black Eagle, who was far ahead of her in the lead, "Sir Eagle, how will we ever find Sarah, if we go so far away from the water?"

With her question, Black Eagle stopped and turned back toward her. Patiently, he waited for her to catch up to him, and when she came within hearing distance, he said, "We have not traveled far from the falls. I am circling the lake and the rapids, looking for something in the environment that I can use to make a shelter that will not be easily recognized for what it is."

"Oh."

He smiled at her. "Are you hungry?"

"Yes," she said at once, not realizing that she was so until he mentioned it.

Motioning to her to come close, he opened a bag that hung from his shoulder, and he offered her the pemmican that was within it. She took a handful and plopping it in her mouth, she chewed. The dried meat, which was mixed with fat and berries, tasted wonderful, more pleasing it seemed than the richest meal she'd ever eaten. It was so good, she observed, "I'm surprised this didn't get soaked."

"It is a little wet."

"Hardly. 'Tis very appealing," she said between bites.

He smiled at her, and bent down to steal a kiss. However, no more had he done so, than he was straightening up. And he was happily grinning. But he wasn't looking at her.

"There," he said, pointing. "There is what I've been looking for."

She gazed in the direction he indicated, but she could see nothing that could bring such delight. She said, "Truly?"

"*Nyoh*, and it is all because of you. Come, I will show you our new home."


It was ingenious. It was simply brilliant. A large elm tree had fallen on its side, leaving a gap of about four feet between its trunk and the ground. Branches were spread out everywhere over the earth.

Looking at it in the raw, however, Marisa was less than pleased. Were they to spend the night inside a tree?

But that had been before Black Eagle had gone on to erect a shelter. First he had cut off some of the tree's upper branches, then he had spread them sideways over the trunk, which had created a lean-to, complete with enough branches over the top so as to form a ceiling. But the real stoke of genius had come in the form of scattering other branches over the ground, around and over the shelter, so that the hideaway literally disappeared into its surroundings.

Further landscaping with limbs, leaves and tufts of grass had hidden the shelter even more so by simply making it appear to be a part of the tree. Inside the shelter, pine boughs became their floor, while tree bark that he had carefully cut from the bottom of the elm tree, provided them with a ceiling.

Their door also consisted of the same tree bark, so, too, the walls of their shelter.

Black Eagle had then gone back to the stream to fill one of his bags with water, while another bag that he carried with him contained enough pemmican to see them through several days.

The shelter wasn't large—it was only about four feet in height—but it was big enough and long enough to allow them to lie down full form. That it was also warm and waterproof made it a bit of a haven in the wilderness.

However, Black Eagle had no more than set up the structure, than he had left, giving her strict instructions to be quiet and to make no fire. It was to be his task, he had told her, to backtrack and erase their trail from the forest floor.

She had meant to busy herself with little tasks, making their shelter more habitable, but in the end, she had capitulated to the tiredness of her body, and it wasn't until Black Eagle crawled into their shelter that she had awakened.

"It is I," he'd said, announcing himself, and scooting in through their doorway.

It was dark inside the shelter, and she realized that she had slept the rest of the afternoon and evening away. Streams of moonlight filtered in through a few of the openings in their ceiling and walls, making Black Eagle barely visible to her. Sitting up and rubbing her eyes, she said, "Welcome home."

"Ah," he said in return, "that it were really true. That we shared a home together, and that I was returning from the hunt, loaded with game to serve us for many a supper in the months ahead."

She smiled. "It does sound quite lovely, doesn't it?"

"*Nyoh*, I wish that it were so. But now that we are alone, and are safe from our enemies—at least for the night—I would look at you more closely. Are you hurt anywhere?"

"No, I don't think so."

"Let me see," he said, as his hands came out to run over her head, over to her face, on down to her neck, her shoulders, her back, down lower still. He threw up her skirts and felt her legs, down her calf muscles to her feet.

"Nothing hurts?"

"No, nothing."

"It is good. I am glad."

She paused, then she asked, "Did you see signs of the Ottawa?"

"*Neh*, but that is not necessarily a good sign. Their scouts will be almost undetectable. I can only hope that this structure I built will avoid their notice. But, we should prepare ourselves by loading our guns, sharpening our knives and hatchets and making ready anything else we will need to protect ourselves."

She nodded.

"When I am out tomorrow searching for your friend, you can do this."

"Yes."

"But now," he said, "much as I would desire to make love to you all night long, I think it best that we get some sleep."

Lying down, he opened up his arms for her, and she went into them easily, as though they two were magnetically attracted. He pulled their blanket up and around them.

What bliss, she thought, to be held so closely and securely by the one that you loved. And so it was on this thought that she fell to sleep.

# Seventeen

"Sarah!"

Marisa awoke screaming.

Musket in hand, Black Eagle followed her up and jumped to his knees. Looking back at her, he placed his fingers over her lips, effectively silencing her, and he knelt there at her side, noiselessly, alert, listening. Several minutes turned into many more, and still he knelt in the same position, alert, awake, his weapons at his fingertips.

Indeed, such a long time elapsed while he remained in this position, that by the time he turned back to her, Marisa was having a hard time keeping her eyes open. He sat back on his haunches, set his weapon down at his side, and taking her up in his arms, he placed a kiss over her lips. Only then did he whisper, "I think we are safe, but enemy scouts may be about. It is a wise man who remains as silent as possible."

She nodded. "I beg your pardon," she muttered quietly. "I had a nightmare."

"That is to be expected."

She shivered, for simply speaking of it brought it back to mind. "It was terrible."

"Do you want to tell me about it?"

"Oh, no," she replied. "There is an old wives' tale that is common amongst the Dutch, and Sarah related it to me, that a dream told before breakfast may come true."

"Ah, then it is as well that you keep it to yourself for now. Do you think you can go back to sleep?"

"I will try, but now I am afraid I might cry out again."

He nodded. "It is a possibility." His arms closed around her to hold her tightly, his chin coming down to rest on the top of her head. "I like the feel of you in my arms," he whispered.

"I, too, enjoy this. But I am afraid," she murmured. "All I can hear in my dreams is the crashing of the waterfall and the sound of the rapids. All I can see is Sarah, being swept away from me, all I can feel is the freezing water, and the muted sounds of the waterfall above me."

"I understand," he said. "Perhaps, then, it would be best to do something else besides sleep. Possibly now is the time to tell you the story I have in the past promised you. Know that waterfalls are not always so fearsome, or so fatal. Sometimes they bring about many good things. This story is about another time, long ago, when a woman fell over the greatest waterfall in the land of the Iroquois, and became the wife of *He-noh*."

"*He-noh?*"

"*He-noh*, the Thunderer," he murmured. "It is he who gives us rain and thunder. Though he is not the Creator, he is yet a giver of life, for without the rain, nothing on this earth could live."

"By Creator, you do mean, of course, God, who lives in heaven?"

"I do," he said, "we call him *Hawenia*, the Creator of all life. But this is the story of another being, the Thunderer. It happened not far from here, in the land of the Seneca, in the village of Gaugwa. Close by to that village is the great waterfall, *Neahga*. Now it happened that there was a beautiful girl whose relatives were dead."

"Like mine?"

He nodded. "Like yours. But instead of living with her uncle, she lived with her aunt. It was the only relative she had."

"Like me."

"Like you," he said, his voice barely raised over a murmur. "Now the girl's name was *Ahweyoh*."

"But that is the name you call me."

"So it is," he said. "There is much similarity between you and the *Ahweyoh* of long ago. Now, *Ahweyoh* was generous and compassionate to all, but her aunt was not kind to her. Some think the aunt was jealous of *Ahweyoh*'s beauty. Others believe that the aunt hated her own brother, thus she took her grievances out on her brother's daughter. Whatever the truth of this, the aunt made *Ahweyoh* wear the oldest clothing, and forced her to do many chores that were unbecoming of her. Still, because *Ahweyoh* was beautiful and kindhearted, there were many who wished to marry her, and would have done so, but for the aunt, who forbid it.

"Now there was a terrible man, an old man who was fat and ugly, who was known to have beat his wife to death. But he had acquired much of the white man's wealth, and the aunt was desperate to have a part of those riches. And so she arranged to have *Ahweyoh* marry this man.

"When *Ahweyoh* became aware of this, she was grief stricken. She refused to marry the man, but the aunt insisted, and was planning the ceremony to take place the next day.

"*Ahweyoh* could not bear the thought of life with this man, and when her pleading fell on deaf ears, *Ahweyoh* decided she would rather die than marry him. And so, late that night she set out in a small canoe, steering her boat toward the rapids that would carry her to *Neahga*. Soon, the canoe was rushing through the rapids, carrying *Ahweyoh* to certain death."

Marisa shivered, and Black Eagle wrapped his arms more tightly around her. In the same low voice, he continued, "Now, long ago it was well-known that the Thunderer lived under the falls of *Neahga*. The people knew it was so, for they could hear his voice. On this night, the sky was clear and so the Thunderer was at his home beneath the falls. He heard the cries of *Ahweyoh*. Looking up, he beheld her, seeing through the rags that she wore, to her beauty beneath, not only of her physical beauty, but he saw into her heart. He fell instantly in love with her . . . much like I did upon seeing you the first time."

Marisa smiled, and snuggled deeper into Black Eagle's embrace.

"The Thunderer saved *Ahweyoh*," continued Black Eagle, "by catching her in his arms as her canoe tipped over the falls. Although he was not quite human, he was a handsome man nonetheless, and *Ahweyoh* fell in love with him, too. Soon, they married, but there was still trouble with her aunt, who plodded to steal her away and force her to marry another. And so to ensure that the aunt was never again able to hurt *Ahweyoh*, the Thunderer abandoned his home under the falls to live in a safer place, a place in the west. Thus, when you see a storm fast moving, coming toward you, look at the direction that it approaches. It will usually come to you from the west."

Marisa sighed, and nuzzled in closer to him. "And did they live happily, to the end of their days?" she asked.

"It is so," Black Eagle said. "They had a son, Thunder Boy. Thunder Boy, because he is half human, often walks upon the earth. Sometimes it is said that *Ahweyoh* becomes lonely for earthly things, and so she joins her son in his walks. If you listen closely in the spring, you can hear the earth echo the call of the lightning. When you hear this, know that all is well, for these are the voices of *Ahweyoh* and the Thunderer as they speak words of love to each other."

A long silence followed the story, until at last, Marisa said, " 'As they speak words of love to each other,' " she repeated. "That is a beautiful story. Tell me, Black Eagle, do you call me *Ahweyoh* because she, like I, had no one to care for her?"

"*Nyoh*, it is so, and also because, like the Thunderer, with one look, I fell in love with you. But there is another resemblance, too. Like the *Ahweyoh* of the past, you chose to lavish your love on someone who is very different from you." He paused, and when he continued, there was a noticeable tremor in his voice as he said, "I think that if we try hard, our life together could be as happy as *Ahweyoh* and the Thunderer."

She smiled. "I would like to wish that, too, but . . ." She went still, then sat up, pushing herself away from him. "Black Eagle, I know you once said that we should marry, but you didn't ask me then. Are you now proposing to me?"

"I am," he admitted simply. "You hold my heart. If I had labored under any doubt of this, the events of today washed them away. The future may be good or bad for us, but it will be a better place for us both, I think, if we face it together."

Marisa wanted nothing more than to say yes. But she knew she could not. She said, "Would that I were free to follow my heart. But from childhood, I have been aware that my marriage is and will be a financial pact between my step-uncle and a man of his choosing. 'Tis my duty to obey him in this, since I owe my guardian my upbringing. Plus, I have promised that I will do this."

"Ah," said Black Eagle, "that would be true in your old life, but what has happened here today has changed that."

"It has?"

"*Nyoh*. Like the *Ahweyoh* of legend, you determined to leave the one who provided your upbringing. And like the *Ahweyoh* of legend, also, the falls did not claim your life. You have a new life now, and in this new life, you are free to determine your own future. You are free now to have me, if you wish it."

Marisa paused while conflicting thoughts consumed her. Black Eagle's logic was not without merit. Indeed, there was much truth to it.

Still, altering the decisions and habits of a lifetime was

not a thing to be done without consideration. So she said, "'Tis true that I have been wrong about the matters that separate us. I have thought too greatly of our cultural differences. But I have come to believe that these things are superficial, and are attached to us with very thin veils. In truth, all it takes is lifting the veils to see that we are much alike."

"It is so."

"I have thought all my life that there was nothing to learn from the Indians of these woodlands," she continued. "I have lived next to your people, and yet I know little about them. This has not been wise. It has made me look upon your people as being somehow less than human.

"Still," she went on to say, "I cannot shed all those things I have held dear for a lifetime."

Reaching out for her, he brought her back into the circle of his arms, where he nestled her head against him. It was a sort of paradise, she thought as her flesh melted into his; the warmth of his body, the feel of his skin next to hers, the security of his arms holding her, was dizzying. If she could have, she would have kept the world away from them, and stayed like this forever.

Brandishing a kiss atop her head, he said, "Nothing has to be decided now. But know this, my life is now yours. Regardless of what you decide, I am now bound to you. You hold my heart."

The passion, the ardor in his words stirred her soul, and tears welled up behind her eyes. Indeed, it was all she could do to simply say, "I love you." And even then, her voice shook.

"And I, you," he responded. Then he sighed. "Do you think you might be able to sleep now?"

"I shall try."

"Perhaps it would be better for you if your dress were loosened," he suggested. "Your manner of dress is constricting, I think."

"Yes, it is."

"Would you like me to help you loosen your clothing?"

She hesitated, but only for a moment. "Yes," she said, "that would be most agreeable and perhaps it might help me to sleep. But a woman's dress is fairly complicated. I can loosen the buttons on this stomacher—that is this piece of clothing that is stiff and unwieldy, here in front of my chest and abdomen—if you will push down the sleeves of the dress while I unbutton it."

He nodded and did so, but his next words to her were ones of surprise, as he said, "There is yet more clothing beneath," he said.

"Yes, that is my chemise," she explained as she pulled the bodice of her gown down from around her shoulders. "If I turn my back to you, do you think you might unfasten my stays? There is a lace that holds my corset in place. Do you see them?"

He nodded.

"If you will but loosen those, I can remove my corset, which will allow me a chance to catch my breath."

His fingers were already at work over the lacings, and his gentle touch, there upon her back, was like magic. Every nerve in her body came alive.

When the corset fell apart, and her breasts spilled out over the shape of it, she felt oddly liberated, as well as relieved. She inhaled deeply.

"Why do white women wear these things?"

"'Tis the style, and one must attain a small waistline somehow. The expense of beauty, I fear, is ofttimes one of discomfort."

"*Nyoh*. Indeed, it seems to be so."

He pulled the garment from her, and it was odd, for it was pitch-black within their lean-to. Yet, she could feel his gaze upon her.

"How strange it is," he whispered, "that we have been often in each other's arms, yet I have never beheld you in the flesh. It is to be regretted that you are forced to wear so many clothes, for one such as you would be beautiful to go without any."

"Without any clothes? Sir Eagle, what you suggest is scandalous."

"It may be, but still there are not many who could retain their beauty without the adornment of clothing. You are such a one."

She sighed. "How you flatter me; it is much too dark in our shelter to see me in the altogether. But I admit, sir, that I like your praise very much all the same."

"No flattery," he admitted. "I speak but the truth, for there is a trickle of light to reveal you. Besides, I can see well enough with my hands."

And with those hands, he was roaming over her bosom and the curves of her stomach as though he would memorize every hill and valley of her form. Again she sighed. "Then come, Sir Eagle, if you wish to see me completely naked, help me to remove my skirts, as well. There is still much work to do before I can safely say that you have seen me in the altogether."

She could almost feel Black Eagle's delight. And though the darkness did not allow her to witness his smile, there was a note of humor in his voice as he said, "I would be most pleased."


She sat before him in nothing but her chemise, her hose and her shoes, which to Marisa's way of thinking was the same as being naked. This, to her frame of reference, was as far as her undressing went. However, it seemed that Black Eagle wished to remove even this last article of clothing, and when he made a motion to take off her chemise, as well, Marisa backed away from him.

"Sir," she said, "what is it you intend?"

"To see you unclad. Are we not removing all of your clothes?"

"But am I not already naked?"

He laughed, the sound soft and deeply masculine. But when she didn't join in with the joke, she could practically hear him frown. He said, "Naked? Do you jest? There is still this slip that hides you."

"You wish me to remove my chemise, as well?"

"*Nyoh*, yes."

"But sir, even a lady long married does not allow her husband such privileges."

"Does she not? I thought I understood the Englishman, but this is a strange custom for a man to have," he said. "Still I would like to take this underdress off of you." He was already pulling the chemise up over her head.

She sighed. But she assisted him nonetheless, holding her arms up over her head.

She'd thought he would simply slip the clothing off. However, he caught and held her arms up over her head, and with her hands caught in her gown, he knelt in front of her, bringing his lips unerringly to the taut nipples of her breasts.

At first touch, excitement filled her, and she felt naughty, sexy, desirable. She was utterly naked, as bare as she had come into this world, and as she knelt before him, her femininity found a safe harbor within his masculinity. It was an empowering experience, and she swayed against his sensual onslaught, a fire rousing to life within her.

Then he removed the chemise completely, and he lay her gently back against their cushion of padded pine boughs. Immediately, the fragrance, not only of fresh pine, but also of his own earthy scent assailed her senses. It occurred to her that she might always, from this moment forward, associate these smells with him.

He bent over her and toward her, coming down to rub his own bare chest against her own. It was a heady experience and she swayed against him, raising her hips to meet his.

He groaned. The sound was like music to her.

While one of his hands held him balanced over her, his other hand kneaded her breasts. And then he set one of his knees into position, there at the junction of her hips, stabilizing him and allowing his kisses to range lower and lower over her abdomen. She cast her head back and opened her chest up to him, letting the fire that this man kindled rage over her.

And he answered her gift, suckling on her breasts, her stomach, down to her belly button. However, when his lips wandered ever lower and lower over her, she became slightly alarmed. His kisses were rambling in a direction wherein lay her most intimate secrets.

"Black Eagle," she whispered, coming up onto her elbows. "What is it you intend doing?"

It took him a moment to answer, though eventually, he said, "To love you."

"Yes, I am most happy about that," she replied. "But how do you intend doing it?"

She sensed more than beheld his grin. "You will see. Lie back. You will enjoy it."

"But—"

His growl interrupted her. It was deep, masculine and incredibly sensuous. And then he had positioned himself over her, there at the apex of her legs. First his fingers found her most private spot, but then his lips followed where his fingers had been.

*Dear Lord*, she thought as she caught her breath. How was a person to bear such pleasure?

It was glorious. It was resplendent. And as her soft, high-pitched moans caught on the air, it seemed to urge him on. All at once, his kisses exploded, his tongue, being the instrument, bringing her to a fine-tuned crescendo. She squirmed, she wiggled, her legs opening to him to give him full access.

It was magic, it was enchanted, she being the recipient of his adoration. On and on it went, until at last, the ecstasy was almost more than she could bear, and she found herself once again tripping over the edge. She moaned, she sighed, and she strained against him as the tempest of release rocked her body. Over and over again, her body pitched with pure elation.

"Dear Lord," she moaned. Incapable of speech for the

moment, there was nothing else she could think of to say. And after a moment, she simply uttered, "Dear Lord," again.

But it wasn't over. He had come up over her, his lips immediately finding hers in an all-out consuming kiss.

"Are you ready for all of me?" he asked.

She nodded. "Oh, yes, please."

Again, he growled, the sound so incredibly masculine, she thought she might melt. At last he became a part of her; it felt right, so very, very right. Briefly, he held himself over her, as he bent down toward her, to whisper into her ear, "Did you enjoy it?"

"Enjoy it?" she repeated. "Do you tease me? How could I not enjoy it? Indeed, sir, I am uncertain that word adequately describes what I have experienced this night."

She felt his smile, as he bent his head against her neck. He murmured, "I am glad."

And then, without further conversation, they were repeating the act of love all over again, he bringing her up once more to that place where all is right with the world. He rocked against her, and she met his every thrust, moving against him with all the adoration she had to give.

Over and over he bore up within her, she meeting his thrusts, and contributing to their spiraling frenzy. His face was only inches from her own, and though it was almost pitch-black within their tiny shelter, she looked up at him, admiration in her gaze as she said, "I love you!"

His response was not verbal. Instead his exertions became fast and furious. There was that fine-tuned sensation again, a fire, an excruciating happiness building up within her, its location centered at the junction of her legs. Exquisite excitement filled her, and as she spiraled into the realm of pure pleasure, she felt him release his seed within her.

Her moans echoed his low-pitched groans. His body came down over her, and yet now and again, he shuddered within her. At last he lay atop her while a few more higher-pitched moans escaped her lips. Inadvertently, she tightened her muscles, there at the junction of her legs, the action eliciting a further groan from him.

He said, "That feels good."

"Yes."

"We will marry," he said simply.

She nodded. "Yes," she said. There was nothing else to say. Indeed, for all practical purposes, they already were married.

This was her life now, her new life.

"Yes," she repeated, loving the sound of the word, loving him. Log cabin or manor house, it mattered not. She belonged to this man. Perhaps she always had.

# Eighteen

Days passed. Days of wonder, of excitement, days that were consumed with searching for Sarah, but they were also days spent making love in the cool evenings, walking hand in hand through the multicolored forests of the Adirondacks, learning new facts about trees and herbs and plants, spotting and admiring deer, moose, elk. Never had Marisa appreciated nature so fully, never had she given so much thought to the miracles she witnessed about her.

Each day was different, each day she discovered some new and awe-inspiring detail about the land that she had, up to this time, taken for granted. Happiness was theirs. Indeed, it was as though she and Black Eagle had momentarily stopped the earth midturn.

Eventually, however, the world could no longer hold off its reality, and as though making up for its negligence, the intrusion into their paradise came in the form of violence.

On this day, Black Eagle had been up, awake and away, as usual. He had left Marisa in their shelter, her task being one of defense: She was to clean and reload their weapons, sharpen their knives and hatchets, and see to any other tool that they might utilize for defense. Black Eagle had left to go in search of Sarah, but before he'd gone, he had given her explicit instructions: remain quiet. If an enemy approached, she was to first go perfectly still, while using her mind to plot an escape. Then, as soon as she had formed a plan, she was to take fast and furious action.

There was to be no going to and from their lean-to while he was away. He'd instructed further, no singing, no talking to oneself, nothing.

Marisa wasn't about to disobey. Besides, she'd discovered that when Black Eagle wasn't with her, her courage waned. Indeed, she would have been hard-pressed to leave their hideaway on any account.

But this was an unusual day. The first moment she sensed that all was not as it ought to be was the mere crack of a twig, like the sound made beneath a footfall. Immediately, she went still, as Black Eagle had instructed.

She waited.

If it were Black Eagle, he would soon make himself known to her with the special call they'd arranged between them. Minutes passed, and still there was nothing, no indication that whoever was out there was Black Eagle.

Instinct made her want to speak out, to query and discover the identity of her intruder. But wisely she kept her silence.

What if it were a bear? A mountain lion? A wolf? Worse, what if it were one of the Ottawa warriors returned?

On this last thought, her stomach somersaulted. Had Black Eagle erased their tracks from their previous day's wanderings? What was it he'd said about constructing their shelter? That it was one thing to fool a white man, it was quite another to trick an enemy scout.

To add to her worry, she was more than aware of the unusual abilities of these Indian scouts. They were uncommon, these scouts. From the telling of it, it seemed to her as if they operated in a world that was half real, half spiritual. If whoever was out there were a scout, would he be able to sense her presence? Would he be able to hear her breathe?

*Crack!*

The sound split the air in two. Again, she froze. The noise had been closer to her this time. Was this to be her last day upon this earth? Her heart raced. In truth, so frightened was she, she dared barely breathe.

Then it happened. Upon looking up through one of the cracks in their bark walls, she beheld the red-painted face of an enemy warrior. He was awful. He was big, bulky and ugly.

Was he one of the Ottawa? If so, it didn't escape her consideration that if he found her, he would kill her. Terror shot through her, and she almost gasped aloud, barely catching herself in time.

Had the warrior sensed her thoughts? Sensed the life on the other side of those logs? What did he see? What did he hear? Could he sense her breathing? Her heartbeat? Could he smell her scent or the remnants of the small fire they'd built last night? The gunpowder she'd been handling?

He reached out toward their shelter, as if he knew it were there somewhere. His hand grasped hold of one the sticks Black Eagle had constructed as part of the structure's deception. All he needed to do was pull on that stick, and their lean-to would be revealed.

She waited for it to happen.

But all at once, the warrior paused and looked off as though he had caught sight of something or was listening to some noise. He straightened.

What did he see? What did he hear? Marisa listened closely, but she could distinguish nothing over the pounding of her heart.

Through the tiny crack in the bark, she watched as the warrior stood up straighter, his eyes fixed on a thing in the distance. And then, as silently as he had come, he disappeared out of her view.

Was he still there? Or had he left the valley?

She waited, and she waited. Coming silently up onto her knees, she took a position beside the crack in their walls, staring out through it. Ah, there he was, off in the distance, leaving their valley in a crouched over run. Marisa sat perfectly still, in thought. She didn't know whether to be glad of his departure, or worried because of it.

What had caused him to go? Were there more of them? Had he gone to get reinforcements? Or had Black Eagle come back somehow? Had he seen the warrior and managed to distract him?

And if Black Eagle had, was he now in danger?

A disturbing thought occurred to her. What would she do if something happened to Black Eagle?

Since coming to this valley, he had been gone from her many times, but she hadn't worried about him. Perhaps she should have been. How would she know if something did happen to him? If he didn't return, should she go and try to find him?

And if she did leave to try to find him, how was she to do it? She had no sense of direction, no way to know how to locate him or how to find his trail, let alone how to survive in the wilderness.

But on that thought came another. If something had happened to him, what would she do? Would she even want to go on without him?

Marisa's thoughts overwhelmed her. It was simply too much loss for her consideration. First Sarah, and now this.

So she sat and did nothing. Worried, frantic, contemplating her life now and in the future. It wasn't at all surprising, therefore, that hours later, she was still sitting in the same spot, still aware that she was alone and still worried. Worse, there were tears falling down over her cheeks. She hadn't even been aware of crying.

Something was wrong. Darkness was approaching, and still Black Eagle hadn't returned.

What to do? Should she stay here? Go look for him?

Anything seemed better than nothing. To stay here when there was the possibility that Black Eagle was hurt or in danger didn't seem right. And yet, what good would she be to him?

Despondent, she looked down, gazing at the weapons she'd been cleaning. Weapons . . . She'd forgotten about them.

That's when it occurred to her: weapons. With these tools that were lying here in her lap, she could be a force to be reckoned with.

That's all it took to decide her. Picking up a knife and its case, she strung it around her neck where she would have easy access to it. She then bent forward to grasp hold of the musket. At last she rose up from the position she'd been keeping for hours and hours.

At first her leg muscles protested, but then, as she stepped out of the shelter and into the dim light of evening, she realized she was glad. Glad to be here. Glad to be well armed and ready to protect her man, if need be.

She didn't know what direction to take, but again, anything was better than nothing.

Black Eagle couldn't be certain what had caused him to sense the presence of the enemy. Perhaps it was a disturbance in the air. Maybe it was the lack of the normal sounds of the forest, for there should have been birds singing or an occasional sighting of an animal. There wasn't.

He frowned. He had left their shelter early in the morning, had been en route to the rapids, there to search another section of the river for Miss Sarah. But suddenly, he had stopped short.

There was another being in the forest. It didn't matter how he knew it, the point being that he knew it.

Meticulous detail helped him find the enemy's trail, but it had taken him much time to discover it. With the necessity of backtracking and erasing his own tracks, it had been well into the afternoon before he'd come upon the distinctive markings of an Ottawa warrior. Black Eagle's heart lurched.

Bending down, he studied the tracks, for they would tell a history of his enemy.

He was a heavy man, perhaps fifty years in age. It was possible, thought Black Eagle, that one of his victims had been this man's son. Such would make sense, because the frenzy that Black Eagle could read in the tracks spoke of an unstable mind. Indeed, the bad mind was at work within this warrior; it was a mind filled with revenge.

There was only the one track, however, which was unusual, and equally dangerous, since a warrior seldom struck out on the warpath alone. To have done so might indicate, again, an instability, a man who would do anything.

But it wasn't until Black Eagle beheld that the tracks were leading to the valley where he had set up camp, that his heart shot into his throat. *Ahweyoh!*

Black Eagle immediately set out in a run, his speed picking up pace quickly as he raced toward the valley, jumping over obstacles, knocking over branches and bushes in his way. Gone from his mind was the need to backtrack and cover his own ground.

He pulled up in the woods, just short of the clearing where he had set up camp. And it was all he could do to keep himself from rushing full force at the enemy he saw there, and engaging the man in hand-to-hand combat. To do so, however, would be folly. The Ottawa could kill *Ahweyoh* first, then turn and kill him.

Alert, Black Eagle watched as the man crept toward the hideaway, watched, at the ready, as the man reached down to pull back the branches that Black Eagle had scattered around their shelter to hide it.

At any minute, the warrior would discover *Ahweyoh.* Would Black Eagle be fast enough to avert a disaster?

Quickly, Black Eagle tried to put the knowledge he had gained from reading the man's tracks to some plan that would defeat him. There was one thing: This enemy warrior was not altogether in his right mind. It was possible that this man had tried to convince his friends to stay on the trail with him, but they, sensing the warrior's madness, had left him alone, going home to their own fires or to rejoin the French.

Could it be that the Ottawa expected his friends to have a change of heart? To join him in his quest for revenge? If that were the case, Black Eagle might be able to distract the man with a sign, some signal the Ottawa might expect from his friends.

Shimmying up a tree to about its midpoint, Black Eagle imitated the mother's call of the dove, a common signal amongst tribes. He repeated the call once.

At last the warrior stood away from the shelter. He looked off to his right, to his left, his sight scanning the horizon.

Black Eagle repeated the call.

At length the Ottawa warrior retreated, angling back into the woods in the direction from where the call had originated. But the danger wasn't past. Far from it.

Black Eagle, watching, would follow the man, if only to ensure his own peace of mind that the warrior posed no further threat.

This had been a mistake.

Marisa was the first to admit it. She should have stayed where she was. She would be of no use to anyone as she was. She was lost. Worse, she was terrified.

Every sigh of the wind, every branch that rubbed against another had her jumping.

What was that? A footfall? Dear Lord, it was pitch-black in this forest. She could see nothing but black shapes in the trees. Was she alone, or was she being stalked?

And if she were being stalked, was it some deer, elk or bear? Worse, was it the Ottawa warrior?

There it was again. The crack of a twig. A footfall.

It couldn't be Black Eagle. Surely, if it were he, he would make himself known to her.

She knew she shouldn't, that she should remain as quiet as possible. But she was beyond fright. She called out, "Black Eagle, is that you?"

No response.

She inhaled, brought up the musket to chest level, and spoke again, "Who is it that follows me? Show yourself."

Nothing. At least not at first.

But then came the singing. It was a man's voice, and the words were indistinguishable. The key was minor. It was an Indian song. But dear Lord, it couldn't be Black Eagle.

The verse was repeated, but this time, it came in English:

> "I have found an English foe. I will kill her.
> I have found an English foe. I will kill her.
> She shall pay for my son's death.
> She shall pay for my son's death.
> I will kill her. Slowly, slowly.
> She will beg for mercy.
> I swear to you, my son, that she will beg for mercy."

This had definitely been a mistake. Involuntarily a warmth ran down her leg and she realized this might surely be the last breath she would ever take. It was really too bad, she thought, because finally she had found love. She wanted to live.

But she was no match for an Indian warrior, and certainly not one who had been trained for war all his life.

However, if this were to be her last stand upon this earth, the least she could do would be to show resistance. Why make it easy for the beast?

Perhaps it was this last thought that sparked a remnant of courage within her. She was frightened, she could barely stand up straight, but raising her musket to shoulder level, and pointing it in the direction of the shadows, she called out, "If you mean to kill me, sir, then come and do it. It must be easy to make war on a woman, since you have little to fear from me."

Had that really been her voice? Had she truly challenged an Indian warrior?

Apparently she had, for the man stepped forward into an opening in the trees. She could barely make out his shape, but of one thing she was certain: In his one hand was a tomahawk and in his other was a musket. He was big, he was burly, and it was useless to believe she would ever be a physical match for him.

Still if she were going to go down, she had best do it in a blaze. She said, "How is it you would prefer to die, sir?"

A knife flew toward her, finding the fullness of her skirt. It caught there, then dropped to the ground.

In reaction, she took careful aim with the musket and fired. But the man had moved out of range and her shot hit nothing better than the bark of a tree.

He leapt toward her with the swiftness and agility of a cat, and within seconds, he had thrown her to the ground, hard, knocking the breath from her. She had no more than caught a bit of air when he pulled her up, forcing her to kneel before him, he standing at her back. Then he said in English, "And how would you like to die, English woman? By fire? By knife? Either way, it will be slow. You will scream much."

Pulling her up by her hair, Marisa had no more than registered the pain in her scalp, when the Ottawa thrust his knife against her throat. Marisa was beyond terror, and she screamed. She kept on screaming, too, until her throat began to ache.

The knife dug into the skin at her throat, and as soon as it did, she fainted. Perhaps it was for the best.

# Nineteen

It was dark by the time Black Eagle returned to their shelter. He had tracked the warrior to the base of the falls, had seen the man embark in a canoe, had watched the Ottawa paddle downstream. Of course it was possible that the man might come ashore and backtrack, but Black Eagle was fairly confident that he had not given his presence away to the man.

Besides, he was worried. He had been gone from *Ahweyoh* for the entire day, and she would be frightened and alone. She might even be worried. He had begun to run, then, had started sprinting through the forest, passing by game that would have been easy for the taking. Perhaps some other time, they would know his prowess as a hunter. For now, onward he sped. Something was wrong. He could feel it.

Upon approaching their shelter, Black Eagle gave the usual meadowlark call to announce his return, but there was no return signal. Every nerve within him kicked into alert.

Coming up onto the shelter in a crouch, it took him but a moment to determine that the shelter was empty. She was gone.

Gone? This he had not expected.

Nor could he ascertain much from the tracks left here. Certainly her emotions were excited. Certainly she was overwrought. But he didn't think her agitation was due to the Ottawa warrior returning to haunt her. His tracks were here from earlier, but there were no fresh ones.

Why would she have left? She would have been safe in their shelter, particularly so because she had been cleaning their weapons, making them ready for use. With these she would have had advantage, she could have made an invincible stand if it had been necessary.

Though he could little understand her reasoning, he set about following her trail, made more difficult by an overcast sky and the darkness of night, which had fallen all around him. But staying on her trail wasn't impossible.

On he sped, his attention on her tracks, but also alert to all around him. Now and again, he bent to trace a deep impression of a track. From these, he extracted what might be her train of thought, and he painted a picture of what he thought might have driven her from their home. Worry.

She was worried for him.

Part of him warmed to the concept. Part of him, however, wanted to scold her for putting herself in danger. But mostly, he simply wanted to find her, if only to hold her in his arms again.

But what was this? Another trail, one following *Ahweyoh*'s. It was a track made by the Ottawa warrior. He was back.

No sooner had Black Eagle determined this than he heard *Ahweyoh*'s scream. His blood ran cold.

He cursed himself, for the Ottawa warrior had outsmarted him. The man must have sensed he was being followed.

With his heart in his throat, Black Eagle hurled himself through the forest, his feet barely touching the ground. He saw them, up ahead. And it was a sight he thought might haunt his nightmares for days on end.

The Ottawa held *Ahweyoh* by the hair in front of him,

his knife against her throat. Even in the dark, Black Eagle could see the blood dripping from the wound.

Was he too late?

The time for thinking was over. Black Eagle propelled himself into furious action. With hatchet drawn, and with a yell like the roar of a lion, he threw himself forward with such speed and force, that the Ottawa, though the bigger of the two of them, was thrown off balance.

Taking advantage, Black Eagle swung his hatchet at the man, hitting him in the forehead. It was a fatal stab. The man lurched backward. Black Eagle followed him down, the hatchet came down again on the Ottawa's shoulder, then, as though to be certain, Black Eagle stabbed him again in the head.

It was over. The Ottawa lay dead. The man would hurt her no more.

Black Eagle turned around toward *Ahweyoh*, fearing what he would find. Was she already dead?

Marisa had fallen to the ground, where she lay still. Too still. Black Eagle paced up next to her and touched her on the shoulder as if he were merely reminding her to rise up.

She groaned.

It was like music to his ears.

She turned over so that she was lying face up.

"Black Eagle?" she whispered.

"It is I," he said, his first action being to place his fingers against the cut on her throat, to see the damage made.

He let out his breath. It was a surface wound.

Unbidden, tears streamed down over his cheeks. She would be all right.

She sat up, and at last they came together, hugging and holding onto one another as though the world might end if they were to draw apart.

He brought his head down to her, nuzzling his face against hers, memorizing the beauty of the fragrance of her hair, her skin, the sweetness of her tears. He inhaled deeply, over and over again, thankful he was alive, that she was alive.

"Is the wound bad?" she asked.

"It is only a scratch. I promise you it is no more than this," he answered. "Come, I will take you back to the shelter and tend to the wound. And then I think it is time that I take you home."

"Home?"

"To my home," he said.

"Yes," she nodded. "Home. It sounds wonderful."

And as they knelt there in each others arms, they both cried.


The scent of the rich fields of corn, beans and squash reached the couple long before they emerged from the forest. As soon as they left the woods, however, they were immersed in the abundant fields of the Mohawk village. There was ripening corn, beans and squash as far as the eye could see, all growing together. Everywhere Marisa looked she saw bounteous rows of yellowish brown and green fields. There were few people working the fields, she noted. Here and there, in the distance, she caught sight of a woman and a child or two. But the fields looked more or less deserted at this time of day.

There was a large difference, however, between the Mohawk fields and those that were generally planted by the English. For one, there were few geometrically spaced rows. For another, all three crops—corn, beans and squash—were planted together. Indeed, there seemed to be no order to the method of planting. Plus, little black tree stumps dotted the fields here and there, marring the ongoing view of green, yellow and orange crops.

There was another alien aspect to the fields, as well. Outposts, little lean-tos raised up high on poles, were stuck deep within the fertile fields. There weren't many of them, perhaps one or two that she could easily see.

"What are those for?" Marisa asked Black Eagle, pointing toward the outpost closest to her.

"Those are used to scare crows and other birds," he

replied. "Children use them and sometimes women, too. They are built high so that one can see far distances and chase away birds or behold an enemy's approach. Sometimes, too, the figure of a man is built into the fields. And to keep the crops safe, a crow is ofttimes caught and held upside down to warn away other crows."

"What an interesting practice," Marisa observed. "But where is your village? All I see here are fields."

Black Eagle pointed upward, toward a cliff set high and slightly back from the river. He said, "We build our villages on high ground and far enough away from the river, so that we can look out over the land. In this way if an enemy approaches, we are sure to spot him before he arrives."

Again, Marisa nodded. "That is wise." She fell into silence momentarily, then, said, "Black Eagle. Forgive me, but I am nervous. What is going to happen to me in your village?"

"You will be taken into a home and adopted by a clan," he said, "and I will come to live with you in your new home, though your new clan might insist that we exchange gifts first, to ensure we are married properly."

Marisa met this news with silence, then, "What if your people hate me?"

"They will love you."

"I wish I could be so certain. Are there not some Mohawks that are allied to the French? Won't they look upon me with ill favor?"

"*Nyoh*, yes, perhaps. But they live much farther north, in Canada. There may be a few of them visiting, but they will do no damage to you while they are here."

It sounded fair enough, but still she was unsettled, and she asked, "Black Eagle, did you have a sweetheart in the village before you left? A lover, perhaps, who will be on the lookout for you?"

He didn't answer right away. Instead his response was a question to her, and he said, "Would you be jealous if I did?"

"Maybe."

He stopped and turned toward her, and taking her hand

in his, he said, "You are now my wife. Perhaps I should be truthful and tell you that there has been a girl or two who has caught my eye. It is only natural that it would be so. But there is no reason for you to be jealous. I made no girl my wife, though I could have. Know that I have not loved another as I love you."

"You never had a special girlfriend?"

"I did once," he answered, "but she married another. My heart, I fear, is free."

"Was free," she corrected. "Then there is no one waiting for you with bated breath?"

"My mother and my sisters, perhaps."

She shook her head. "There is something here I can little comprehend. You are a handsome man, and kind. I cannot visualize a village without a woman clever enough to have made herself a part of your life."

"This might have happened, it is true. But the one I would have chosen to be my wife belongs to another. And I fear that my heart had barely recovered from that when the hostilities between the French and English came to our land. The hatred between these two sets of white men has disrupted our village life."

He turned his face around, his gaze centered upward, looking toward the high ground where he'd said their village was located. "We Mohawks," he went on to say, "are caught between these two great forces and many are the times when the English or the French have come to our village to seek our assistance to help win their war."

"Yes," she said, "I can imagine that the two powers would affect you adversely."

"It is so. Long have we been at war because of the white man. Hundreds of years have passed since he came here with his wars," he said. "There was a time—though so long ago that not even our old people can remember it—when we made our own goods, manufactured our own bowls for cooking, our own pottery, our own clothes and produced our own weapons for hunting or for war. When we did this, we Indian Nations were on an even footing with one another. We were at peace. Or so it is said. But with the coming of the white man, who brought to us his guns for killing, his metal for cooking and his trinkets to satisfy the women, our people have had to fight to stay alive. For it is well known amongst all the Indian Nations that whoever has the best arms can dominate all the tribes. No one wants to be a slave."

"No, I should say not."

"Once, many hundreds of years ago, it is said that my ancestors were enslaved by a tribe known as the Adirondacks. These mountains that shelter us still carry their name. At that long ago time, we had to pay them tribute. It was a hard time for my people. But we escaped them, enduring hardship, for there is one particular we Iroquois treasure above all else, and that is our freedom."

Marisa barely knew what to say. It was a history and a viewpoint she had never known. At last, she ventured, "Then do your people hate the white man for bringing so much war?"

"Hate? Never. Instead we have allied ourselves to the white men who have treated us well. At first those people were the Dutch who settled close to Mohawk land. But then the English came and conquered them, and the treaty we had made with the Dutch transferred to the English. We have never broken it."

"And you are close to Sir William Johnson, personally, are you not?"

"I am. I have spent many hours in his home."

"And does he come here often?"

"He does. He is a part of our tribe. Some have even called him our white sachem."

"A white sachem," she repeated. "How strange that it should be so."

"Strange, perhaps, but true. He has married among us, his children run in our fields, eat at our fires. Once an Iroquois adopts a person into the tribe, they become Iroquois, with all the rights of an Iroquois. It is as though they are reborn among us."

"I see," she said.

"Like you. You have a new life now, and I think that you are going to be the cause of great happiness to some family who has lost a son or daughter." He reached out to caress his fingers over her cheek.

She smiled and leaned in toward his touch. "I hope so. But still I worry about my welcome. I know women. And I fear that the one that you once loved may be upset that you have brought me."

"Perhaps, but I think she will be content that I have found another and that I, too, am at last happy."

"Maybe," answered Marisa with a sigh, "but there are some women who, though they do not want a man for themselves, will yet do all possible to keep another from having him."

"Humph!" he grunted. "We will have to see. But if it becomes evident that this is so," he said, "there is not a person in whatever clan it is that adopts you who would not come to your defense."

"Perhaps," she said. "I am still apprehensive."

He bent toward her and brushed a kiss against her cheek before he said, "I will be there for you. Know that you have become and are now the most important person in my life."

"Truly?"

"Truly," he murmured the words against her cheek, before planting a sweet kiss against her lips. "Now," he said, straightening up, "come, our scouts have already spotted us and have given me the signal to enter into the village. Come, they will have told the people that we are here, and there will be many who will be curious to meet you."

Marisa inhaled deeply. Was she ready for this? Hardly. However, there was no going back.

Turning, Black Eagle led the way up the well-worn path to the village, and setting her pace to follow him, she trod along behind him.

\* \* \*

The view was spectacular. The village was positioned on a cliff overlooking Mohawk fields and the Mohawk River, which flowed and gurgled over rocks and boulders in an ever continuing cascade of white waves. In the distance, mountains and hills, rich with autumn color, rose up both east and west of them. Set against a blue sky, the site for the Mohawk village was surrounded by breathtaking beauty.

It gave her hope. Surely people who appreciated such aesthetics couldn't be completely savage.

The first sight of the village that met her view was that of a wooden stockade. Sharp wooden poles, driven into the ground, and tied at the top, enclosed whatever of the village she was about to see.

The entrance to the town was unusual, as well; it consisting of overlapping logs instead of a gate. At this entrance, she noted, was yet another outpost. Men stood there, heavily armed.

At the sight, Marisa cringed. But Black Eagle, who was in the lead, couldn't see her reaction. He paid the guards no attention. Marisa, however, was having second thoughts about the wisdom of coming to Black Eagle's home. What had seemed a good idea in theory was, in the flesh, rather daunting.

Black Eagle turned back toward her. He queried, "Are you ready?"

What could she say? There was no possibility of retreat. Not only could she not find her way back through the forest, but until she discovered what had motivated Thompson's behavior, Albany's safety remained in question.

Indeed, all she could do in response to Black Eagle's query was to smile, and say, "Ready? Indeed, I fear I am not. But lead on."

He smiled at her and winked. "Come."

# Twenty

A sentry post, consisting of a lean-to set atop four sturdy poles, sat at the inside position of the stockade's entrance. However, instead of a gate that opened and closed, the village entrance consisted of overlapping rows of spiked poles. Men stood on guard here; they were big, dangerous looking men. They were heavily armed. That each of them stared at her, not in greeting, but as though she were an enemy, was intimidating.

Marisa gazed at them, then away, swallowing hard. However, a quick look forward had her noting that she was lagging behind Black Eagle, and she hurried forward. As she and Black Eagle rounded the corner of the overlapping logs, the village at last came into view.

Like a scene gradually opening up before her, she first noticed colors, the greens of crops and grass, the browns of dried grass and buildings; the oranges, yellows and golds of produce set on the ground, as well as the various tree leaves turning color. The village, she decided, was not without beauty.

It felt warmer here, also, she observed, and it was a busy place, though oddly quiet. Women sat in groups, working and talking softly. Scantily dressed children were running freely, playing and speaking to each other, but even they were not overly loud. Older children were seated around their elders, helping with the work. There was drumming in the background, but it was muffled, as though it were coming from within a building.

There was a definite scent of smoke in the air, as well as the farm-rich fragrance of corn, beans and husks. And somewhere in the village, someone was barbecuing meat, or perhaps it was a soup that she smelled. Whatever it was Marisa's taste buds came alive. Her stomach growled, reminding her that the steady diet of dried corn and meat that she had been consuming was not the only food to be had.

She and Black Eagle were pacing down what appeared to be a major street. Here and there, trees and other flora decorated each side of the passageway, adding yet another layer of beauty to the enclosed village. Interestingly, except for the manner in which the people were dressed and the fact that they were obviously of a different race than she, the Mohawk village might have looked like a village anywhere.

Along the street were a few log cabins, but mostly the buildings consisted of very long structures, which looked to be made of logs and bark. In many aspects, she thought, they resembled barns.

Glancing under her lashes from one side of the street to the other, she noticed that conversations stopped when she passed and that many curious glances followed her. Although no one overly stared at her, she could feel their eyes upon her as she passed by them.

Through it all, a thought kept running through her mind, one that she couldn't shake.

*Will I be required to run the gauntlet?*

In Albany, hadn't she heard rumors that this was required of all captives? It was an ordeal, a circumstance where villagers lined up and forced a captive to run between them, beating a person as they ran through.

Was this to be her fate?

Briefly, Marisa shut her eyes and swallowed, hard.

Why hadn't she asked Black Eagle about this when she'd had the chance? Why hadn't she remembered the rumor until now?

Suddenly, and perhaps without cause, she felt as though she could not have been more on display if she had been walking naked through the village. To counter the feeling, she kept close on Black Eagle's heels. Perhaps too close.

A few times, she had come in so near to him that she had tripped him. But he had said nothing. Instead, he had merely turned to her and smiled, as though to give her courage.

At last they came to a particular longhouse where Black Eagle stopped. She was staring at the odd-looking bark structure when Black Eagle turned to her and said, "Remain here. I will be gone a moment only."

Marisa nodded, but she must have looked as worried as she felt, for he added, "No one will hurt you. You will see."

Again, she nodded, but as he left her to enter into the dwelling, she began to wring her hands.

A child who was dressed in a garment of dark blue, which was heavily embroidered, came up beside Marisa and chattered at her in a language Marisa didn't understand. Marisa paid the little girl no attention.

The child, however, was persistent, and pulled on Marisa's dress. At last, Marisa gave the little girl her attention, noticing that except for a different manner of dressing, the little girl looked like children everywhere. Two braids were caught at the sides of the child's face and in her arms was a corn-husk doll, a doll whose head was missing a face.

The child was prattling off words at such a rate, however, that Marisa felt slightly dizzy; she was also offering Marisa her doll, which Marisa steadfastly refused to take. Marisa did make the effort to show the girl that she didn't understand her words, but it seemed useless. The little girl persevered, pushing her doll into Marisa's hands.

At some length, Black Eagle returned and spoke to the child, then said to Marisa, "She welcomes you to her village. You'd best take the doll. To not do so is an insult."

"Oh." At last Marisa accepted the child's gift. "Would you tell her thank you for me?"

"*Nyah-weh*," he said to the child.

The girl smiled, and leaning in close, placed her hand within Marisa's.

"I think you've made a friend. Come," said Black Eagle. "I will introduce you to my mother."

"Your mother?" Marisa gasped, and held back. "I'm to meet your mother so soon? Without even changing my clothing or bathing first?"

"She will understand. Come."

Marisa sighed, wishing at this very moment that she were anywhere else but here. Nor could she make herself move to follow Black Eagle.

He stepped toward her, and taking a lock of her hair within his fingers, Black Eagle studied it as its burnished color glowed beneath the direct rays of the sun. He said, "Even unbathed and with clothes torn and dirty, you are the most beautiful woman I have known. Yours is a beauty, not only of the physical realm, but also of the heart. You have nothing to fear. My mother will be pleased to help you to bathe and to change. She will be honored." Black Eagle paused, then went on to explain, "There will be a council tonight to decide what clan will have the distinction of becoming your new family."

"My new family?" Marisa gasped. "I know you said something about that, but I . . . I don't understand. Why do I need a new family? Please tell me again. I thought I was to stay with you."

"We will be together," he said, "but to have your own family—a family that is not mine—is for your benefit. While you could live with my clan, you might find that things are not always to your liking."

Marisa's head was spinning, and she took a step backward. Her own family? Adoption? A clan?

Shaking her head, she said, "Please, Black Eagle. I must apologize if I seem ungrateful, but I don't understand why we couldn't simply have our own home, our own house."

He nodded toward the longhouses. "We could," he said, "but we would seem odd here in my village. We Iroquois call ourselves the *Haudenosaunee*, or the People of the Longhouse. No two people here in our village live alone. We all reside in the longhouse of our separate clans."

"Married people, children, elders, all reside with each other in the same house?"

"It is so. Each has his own quarters within the longhouse, however, and no one would ever think to disturb a person in his own part of the house."

"I see." Slowly Marisa let out her breath. She still had questions, however, and she argued, "But if all this is so, why couldn't I come and live with your clan instead of being adopted by people I don't know and have never met?"

"Because it would be unfair to you. It is true that we could live this way and no one would prevent it, but you might become unhappy."

"Unhappy? Unfair to me? How can that be? It seems natural to me to live with your husband's people."

"It might seem so at first, but all things here in my village are based on family or clan. What if we were to have an argument? Who would you go home to? Who would take your side? While it is true that there may be someone within my clan who might aid you, there could as easily be no one. But if you have your own family, it is certain that you will find a champion with them. They will treat you well. I promise." Black Eagle smiled at her and bending toward her, he whispered in her ear, "I know it is all strange to you, but you must persevere through this. Good things will come from this. You will see."

He planted a kiss on the delicate flesh of her ear. Then straightening away, he said, "Come. I think my elders will insist that a ceremony take place today. My mother will help you. It seems that Pretty Ribbon has decided to help you, also."

"Pretty Ribbon? Is that the child's name?"

He nodded.

"Pretty Ribbon. What a fascinating name." She smiled at the child, then said, "Very well. I will put my trust in you, then."

"I am honored."

"But Black Eagle," she continued, "this is not easy, and I am worried about what is to happen to me."

"I know you are. But I am here." He smiled at her, and so handsome was the look of him, her heart lurched up into her throat. It was a half grin he gave her, and although she realized he meant it as goodwill, and to bolster her spirits, that smile of his was incredibly sexy. It served to remind her not only how much she loved this man, but how much she trusted him.

Squeezing her hand, he repeated, "I am here." And turning to again take the lead, Black Eagle escorted her deeper into the village, with the little girl, Pretty Ribbon, holding Marisa's hand and skipping along beside her.


Marisa's mind was wandering.

Though her back was toward it, she knew the sun had journeyed to the west, if only because its orange and pinkish rays were coloring the dried grasses at her feet. In the distance from where she stood, fires had been lit. Women were busy cooking a celebration feast . . . for her.

The adoption had begun.

It was strange. She had been in the village no longer than a few hours and already she was being treated as though she had been born into the tribe.

Earlier, Black Eagle had indeed taken her to his mother, who had appeared pleased at the prospect of gaining a new daughter-in-law. She had been kind, considerate, acting as though there were nothing more important than ensuring her son's and her new daughter-in-law's happiness. This had done much to settle Marisa's nerves. It was especially so because Marisa kept expecting harshness from the woman, or from some other source, perhaps even abuse.

But it never came.

Black Eagle's mother, Blue Necklace, had escorted Marisa to a private place in the river to bathe; the little girl, Pretty Ribbon, had flounced along after them, happily talking to her doll. As Marisa had bathed, Blue Necklace had taken Marisa's own clothes and had set to washing them, hanging them to dry. Then the woman had set out a fresh set of other garments, Indian made, for Marisa's inspection. Next she had begun plaiting Marisa's hair.

What was intriguing to Marisa was that she had not been required to lift a finger to help. It was all done for her, as though she were a very special guest of honor.

Blue Necklace had kept up a steady stream of chatter, as well, bestowing Marisa with warm smiles and a gentle way. Interestingly, Black Eagle's mother seemed younger than what Marisa might have thought she would be. She was probably not over forty-five years in age, and she seemed to be a young forty-five as well.

A few basic hand signals had been used to communicate between the two women as Blue Necklace had sat, braiding Marisa's hair. As soon as that task had been completed, Blue Necklace had taken Marisa's hand and led her to the exquisite Indian costume she had earlier laid out. The dress was simple, made of trade cloth, but what fashioned the dress to be so handsome was the intricate embroidering that had been accomplished over most of the dress's surface. Its basic color was that of gold, with threads of blue and green and red sewn directly onto the gown, the embroidery stitching producing figures of water lilies.

*It is as though the gown was created especially for me.*

The sleeves were puffed at the shoulder and fell just below the elbow, and the bodice fit tightly, it, too, being embroidered with green and blue thread. Similarly made leggings fell down to moccasins, which matched the dress. Most amazing to Marisa, however, was that the gown fit.

"*Weh-yeh!*" said Blue Necklace.

Marisa shook her head.

"Beau-ti-ful . . . you . . ."

"*Nyah-weh*, thank you," said Marisa, and she had smiled at this woman who treated her so kindly. Then to herself and under her breath, Marisa had commented, "I wonder if all this kindness is in preparation for me running the gauntlet? As one might feed a turkey well before slaughter, am I to be dressed so that I might produce a spectacular image as I am forced to run through a line of villagers?"

"You . . . come . . . ," said Blue Necklace, and taking hold of Marisa's hand, she had led Marisa from the stream, back into the palisaded village, back along the main pathway that led through the village to the longhouse where Black Eagle had first taken her.

"Come." Again Blue Necklace had urged Marisa along with her, and lifting up the bark door of the longhouse, she had brought Marisa into the inner sanctum of the longhouse.

It had been dark on the inside, since the only light appeared to be from either the doorway or the smoke holes at the top of the structure. There were no windows.

The corridor had led from one end of the structure to the other, and it was long. There were hearths set in regular intervals down that corridor, spaced perhaps twenty feet apart. At that time, there had been a few of the older women seated around those fires, tending to them, and many of these women had been holding a child in their laps.

It had been yet another busy place, and a little noisier than the outside, since small children ran to and fro. She remembered that drums had been beating there, as well, and that men had been singing. Incredibly, the buzz of conversation had made the space seem homey.

Glancing around, Marisa had estimated that the longhouse was probably one hundred feet long and maybe thirty feet wide. It was a tall structure, perhaps twenty feet high. As Blue Necklace had led Marisa down the main passageway, Marisa had noted that on each side of the corridor were separate compartments, each partitioned off from the next with sheets of bark. There had been corncobs strung up to dry, gourds that had been set in neat rows on the floor and cooking utensils and other articles had been stored neatly next to the hearth.

Smoke holes in the ceiling let the smoke from the many fires escape, yet not all of the smoke left, she'd noted, for the interior was still smoky and warm. Plus, there had been food cooking, and Marisa had been pressed to contain her excitement. Were they going to eat?

About five hearths into the longhouse, Blue Necklace had signaled to Marisa to take a seat, which Marisa had done at once. Blue Necklace had then heaped upon a plate as many corncobs, corn cakes, ribs and succotash as Marisa had desired. It had been a feast. It had smelled delicious, and it had tasted even better.

Blue Necklace had watched her, smiling, and although she had allowed Marisa as much time as she needed to satisfy her appetite, as soon as Marisa had finished her meal, Blue Necklace had escorted her out of the longhouse, bringing her here, to the central point of the village.

People had gradually gathered here. Many speeches were being made, even as she stood before them, waiting, and many men had been talking for quite some time. Once again, Marisa felt as if she were the center of attention, especially so since she stood next to the speakers. What was being said? Did any of it have to do with her? But most importantly, did adoption consist of running the gauntlet?

Time passed, and when no actions were taken against her, Marisa began to study her audience. There were hundreds of people here, each one dark haired and dark skinned. A predominance of the men wore the Mohawk hairstyle proudly, with feathers attached at the back. However, there were other men who had cultivated their hair to long lengths, although these men tended to be older. The women appeared to favor three different hairstyles, either that of letting the hair hang loose and long, or that of two braids at the side of their face or one braid down the back.

But what set this meeting apart from any town meeting she had ever attended, thought Marisa, was that every person here seemed inordinately interested in what was taking place. No one interrupted the speaker, no one spoke when another was talking. Nor did their attention seem to vary.

Then she saw him. Black Eagle was winding his way through the crowd, toward her. At last here was a familiar face, someone dear to her. She felt herself come alive, and her heart warmed to him.

He was wearing what appeared to be white buckskin, she noted, heavily fringed and embroidered with flowing patterns of beadwork. Over his jacket, he wore a beaded baldric and in his hand was his ever-present musket. He still wore pouches of ammunition strung over his shoulder with straps, and in one of his sashes was his tomahawk. His leggings were skin tight and fell down to cover his moccasins. His step was light, and reflected in his eyes was a keen intelligence. One she recognized so very well. He was looking directly at her, and his gaze was soft, gentle.

As he drew level with her, he smiled, and murmured, "Have you understood what is happening here?"

"No. I fear I have not," she whispered back.

"Then let me tell you what is occurring. You are being adopted by a family of the Turtle Clan."

"The Turtle Clan?"

"*Nyoh*, yes. Look outward from here. Do you see the four people lined up there to your right?"

She nodded.

"This is your new family. I am here to introduce you to them, one by one, but I think you know one of them already."

As an ancient-looking woman stepped forward, there was a little girl caught onto her arm. It was Pretty Ribbon, the little girl who had befriended her almost as soon as she had stepped foot inside the village. Marisa was at once delighted.

"This is your clan mother," spoke Black Eagle. "She is the matron of the Turtle Clan."

The two women acknowledged each other with a nod, and the clan mother presented Marisa with a gift of corn. Marisa graciously accepted it.

"You already know Pretty Ribbon, and behind Pretty Ribbon is her mother, Rainbow, and Pretty Ribbon's elder sister, Laughing Maid. You are replacing their brother, who was lost recently in Sir Johnson's battle with the French."

"I'm to replace a brother?"

"*Nyoh*, yes. Taking another's place does not require you to be of the same sex."

"How fascinating." Marisa said, as she smiled and nodded to her new sisters. Pretty Ribbon, however, could not long keep her enthusiasm to herself, and Marisa caught her hand, as the child placed it within her own.

Laughing Maid, the elder sister, stepped forward, and in her arms was a wooden tray full of food. With some ceremony, and words that Marisa could not understand, she placed the tray into Marisa's free hand. Again, Marisa accepted the gift, but as soon as she had an opportunity, she murmured to Black Eagle beneath her breath, "What are all these gifts about?"

"Your family and I are ensuring your safety. First you required a new family. And now that you have that family, we are to marry."

"We are to marry?"

"Yes, you and I."

"On the same day that I am adopted by people I little know? Is this not happening a little fast?"

"It is considered necessary," he explained. "No one here is foolish enough to consider that we have not indulged in lovemaking. It is evident that we are in love, and we have been much alone. Therefore, your family thinks it best that a marriage takes place between us with all possible speed. Already your family acts in your behalf."

Marisa had barely enough time to digest this information, when Blue Necklace stepped forward to place a tray full of food into Black Eagle's hands.

Black Eagle inclined his head toward his mother, then

said to Marisa, "And now we exchange these food trays, and when we do, we are married. Are you ready?"

Marisa nodded, and releasing Pretty Ribbon's hand so that she could hold the trays without dropping them, Marisa exchanged her tray with Black Eagle's. Black Eagle let out a deep breath, smiled at her, and said, "And now you are my wife."

"Wife," she repeated, almost to herself. *I am this man's wife.*

Looking up at him, and staring into his dark, dark eyes, it occurred to her that her life had taken a sharp turn. However, from all indications it seemed that it might be a turn for the better. Only time would tell.

At least, she thought, she had a family who appeared to want her and a husband who loved her. As Black Eagle had once said, she had a new life.

Marisa was touched by their kindness, and she might not have been quite human were there not a tear or two at the back of her eyes. But she didn't cry. Instead, she smiled. And it was not lost on her that this was the first time she had done so since coming into the village.

All she said to her new husband, however, was, "I love you."

Nonetheless, it might have been an eloquent speech, for his reaction was a heartwarming smile, and taking her on his arm, he led her away, toward their new home in the longhouse of the Turtle Clan.

# Twenty-one

After a month of being in the Mohawk village, life had settled into a routine. To the mornings fell the activities of collecting water, and food preparation. There was corn to grind into flour, berries to be picked and dried, stews and soups to be made. Black Eagle often added to her chores, as well, by bringing home game; it had to be cleaned, cut up and eaten or dried for storage.

Afternoons passed leisurely in much the same way. Always, there were chores, but there were so many people to help and to talk to, that the time passed quickly.

And then there were the evenings. Marisa looked forward to the nights. Usually the evening hours started with a wash and a swim in the river. Then it was back to the longhouse to eat and to sit around the fire with family. But mostly, many evenings meant cuddling with Black Eagle.

At present both Marisa and her sister, Laughing Maid, were returning from their twilight swim, where they had both played a rousing game of ball. There was a slight chill in the air, a warning that winter was coming, but Marisa was laughing and drying her hair, as was Laughing Maid.

"I hear that your husband has returned with another deer," said Laughing Maid in the Iroquois tongue.

"Another one? It has only been a matter of days since I cleaned the last one," Marisa replied in the same tongue. It was interesting to note, she thought, that when one had good reason, one could quickly learn to converse in another language.

"I think your husband is very daring. He goes out alone many times, which is unusual. I think he is trying to show you he is a good provider."

"*Nyoh*, I believe you are right, although he has no need to try to impress me. He will always be a hero to me."

"A hero. Yes. Do you think you could tell the story again tonight? The story of how he rescued you?"

"I could try, although he tells it better than I do. There are some parts that I don't remember well."

"That is to be understood. You almost drowned. But if you tell it while we work, I could help you to skin and clean the deer as I listen."

"That would be very well," said Marisa, "very well, indeed, but can you spare the time?"

"The harvest is done, and since we have more than enough food to last us through the winter, most of my work is over. I have little to do but to wait for the Harvest Festival."

"The Harvest Festival. Yes, I've heard others talking about it. What happens at the Harvest Festival?"

"You will like it. It is the time when we thank the 'three sisters,' corn, squash and beans. During the day, many of our wisest men will give speeches of thanksgiving. And at night, there will be dances and games. Few people sleep, for the fun goes on the night through. Truly, you will like it."

"I'm sure that I will," said Marisa. "Is there anything special I should do for it?"

"You can help with the food preparation. There will be much feasting. And at night, you can wear your best dress. The evenings are when lovers meet and plan their futures."

"Ah, but I already spend most evenings with my husband."

"Yes, but you will still need a special dress. I will help you with that."

"That would be most pleasing," said Marisa, falling into step with Laughing Maid.

As the two women approached the village, they were met by Pretty Ribbon, who came immediately to Marisa's side and took her hand.

"Sister," said Pretty Ribbon, "I made this for you." The little girl presented Marisa with a bouquet of wild flowers, tied together with a piece of bark.

"Oh, they're beautiful," said Marisa, and she bent down to give the little girl a hug and kiss. "How lucky I am that you are my sister." She hugged her tightly.

Under the compliment, Pretty Ribbon beamed. "The clan mother says that if I ask you, I might be able to try on your white man's clothes. Then we can see how I might look if I were a white person."

"Ah," said Marisa, "but you have no need to be a white person. You are perfect exactly as you are." Oddly enough, Marisa meant it. It had been a little over four weeks now that she had been adopted into the Mohawk tribe, and Marisa would have been hard-pressed to recall a happier time in her life.

Although it was true that an Indian woman's work was hard and constant, it was never daunting. One was not harassed to do more than she could easily do, and there were always helping hands if one fell behind. To add to her pleasure, however, Pretty Ribbon had become Marisa's almost constant companion, and oddly enough it was the little girl who had helped Marisa to learn the language.

"I would still like to try them on," said Pretty Ribbon.

"And so you shall," said Marisa. "Come, let us return home. I am told that my husband is back from hunting and that he has brought in even more deer meat."

"He has," said Pretty Ribbon. "Can I help you to feed him?"

"Of course you can. Come, let's hurry." And Marisa, taking both of her sister's hands, said, "Do you want to race?"

Laughing Maid grinned, but Pretty Ribbon wasn't too keen. She said, "I am too little. I always lose."

"Yes," said Laughing Maid, "but look at how hard you try. You are faster than any of the other girls your age."

"I am?"

"*Nyoh.* Yes, you are."

That decided it. "Then let us race," said Pretty Ribbon. Smiling up at her two sisters, she said, "Go!"

And with much laughing, the three sisters flew on home, and surprisingly enough, Pretty Ribbon won.


Was she happy?

As Black Eagle stood next to his fellow runners on the race track, he chanced to look toward the sidelines of the track, catching his wife's eye. He witnessed her smile, and he returned it, watching her even when she glanced away.

She seemed happy, he thought, but he was aware that his village provided a life greatly different than what her own had been. Could she be content here with him? Without all the material wealth to which she was accustomed? Or would there come a time when she would yearn for the company of her own people? Material things?

He wished desperately that he had been able to find and save Miss Sarah from the falls. Her loss had come at a bad time, not only because she had earned his respect, but because she deserved better than to die at the hands of a traitor.

That she would have provided good company for his wife was also good reason to lament her loss. Hopefully his wife's new sister, Laughing Maid, would render companionship for *Ahweyoh*, as well. That Pretty Ribbon was enamored with her new sister was also evident. The child rarely left *Ahweyoh*'s side.

Nonetheless, he worried. Was it enough? He hoped so.

Bringing his attention back to the present, he noticed that *Ahweyoh* had raised up her glance to meet his, and that she was now staring back at him with such blatant seduction that Black Eagle was stunned at first, yet responded, as any healthy male might . . . and instantly. His loins stirred to life, reminding him that he had the entire evening to hold his wife in his arms, if he wished to wait that long.

However, this was not a good thought to recall at the start of a footrace. He needed his wits about him if he were to win this race. And it was important that he win. After all, his family had placed bets on his success.

Shaking his head, he turned around, presenting the people on the sidelines with his back, as he endeavored to calm his body and bring his attention back to the matter at hand. The fields had been cleared for the race. Later, the same ground would be used in the game of lacrosse. He would be involved in that game, too.

But for now, he had to concentrate. He wished to win this race, not only for himself and his reputation, but also to impress his wife. He sighed. She seemed to always be in his thoughts.


It was the second day of the Harvest Festival, the first day having been rained out. Today, however, had dawned a warm, clear and bright day.

Marisa stood on the outskirts of the footrace. Black Eagle was there, stripped down of all his clothes, save his breechcloth and moccasins, as were all of the participants. But none looked better, sexier or stronger than Black Eagle. Indeed, when he caught her eye, she smiled, then looked down, feeling self-conscious. But why?

After several weeks of being in the camp, she had observed a certain independence in the Mohawk women. They were not a timid people, nor were they cowed by their men or subservient to them. While never encroaching on a man's realm, nor detracting from his natural strength or power, the women yet retained much strength of their own.

Perhaps she had some of that grit, too. Setting her shoulders back, she brushed her hair from her face and looked up at Black Eagle once more. She smiled, presenting him with silent seduction. Gone was her reserve, and quite deliberately, she bestowed upon Black Eagle what had to be a "come-on" look. She watched, then, as he so obviously received her intent, watched also a part of his body that was not within his conscious control twitch to life. Fortunately for her, but unfortunate for him, the breechcloth he wore provided little cover.

She grinned, feeling extremely feminine, yet powerful in her own right. His reaction was exactly what she had hoped for, but what she hadn't counted on was an answering response that echoed within her.

"Your husband is the fastest runner in all the Mohawk Nation." It was Laughing Maid speaking. All three sisters stood together at the side of the track. As was becoming commonplace, Pretty Ribbon was hanging onto Marisa's hand.

"The fastest runner? Truly?"

"*Nyoh*, we will see today if he will hold onto the honor. Look, they are about to begin."

A shot fired and all the men who were participating in the race leapt forward. The crowd around her sent up cheers. At first, Black Eagle lagged behind several of the others, but it wasn't long before he had started to pull ahead.

"Go Black Eagle!" she cried in English, adding her voice to the shouts of those around her.

And then all of the runners disappeared into a valley. Momentarily, the participants were hidden from view.

The track was long, perhaps a two or three mile run. Several fields had been cleared to make the track, and later today it would be used for other games, as well. However, these fields dipped into and out of the forests, and perhaps this made the race more interesting to the runners, but difficult for the spectators. The track did make a large circle that would eventually bring the runners back to the starting point, which was also the finishing line. But that didn't make the spectator's anxiety less.

"Look there!"

"I see them!"

The runners were coming back, headed toward them from the opposite direction. Who was in the lead? Was it Black Eagle? She edged forward, straining to see.

It was Black Eagle in the lead, along with another youth, one whose name she had never learned. The two were coming into the finish line neck and neck.

As they sped across that line, it was evident that Black Eagle won. But perhaps he had done so only by a nose. The youth had been right on his heels.

The crowd yelled and cheered, and several well-wishers rushed forward to congratulate not only Black Eagle, but the youth who had put him to the test. Among them was a beautiful, young Indian woman. Marisa took note.

"It is good that Black Eagle won," observed Laughing Maid. "The boy who almost beat him is the brother of White Doe."

"White Doe?" asked Marisa.

Laughing Maid nodded toward the pretty woman.

"Who is she?" asked Marisa.

"She is the one who broke your husband's heart by marrying another. It is said that she was in love with Black Eagle, but because his family was poorer than Good Shield's, she passed Black Eagle by. It is said that she still loves Black Eagle, and were Black Eagle a little less proud, that she would allow him to have an affair with her."

"Is that possible here, where everyone knows everyone else?"

"Of course it is possible. But do not worry. Black Eagle is an honorable man, and Good Shield is a faithful husband to White Doe and a good father to their children. It may only be gossip, also."

"Yes," said Marisa. "It is probably no more than gossip. People do like to talk."

Still, as Marisa looked at the woman, it was a less than amicable glance. She said, "Perhaps I will go and congratulation my husband, as well. Come, Pretty Ribbon, let's go and give my husband a kiss."

When Pretty Ribbon nodded, Marisa pushed forward, through the crowd, eventually elbowing her way to the center of attraction. As she approached Black Eagle, she noted that White Doe stood by his side, smiling up at him, as though she deserved his extra-special attention.

*We'll have none of that*, thought Marisa, and coming directly up to Black Eagle, she stood unashamedly before him. Standing on tiptoe, she reached up to place a kiss on his lips.

He responded immediately, pulling her in close to him, deepening the kiss, acting as though none of the other people who stood around them existed. She whispered, "Congratulations!"

But his only response was a low growl, as his tongue took advantage of her open lips and invaded her mouth. She responded with much the same fervor as he, and the kiss went on and on. Even the people around them began to comment:

"They are newly married. It is only natural."

"They are in love."

Several people laughed.

Eventually, he broke off the kiss, but only to pull her even closer in his arms, and bringing his head down to inhale the fragrance of her hair, he said in English, "Perhaps I should ask White Doe to stand by me every day of my life."

Marisa broke apart from him. "Oh, you! You knew!"

He grinned at her. "Of course I knew. And I like it. Pretty Ribbon, can you go and find your other sister? *Ahw-eyoh* and I are going to our quarters."

And when Pretty Ribbon nodded, Black Eagle said to Marisa, "Come. There are some things we need to do."

Marisa grinned.

* * *

Lifting up the bark door of the longhouse, Black Eagle escorted his wife into its dark interior. Since most everyone was at the festival, the dwelling was almost deserted. He had no more than closed the door, when he backed her up against one of the posts and stole a kiss.

"You flirted with me before the race," he stated between kisses, speaking in English.

She laughed. "Yes, I did."

Reaching down to grab hold of her buttocks, he pulled her in toward him. "Do you not realize," he asked, "that it is difficult to race when your blood is pooling in the center of your body?" He kissed her again.

"Oh?" She wiggled out of his embrace and ran down the corridor to their own quarters. He followed.

"*Nyoh*. And now comes your punishment."

"Ah! And what punishment is that?"

He caught up with her and brought her into his embrace again, but this time he tickled her ribs.

"Stop that!" she demanded, but she laughed nonetheless.

He repeated his teasing, running his fingers up and down her sides. She squirmed.

But he didn't release her. Instead he kissed and tickled her at the same time.

At last she freed herself, and laughing up at him, she opened the bark partition that separated their quarters from the others. She flung herself onto their bed, but the landing was soft, since the bed was made of corn husks.

With another "come-hither" look in her eye, she said, "Can you not think of any other kind of punishment for me?"

He growled at her before he followed her down onto the bed and he kissed her. "Take that," he said.

She giggled.

"And that," he whispered as his tongue licked her lips.

"Oh, my dear husband, these are, indeed, cruel and unusual punishments."

"There are others that come to mind," he said, "I can think of many penances I would like to demand from you. But for now I find that instead of retribution, I would rather play. Not the lacrosse game I am supposed to take part in yet this day. I fear it would not go well, anyway, because I am distracted by . . ." He gave her a knowing look. "Things, and I think that I should like to do nothing better than spend the day with my wife. After all, I am free to decide what kind of games I care to play."

She was already untying the blouse of her dress, and crawling up onto her knees on the bed, she slowly lowered her blouse until it fell off of her, her glance at him pure enticement.

She said, "And what sort of games were you thinking of playing, Sir Eagle?"

He sighed, sat up to pull the bark partition back into place and said, "Fun, exciting and thrilling games."

*Ahweyoh* was already leaning her hips in toward him and moving against him in a way that made his blood boil. He came up onto his knees before her, and said, "Do you know what you do to me?"

"I think so, but—"

Whatever else it was that she'd been about to say was lost to the air. He caught her and kissed her long and hard, grinding his hips in against hers. Then he nudged his face into the crook of her neck, and he murmured, "Does that give you an idea of how I feel when you seduce me?"

She laughed. "Why, sir, I don't know what you mean. I am a young maid after all. I think you will have to be more explicit."

"That is possible. That is entirely possible." His hands felt her everywhere, but this time minus the tickling. Instead, he intended seduction. She sighed, and in response he felt himself grow bolder.

He pushed her down so that she was lying beneath him. Already his hands had spanned her full breasts.

What happiness! What joy! He brought his head to her chest and with his lips, he did adore her. First he lingered over one breast, then the other. After some time, he raised himself up and said, "Your flirtation at the race comes at a bad time since I have been away several days on the hunt and I have been very much missing my wife."

"Oh?" She drew her shoulders back, and with head thrown back, gave him full reign over her. "Missing her how?"

He looked up at her and smiled briefly before continuing his adoration. "You are a seductress."

She giggled. "I should hope so. I would hate for you to have to pine after White Doe."

He shook his head. "White Doe made her choice long ago, and she is married to a good man. In truth, I am glad she did not choose me. If she had, I would not now know your warmth, and I would be less a man because of it."

"Less a man?"

"What good is a man without a good woman beside him? Would he have the warmth of children around him?"

"But she would have given you that."

"So she would have. But she wouldn't have made my heart sing. She wouldn't have inspired me to arise each day to do nothing more than make her smile. Indeed, I would be only half alive without you, the woman of my dreams."

She stared at him for some time before she said, "I love you."

"As I love you."

"But, sir, long have I been attracted to your golden tongue. I fear you have seduced me with your stories from the start of our acquaintance."

"Seduction? Perhaps. But stories? I merely say the truth as I see it," he said. "However, we talk when I wish to be making love."

"True."

His hands were already at her skirt, and he pulled it off her with ease. He caught his breath. There she lay before him, pale, naked, luscious.

He said, "I am a lucky man."

"Perhaps," she answered huskily, "but more than that,

you are a good man. You are the man I love. The man
whom I hope I have seduced into spending the afternoon
with me."

He grinned down at her. "I fear that you have captured
me for the whole day, and your whole life."

"Do you promise?"

"I promise." He smiled, but at the same time a sadness
filled his heart. Was there a reason for it? Maybe. He said,
"Ah, I much prefer Mohawk clothes to the white man's.
They are easier to remove."

Again, she laughed. "At your service, sir."

He commenced to loving her; he felt her everywhere,
down her sides, over her chest, to her belly, her hips, around
to the heart of her sexuality. Her skin was soft, her scent
sweet, and it drove him to distraction. He had never felt
more ready for a women.

His lips soon followed where his fingers led. That she
wiggled against him, teasing him, sent him practically
reeling. In truth, so inspiring was she, he found his breath
catching in his throat.

But he cautioned himself against too much action, too
soon. Slowly, slowly. He would give her all the pleasure
it was within him to give. In this way, regardless of what
the future held for them, she might always remember their
lovemaking . . .

He had no way of knowing how long she would be with
him. He hoped a lifetime, but he didn't fool himself. Life
held no guarantees.

Perhaps it was a vision of things to come, but already he
feared her loss. If she ever desired to leave and go back to
the whites, he would take her. It would destroy him to do
so, but he would do it.

There was also the white man to consider. To his people
a woman was free to make her own choice. But this was
not so in the white man's world. It was as if the white man
thought of his women as possessions, instead of as mates.

Indeed, if the whites knew she were here, her desires
would not be considered. Nor his. They would take her.

But enough. She was here now. And she was his wife.

As he slid his lips down her breasts to her belly and beyond, he whispered, "I worry."

"You do?"

"You have been here now for a full moon, and I am uncertain. I wonder, are you happy?"

"Very."

He came up onto his elbows over her. "Do you tell me true?"

"I am very happy, my husband. And with good reason. I have a family of my own. I have a husband whom I adore and who loves me in return. Though a woman's work here is great, I admit, it is not all consuming and everyone is so kind to me. Plus, I feel an independence here that is hard for me to explain. This experience is new to me. Are all your women considered . . . equal?"

"We are all of us human beings," he said, kissing the inside of her leg.

"Yes, but there are those who consider themselves to be above a mere human being. I used to think this, too. I no longer do."

He came up onto his elbows over her, and gazing up at her, he said, "The white man's beliefs are ofttimes foolish. What is a man without a woman? He has bad clothes, bad food, no happiness and no children. Why would a man seek to enslave that being who completes him? Only a man who has lost his reason, who himself is less than a human being, would seek to do this."

"Do you mean it?"

"It is what I think. It is what most of my people think."

"That would explain much. It would also offer a reason why I feel so free here. It's very empowering. I only wish Sarah were here to experience this. She would . . . She would . . ." Her voice broke.

"I, too, feel Miss Sarah's loss," he said. "After the festival, we will have a condolence ceremony to console you. I would have asked for it immediately, but such ceremonies must be done properly with full ritual and this is not easy to accomplish in the fall when there is so much work to do in preparation for winter. But when the winter moons are upon us, we of the Mohawk tribe will console you."

"You will?"

He nodded.

There were tears in her eyes; tears she tried to hide from him. But he wouldn't let her. Instead he raised himself up over her, kissed her lips, and bringing up a finger, he wiped her tears away.

She said, "Thank you, Black Eagle. You are good to me."

"And I hope to be even better to you. Now lie here still, and enjoy."

"Lie still? How is that possible, when you make me want to burst with joy?"

He groaned. "You flatter me. But"—he smiled—"I would not have you talk any other way." And coming up over her, he looked down at her, trying to see to her very being, and when he kissed her, his tongue invaded her mouth with such intensity and ardor, he might have been branding her. In truth, maybe he was. She was his. He would have the whole world know it.

Downward his kisses spread, centering over her body, his lips ranging lower and lower until at last he found the feminine haven he had been seeking. Her sighs and moans were pure enchantment and he kissed her directly there, where he knew her desire culminated.

He loved her. Somehow the words in neither tongue seemed fiery enough. He truly *loved* her. And her heated response affected him like fire to kindling. He gloried in her response, watched as she met her pleasure.

Ah! Sweetness! Pure sweetness!

He wanted her. All of her. It was time.

Rising up onto his knees, he brought her legs up and onto his shoulders, pressing his masculinity against her and making himself a part of her. Staring down at her, looking deeply into her eyes, he gazed into her soul. He knew exactly who she was. And he loved her.

He was rigid and hard, he was halfway to satisfaction,

yet first he would tell her a matter of importance, and he said by way of a pledge, "I little know what the future holds. Our way may be hard, but I would keep you with me. Always."

There were tears in her eyes as she said, "How I love you."

"And I love you, my wife."

The stimulation was almost more than he could easily stand. But he refused to meet his own pleasure until she was consumed with hers. He watched as the excitement built up within her, witnessed the beauty of her struggle as she reached toward pleasure. Still he held back until he felt the beginnings of her release and then he joined in with her, thrusting deeply into her. Ah, what beauty. What pleasure.

Over and over the elation washed through him, his thrusts deep into her as though he would make his claim upon her here and now. All he had, all he would ever be, he gave to her. Freely.

He only hoped it would be enough.

# Twenty-two

Afternoon passed to night, night to morning, and still they lay abed, surfacing only occasionally for sustenance. No one bothered them, not even when Black Eagle failed to show for the lacrosse game. Indeed, the morning hours of the next day found them awake, then snoozing, awake again, then more snoozing.

And still they loved. It was as though they both knew it might never last, as though by unspoken yet mutual agreement, they would horde their time now, even if it meant blocking out the rest of the world.

Black Eagle lay against her, and he was exhausted. But he would not leave his wife's side. As long as she needed him, he would muster up the wherewithal to satisfy her . . . somehow.

It was *Ahweyoh* who was the first to mention that perhaps they might seek out the company of others. She said, "I hear there is dancing at night during the festival."

"There is."

"Is it the sort of dancing that I can do?"

"I could teach you, or your sisters could. Are you wanting to attend?"

"Perhaps. Tell me, my husband, do you think we might have made a child last night?" She grinned at him.

His heart swelled. He said, "I would be the happiest man on earth if we did, for I can think of no better joy than raising a family with my wife, she whom I love with all my being."

"I want a child. Somehow a child is . . . permanent."

He nodded. "Yes. A child is permanent. Perhaps a child might bridge our two worlds, as well. But I fear that this might not be good for the child. As soon as possible, we should find a safe place where we can stand together, if only for the sake of any children we might bring into the world."

"What are you saying? That you fear for our future? Because if so, let me assure you again that I have never been happier."

"It is not you I fear, but rather what the white people will do if they know you are here . . ."

She frowned. "Then we shall not let them know."

"Yes." He nodded. "*Nyoh*. We should not let them know."

She smiled. "I am so happy. It is hard for me to think seriously, though perhaps I should."

However, though she might talk of seriousness, she yet giggled, and coming up on top of him, she tickled him on his ribs. But he didn't laugh.

She frowned at him. "You should chuckle or at least smile," she said. "Aren't you ticklish?"

"Of course I am. But I am a man. I can endure all kinds of torture."

"Oh, can you? Then how about this kind of torture?" And so saying, she slid down his chest, lower and lower over his belly and on downward until she was caressing and kissing the very essence of his masculinity.

He grunted, the sound low, masculine and deep in his throat. How had he ever come to be so lucky?

On that thought, he sighed. And his last conscious reflection, before he surrendered himself to her charm, was to avow to himself that so long as he existed he would love and protect this woman. Forever he would give of himself to her, all of his love, his loyalty, the crux of who and what he was.

And if future times might become unbearable, they would survive. Indeed, they would survive.


The central fire was ablaze when Marisa and Black Eagle at last joined in with the rest of the festivities. The rhythmic beat of the drum was low, was contagious, and people, old and young, were dancing. Many were singing, and the hum of talk and laughter filled the night air. The happiness of the people was a tangible thing, and it abounded around him. How could anything ever come to take this away?

It seemed impossible.

Black Eagle watched with delight as his wife caught and held her sister, Laughing Maid's, eye. He watched as the two shared a smile.

It was good. Not only were these women sisters, they were friends.

Pretty Ribbon soon found them. This, too, was good.

The little girl's devotion to *Ahweyoh* was pleasing, he thought. And in truth, he owed the child his gratitude, for it was because of Pretty Ribbon that *Ahweyoh*'s transition to their village life had gone so smoothly. He would honor the girl in some way.

His wife bent toward Pretty Ribbon as the child grabbed hold of her hand, and she hugged the little girl. Taking her in her arms, he heard her say, "I love you."

His heart swelled.

Pretty Ribbon grinned back at *Ahweyoh*, and said, "I made something for you. Come and see!"

Though he didn't wish to eavesdrop on their conversation, he would have been hard-pressed not to witness *Ahweyoh* nod her agreement. Soon, she stood to her feet, and turning toward him, she said, "I am going to see what Pretty Ribbon has for me."

Black Eagle inclined his head. "Yes. Go. I will join the drumming and singing. I will be over there." He indicated the drum with a flicking motion of his head, then smiled at her. "These songs are a part of who we Mohawk people are. When you have finished, if you would come and stand behind me as I sing, I would be honored."

*Ahweyoh* beamed at him. "I will. I, too, would be honored."

They shared a smile that was intimate, perhaps even passion filled, and then *Ahweyoh* turned to leave, the little girl still clutching at her hand.

Black Eagle watched his wife for a while. Yet again, a sadness invaded his heart. Why did he have a bad feeling about this? Why did he worry about their future so greatly? And why couldn't he shake the feeling?

It was most likely nothing. Conceivably he worried needlessly. They were here. They were safe in his village.

At least for now, things were good. Maybe the drumming and singing would clear his mind.

He could only hope it would be so.


Pretty Ribbon half pulled, half led Marisa to the place where she had hidden a gift. It was in an opposite direction to where Black Eagle had indicated she would later find him. With a heartfelt look at him, she bid him adieu, and willingly let herself be led by the child.

As Marisa passed by several women whom she knew, she acknowledged them with a greeting. It was much returned.

"What have you made for me?" Marisa asked Pretty Ribbon at last.

"You will see. Come."

"Yes, I'm coming."

Pretty Ribbon dragged Marisa onto the outskirts of the fire's circle, leading her up onto a grassy knoll. It was pleasant here, Marisa thought. It was here at the crown of the hill where the west wind blew up behind them, reminding *Ahweyoh* of the story of the Thunderer and *Ahweyoh*. Marisa smiled.

Gazing upward, even the clouds and stars looked closer. As Marisa inhaled deeply, Pretty Ribbon said, "Here it is."

Marisa bent down onto her haunches to see what was so important. Whatever it was, it was hidden beneath a rock. Cautiously, she lifted up the rock to find a folded up piece of hemp parchment. Pictures were scribbled all over it.

"I drew it myself," said Pretty Ribbon.

It was not exactly easy to see in the darkness, yet if Marisa squinted, she could discern certain qualities of the picture. It was a drawing of herself and Black Eagle, as seen from the eyes of a child. There he was, captured on parchment, a dark and handsome stick figure; there she was, a red-haired, pale stick figure. They were drawn holding hands. And by her side was another, tinier stick figure. A dark-haired child with two braids.

"That's me," said Pretty Ribbon pointing.

"Why it's beautiful," praised Marisa. "You are quite an artist. I love it."

"It is yours. I made it for you."

"You did? What a wonderful present. I will always treasure it. But where did you get this paper?"

"Oh, from him." Pretty Ribbon pointed back into the crowd, but Marisa couldn't see who it was that she indicated.

"Who?"

Again Pretty Ribbon took Marisa's hand. "I'll show you."

And before Marisa could think to object, Pretty Ribbon was pulling her back into the crowd, winding her way between the bigger adults, until she had brought Marisa face-to-face with a white man. It was a white man Marisa knew, though just barely. It was Sir William Johnson.

Shocked, Marisa stopped still.

At the insistent touch of the child, William Johnson

spun round toward them. At first he barely acknowledged Marisa, and he turned his back on her. However, after only a few seconds, he swung back around.

Squinting and frowning at her, he said, "Lady Marisa? Be that who ye are?"

"Sir William," she acknowledged. "Yes, of course you would attend the festival. You are yourself, Mohawk, are you not?"

He didn't answer the question. Instead, he asked one of his own, and said, "But what has happened to ye?"

"I live here now."

"Here?" Adopted as he was into the Mohawk Nation or not, he seemed taken aback.

"Yes," she repeated, "here. I had trouble on the way to New Hampshire," she went on to explain. "We were attacked, and I have lost my maid to the falls, I fear. She was my best friend. I, myself, was rescued by a Mohawk man. I owe him my life. He brought me here."

"I see." Sir William nodded, yet it was clear that he was lost in thought, for his gaze at her seemed distracted. He continued, "Then I shall rescue ye further. I shall take ye home."

"Please no, Sir William. I am home, and I would beg you to forget that you have seen me here. I have married into the tribe now, and I wish to remain. My old life is gone. But I have a new life, and my new life is here."

Sir William remained silent for far too long. At length, he said, "I understand yer fascination with these people, for I share it with ye, lass. But I fear I canna let ye stay. Ye are a white woman."

"Yes I am, and you have a Mohawk wife, who has left her people to stay with you."

That Sir William seemed taken aback by her defense was a surprise, and they stared at one another for several more moments. "Ye dinna belong here," he said after a while.

"Perhaps, but if your reasoning has to do with the color of my skin, then it is clear to me that you do not belong here either."

"But, lass, I am a man."

"Yes," she said, "obviously, and I am a woman."

Their looks clashed with one another. Then, as though resigned, Sir William said, "Touché. I forget the urges of youth sometimes. Stay by all means if ye must, Lady Marisa." He placed his hand on her shoulder. "Yer secret is safe with me. But should ye ever desire to leave, ye have only to send me a note."

"I will remember," she said, and glancing to her left, toward Black Eagle, where he sat amongst the other men, she caught his attention. Curiously, he looked up at her, then at Johnson, his gaze taking in Johnson's hand on her shoulder. And even though there was a goodly distance between them, she could feel the heat of his regard.

Within only a matter of moments, he had left his place at the drum, had come up behind Marisa and she heard him say, "Sir William, my heart is happy to see you. I think you have already met my wife."

Sir William gazed from one of them to the other. At length, he said, "Ye are her husband?"

"I am."

"Aye, lass, ye couldn't have done better. Black Eagle is like me own son, and it is good to see ye. It has been several moons. I fear I did not know ye had married."

Black Eagle stepped forward, coming to her side. He smiled at his friend, and placed his hand on Johnson's shoulder. He said, "I sent a runner to you. Did you not receive my message?"

"I did, son. But there is a war going on."

*"Nyoh."*

"I take it that ye are the brave who rescued this lady, then?"

"I am."

Sir William nodded. "Ye realize that if this marriage is known, there will be trouble."

*"Nyoh."*

"Ye should let her come with me. I know 'twould tear ye apart. But 'tis best."

"No!" It was Marisa speaking. "I do not wish to go!"

Her declaration was met with silence, an uncomfortable silence at best, until at last Black Eagle said, "That is your answer, Sir William. I will not force my wife to do something she doesn't wish to do."

"Then I will try to keep this silent, son. I will do my best. But ye might be advised to go west. Ye are close to Albany here. Too close. Word will leak out eventually. There are traders in yer camp, and there will be more and more English who will come here as the war rages on around Mohawk land. Aye, if ye wish to be together, my advice would be to go west."

"*Nyuh-weh*, thank you," said Black Eagle. "I hope that your family is well. How is your sister, Catherine?"

"I am afraid she is missing her husband, who, if ye will remember died at the Battle of Lake George."

"I remember it well. I am grieved for your sister. It is true that women sometimes miss their husbands too much."

Though it was evident to Marisa that the two men were close friends, neither seemed willing to negotiate separate viewpoints as regards her. However, the offering of an olive branch came from Black Eagle, and he said, "I would be honored if you would come to my home before you leave. I would like to make a feast for you, since you missed our wedding."

"That would be a fine thing, son," said Johnson. "That would be a fine thing, indeed."

Black Eagle nodded. "It will be done. My wife and I now go to prepare."

As they turned to leave, Johnson smiled at them both.


"Yer to get her, man!"

"I cannot. My uncle forbids it. My only purpose in seeking you out, Sir Rathburn, is to inform you that your niece is in good health and is being well cared for, although apparently she lost her maid in an attack upon them. My uncle is aware that you have offered a ransom for her return, and he begs you to release it, and to ease your mind as to her fate. She is happy and wishes to remain where she is. Therefore, the bounty is unnecessary."

"'Tis very necessary. Do ye think I am the sort of man to leave her with Indians? A lady?"

"It is her wish," said Guy Johnson, Sir William's nephew. "Perhaps in time Sir William or myself can convince her to leave the Indians and return home of her own free will, but if she does not wish to leave them, the Indians will defend her to a man."

"Aye, of course. But, perhaps if we sent an army to rescue her . . ."

"And lose the Mohawk alliance with the English in a time of war?"

"Aye. Aye." John Rathburn frowned. "'Tis not yer problem. 'Tis mine."

"I beg you, do not do anything foolish. We cannot risk turning the Mohawk against us. An army sent into their camp, regardless of the reason, will upset them. Simply take to heart that she is not dead, that she is well, alive and happy, and let your own heart rest in the knowledge."

"Aye. I thank ye. Tell yer uncle that I appreciate his bringing this to my attention."

Guy Johnson nodded. "And now if you will excuse me. There are other matters I must attend to."

"By all means. By all means."

The two men rose, shook hands, and Guy Johnson turned to leave the Rathburn study, perhaps to report to his uncle his success with the head of the Rathburn estate.

However, little did Guy Johnson know that when he departed, he left John Rathburn sitting at his desk, frowning, twiddling his thumbs and deep in thought.


The days had turned colder, the bright autumn leaves were falling in greater numbers than they had been only a few weeks prior and the men were organizing hunting parties. Black Eagle was amongst them.

Winter was around the corner and the time to hunt was now. As was typical, the men planned to be gone for many months, since most of them would be traveling great distances. Some would go to the Ohio Valley, some would go north and east to Lake Champlain. Others might travel to the Susquehanna River in Pennsylvania and still others might traverse all the way up into Canada or to the Niagara Falls in the country of the Seneca. All told, their men would be away from the village for more time than Marisa liked to consider.

Parting for such an extended time period had been difficult for both Marisa and Black Eagle, and Marisa had begged to be taken with the men. But the way was too far and Marisa too inexperienced, and the fact that none of the other women would be accompanying their men on this trip made the likelihood of her going almost impossible. In the end, both Marisa and Black Eagle had decided it was better if she stay in the village, hard though it might be on them. Maybe next year she could accompany him when she was more accustomed to travel and when he might not be journeying so far.

She missed him terribly, of course, and even the constant work and the prattle of the other women couldn't make up for his absence. Nights were the hardest. If not for Pretty Ribbon, who kept Marisa constant company, it would have been even harder.

Gradually, however, as Marisa became more accustomed to village life, the rhythm of the days seemed to flow one into the other, and life began to follow a pattern. Also, she was surrounded by family, who watched over her carefully and ensured she always had enough company.

But today there was excitement. Today they were to leave the village and go out into the woods, nut gathering. The nuts would be ripe now and they were needed for many different things. The oil from the butternut, for instance, was fed to babies; some nuts were soaked and pounded into flour, or boiled. Others went into the corn bread for flavor or mixed into puddings. Nothing was wasted.

It was all new and interesting to Marisa, who hadn't known the woods abounded with so much nutritious food. Apparently, there were all sorts of nuts to be found in the woods, as well; there were black walnuts, hazelnuts, acorns, butternuts, hickory and chestnuts. Indeed, the work would be long and intense, and most of the women and girls in the village would, themselves, be gone from the village for several days. This included Marisa and her sisters.

"I like hazelnuts best of all," said Pretty Ribbon as she skipped along beside Marisa. Equipped with bark baskets in hand, the women and two guards had already entered the woods. "What nut do you like best?"

"Hmmm, I think I like roasted chestnuts. Yes," said Marisa, "it would be roasted chestnuts."

"Oh, look!" It was Laughing Maid speaking. "Do you see? Over there, in the clearing—it's the biggest walnut tree I have ever beheld. Let's see if we can get there before the others find it, and let's fill our baskets. There must be hundreds, maybe thousands of nuts in that one tree, alone. Won't our clan mother have great praise for us if we come home with all of our baskets filled? And so soon."

"Yes, let's try."

Pretty Ribbon, however, wasn't pleased. She held back, saying, "I think we should wait for the others."

"Good," said Laughing Maid. "You wait for them. Tell them where we have gone."

"I want you to wait with me."

"Do not be such a child. You'll be fine. Tell them where we've gone."

Pretty Ribbon seemed mortified at the reprimand, and she nodded quietly.

"Don't worry, Pretty Ribbon, we'll be back in only a moment," said Marisa, and the two elder sisters set off at a fast pace toward the walnut tree.

"There is always a contest amongst us to see who can

gather the most nuts. I have never won. Maybe this time I will."

"I'll help you," said Marisa. "I'll fill up your basket first before mine."

"No," said Laughing Maid. "That would be cheating. The contest is won on your own merit or not at all."

"Oh," said Marisa as she rocked back on her feet and exhaled. Never had she been amongst such honest and hardworking people. Invariably, given half a chance she might yet lead her sisters astray. Luckily when her suggestions were a mite off-color for them—seeming right to her, but breaking some moral code for them—someone usually corrected her.

"Let's hurry," said Laughing Maid.

As they ran toward the tree, they didn't hear the men, who had been waiting. Nor did they sense the men's presence until too late.

They struck the two women from behind furiously and fast. One of the brutes hit Laughing Maid so hard that with a scream, she fell to the ground. Marisa's scream split through the forest, but these men were fast, and stuffing a dirty handkerchief into her mouth and grabbing both of her hands, one of the bullies picked her up and ran.

Marisa tried to scream again, but it was useless.

Who were these people? They weren't Indians. She could smell the dirt and grease on their clothing, inhale the scent of their body odor. These men didn't bathe so often. They were definitely not Indians.

As she was jostled on the shoulders of her attacker, she wondered if any of the Indian guards would follow. The guards themselves were only teenagers, since most of the men within warring age were away from the village. Plus, with a war on, most of the older teenagers were away, and what was left of the male population in the village were the old men and children.

Because of this, it was doubtful anyone would be able to put up a rescue party.

What was Black Eagle going to think? she wondered.

Would he believe she had run away? Surely not. Pretty Ribbon would put his mind to rest on that account.

What would he do? Would he come after her? Would a runner be sent to tell him what had happened? And how long would it take for a runner to get to him, and for Black Eagle to respond?

Would he be required to save her yet again?

"Don't worry, miss," said her attacker. "We got ya."

Oh, how she wanted to talk back to this bully, how she wished she could give this man a piece of her mind. But she was gagged and her hands were bound. She could hardly swallow, let alone talk.

She was not left long to wonder who had stolen her, however. After running only a short distance, the man entered into a camp of soldiers. But they weren't British soldiers. They were the American militia.

The burly brute who had flung her over his shoulder dumped her on the ground not so gently, and getting up to her knees, she smoothed her hands over her wrists. Next to her was the man who must have been the "in-charge" of this group.

"Please excuse the roughness of the rescue, Lady Marisa," he said, "but we had no choice. We had to steal you fast and leave with you fast. Name's Brent. Colin Brent. Our orders are to get you and return to Albany with you as quickly as possible."

With her hands freed, she took the handkerchief out of her mouth, and began, "You didn't have to hit Laughing Maid. I have no idea if she's alive or not. Why did you do that?"

"Sorry, ma'am, but we have to work fast."

"Well, I'm sorry to inform you of this, but I don't wish to leave, thank you very much. So if it's all the same to you, I'll be leaving you now to go back to the Iroquois village. Goodness knows if you hurt my sister."

"Your sister?"

"Yes, my Iroquois sister."

"Don't know nothing about no sister, but I can't be

letting you go, ma'am. There's a reward on your head, and the next man might not be so polite. Can't stay here either. We gotta be moving. I have my orders." He nodded to the bully who had carried her here. "Get the lady, Coleman. We gotta get out. Fast. We're leaving now."

"I'm not going."

"Sorry, ma'am, but you are. If I have to I'll bind and gag you."

She folded her arms over her chest. "I'm not going."

"Coleman, get moving, over here. Now. I'll need you to bind the lady, put her on the horse and tie her on. We're leaving."

Of course she didn't have any chance of escape, but she wouldn't have thought much of herself if she hadn't tried. Without giving warning, she started running, back in the direction from which they had come.

But she was no physical match for these men and she was unarmed. The bully named Coleman caught her easily, tied her up and set her on the horse.

And she really didn't need him telling her, "It's for your own good, miss," to anger her.

Her reply was, "I am married. You remember that."

And then they were away, moving quickly, heading back to Albany. When she screamed, they gagged her. When she plummeted her hands on the horse, they tied them onto it, too.

Her heart was breaking, her emotions were shattered and her will was frustrated. Looking back in the direction of the village, she made a vow. Somehow, in some way, she would go back there.

# Twenty-three

Black Eagle leapt and sprinted over the pathway so quickly, he might have been a deer in flight. Flintlock in hand, with one other strapped over his shoulder, did not slow him down. Indeed, their weight served as a reminder of why he required them and spurred him onward.

They had taken his wife. They had knocked Laughing Maid unconscious and according to the last report he'd received from runners, she had still not revived.

His powder horn was full, and there were a multitude of lead balls in his pouches. Thrown over his shoulder was a bow; a quiver full of arrows was strapped across his back. His tomahawk was fixed securely in his belt. He was ready to fight. He wanted to fight.

The path over which he ran was clear, purposely kept that way by the Six Nations. Sometimes the trail was called the corridor that linked the eastern door of the Mohawk country to the western door of the Seneca, the comparison being that of the corridor of the longhouse. Ahead of him, a branch had fallen in his way, but he flew over it easily, not stopping to go back and remove it from the pathway. His mission was too important to slow down or to stop.

The woods around him reflected the anger in his heart.
The leaves had fallen, the trees were stripped of their
dignity, the grass was dry and brown and the coldness of
winter was soon to come. The forest echoed with shouts
of injustice. No one had come to the village to negotiate.
No one had spoken a word. She had been kidnapped, and it
had been cruelly done.

Could there have been less dignity in the act?

He would speak to Sir William. Such outrages must cease.

Darting quickly through a stream, Black Eagle set his
pace again to a furious sprint, ignoring the sounds and the
scents of the forest. They held nothing for him at this time
of year.

He would recover her, he would discover the truth
behind the attacks on her person and he would see to justice. Indian justice. Indian revenge.

Whoever had done this, whoever was doing this was
a person of evil. And whoever this was, they had now
insulted him. But they would be no more . . . and soon . . .

"Ye must eat something, Miss Marisa."

It was cook speaking. It was cook who had brought a
tray up to Marisa's rooms.

"Yes, thank you, Mrs. Stanton. But please, cease calling
me Miss Marisa. I am married now."

"Beg pardon, miss . . . ah, Lady Marisa."

Marisa exhaled on a sigh. "Thank you Mrs. Stanton, and
forgive me if I seem uncaring. I am not. I appreciate all that
you have done for me in these difficult weeks. But I have
changed. My maid, my best friend, is gone. My husband is
lost to me. All I have ever cared about is gone. Worse, my
step-uncle is seeking to rush me into marriage. He would
have me become a bigamist, I think."

Mrs. Stanton tut-tutted. "Forgive me for asking, but
couldn't ye pretend to go along with yer uncle? At least so
as to secure yer freedom. 'Tis not right to keep ye locked in
yer room. All the servants think so."

"But to leave the room, I have to agree to the marriage, and I cannot. I am already married, whether my step-uncle acknowledges it or not. Besides, the man my uncle has picked for me is three times my age, he speaks with a lisp and he is so skinny, he would fit into the head of a needle. Besides, if I were to agree, my uncle would rush me into marriage at once, tonight."

"'Tis a bad lot ye have. Forgive me for saying this, but . . ." She hesitated.

"Yes? Please go on."

"If ye are to change yer lot, ye will need yer strength. After all, what is a locked door, when a body is healthy and has an open window?"

"I have thought of that. But there are guards posted around the house, as well as at the bottom of my window. I have seen them there."

"Aye, and they are bought with the finest gold in all the land," said Mrs. Stanton. "But gold doesn't make a man loyal . . . forgive my forthrightness."

"Be at your ease, Mrs. Stanton. I enjoy your frankness and your company."

Mrs. Stanton placed her hands on her hips, standing akimbo as she said, "I should know about the guards. I feed 'em."

"Truly?"

"But your uncle doesn't. He thinks men can be bought. Maybe some can, like that Colonial militia that came and took ye from the Indians. They were happy to be bought. But there were some that thought they be doin' ye a favor. They had goodness in their hearts."

"I disagree, Mrs. Stanton. They tied me to a horse, they gagged me, and not one of them came to my rescue."

"'Cause they thought ye would leave."

"I would have."

"But don't ye see, some thought they were doin' good. Them's the ones I can help ye with."

Marisa slanted Mrs. Stanton a respectful look. "You would help me?"

Mrs. Stanton nodded. "'Tisn't right what yer uncle be doin' to ye, child. Now, I may not be the smartest woman in all of Albany, but I have a plan I think might work."

Marisa gazed at Mrs. Stanton with newfound respect, and she said. "You have a plan?"

Mrs. Stanton nodded. "Now, come here, child and I'll tell ye what I think. But if I do this, ye must promise me that ye'll eat."

"I promise."


Marisa and Mrs. Stanton had set their plans well. According to Mrs. Stanton, the best time to sneak away, using the window, was late at night, after the evening meal. The guard on duty at that time was a young man who appeared to be sympathetic to Marisa's plight. Plus, he was always hungry.

Their plans were simple. Mrs. Stanton was to lure him to the kitchen on the pretext of a meal. Marisa was then to set into motion, to climb down from three flights up, using the rope she had been carefully making from her good, strong hemp sheets.

Marisa had already donned her best riding habit in preparation for her escape; it was a dark blue material that would also act as camouflage. She had also caught up her hair in a dark blue, silk and lace kerchief.

She had set her plans well. She would go directly to the woods, bypassing the livery; it would be the first place they might look for her.

Besides, after being so long on the trail with Black Eagle, she felt more than able to traverse the distance on foot. Taking a cue from Black Eagle, she had attached an extra pair of slippers to a strap that hung from around her shoulders, and in one of her bags she had placed a knife, carefully sheathed, having been donated by cook.

Three weeks. For three weeks, she'd been back in Albany. And for almost as long she'd been locked in her rooms.

At first her guardian had seemed happy at her return, but this had quickly faded when she had adamantly refused his plans for an upcoming marriage. Indeed, the several times she had attempted to escape the Rathburn estate, John Rathburn had locked her in her quarters. Amidst threats, he had posted a guard below her window and had demanded her complete agreement to marry, or she would never leave her rooms.

Thus, two strong wills came into conflict.

But John Rathburn was not to be crossed so easily. With or without her agreement, he had arranged the marriage to take place in their home, complete with groom and preacher and guests. He had arranged it thinking that Marisa would be so cowed that she would fall in with his plans.

How wrong he'd been. Marisa had refused to say the necessary words to seal the arrangement. And luckily, the preacher could not be bought.

Only these last few days had been good. For the first time in weeks, she was eating, she was well nourished and she was excited. She knew exactly what she would do.

Stepping to her window, she looked up at the night sky; this, too, was good. It was a cloudless night, although there was no moon. The stars would be her guide.

Her plans were thus: First she would enter the forest and find the tree where she and Black Eagle had first experienced their love for one another. There she would hide until her uncle's bullies had either gone or had stopped looking for her. Then when it was safe, perhaps tomorrow evening, she would be away.

She was frightened, it was true, but anything was better than being held prisoner.

Taking a deep breath, and saying a prayer, she lowered the rope made of sheets, securing it to the foot of her bed. Standing on a chair, she climbed over the windowsill, hauling herself down, slowly.

There was a second floor window directly below hers and she prayed there would be no one there to see her. Her luck held. The window was pitch-black.

Downward she climbed until at last her feet hit the ground. She was so frightened, she was shaking. But taking courage, she turned swiftly around and started to run toward the woods.

She had taken no more than a few steps, however, when a dark shadow stepped out from the bushes in front of her. Immediately her stomach turned, and fear washed through her. She knew immediately who it was. She recognized that stench.

It was Thompson. So Thompson was alive. And she was in trouble.

"Goin' somewhere, miss?"

"Yes," she said. "Home."

"Aren't ye there, lass?"

"Hardly. Step out of my way or I will kill you. Lord knows I want to kill you. My maid is gone because of you."

"Good," he said. "Good. I be glad to hear that one of ye is gone. Now for the other one."

"That will be a little hard for you. I have a gun pointed directly at your chest." She didn't, of course. All her firearms had been taken from her. But under the cover of darkness, and with her hand in her purse, perhaps Thompson might never suspect. And so she continued, "If you want to live, I suggest you get out of my way."

Unfortunately for Marisa, Thompson was far more experienced, he was much larger than she was and he was an assassin. When he made a move toward her, he quickly overpowered her, taking away the only weapon she had, the knife given to her by Mrs. Stanton.

"Now, miss, we'll be seeing what's what. Come along."

Marisa tried to extricate herself from Thompson's grip. But it was useless. No matter how much she fought him, she was helpless to overpower him, and he dragged her toward the house.

Marisa sighed. Another attempted escape foiled. She might never have another one.

* * *

Albany. At last Black Eagle had arrived. Immediately, he sought out others from the Six Nations who made Albany their home. From them he learned much.

She was here. She was kept prisoner in her room. She had tried to escape twice.

It was enlightening. Quickly, he laid his plans and set out to put things in order. The tree would be their hideaway. There they would stay until it was safe to leave.

He sprinted to that place now. Moving quickly, he stocked the tree with skin-covered pouches of water, also bags full of dried meat and corn. Over the floor, to cushion her, he left his blanket.

And now for the most important element of his plan, his wife.

It was evening. The shadows would hide him well enough so that if he were careful, he could steal onto the grounds of the Rathburn estate. He had learned where her window was. He would go there now.

Curiously, he found the place unguarded. But there was a rope of sorts hanging from her window. Had she already escaped? Was he too late?

Looking around the grounds for telltale tracks, he saw that she had left here, perhaps only minutes ago. He wasn't too late.

He followed her trail, observing when she was joined by another set of prints. He recognized these, too. Thompson. He was back. He was alive.

Crouching down low, Black Eagle followed their path, which led directly to the mansion. Still amused that he had not encountered any guards, for it was said that the house was well protected, he stole up to a window and looked in. But he could see nothing.

The window, however, was not locked. He let himself in and crept forward. Where were they?

If Thompson were with her, and it appeared that he was,

her life was in danger. He must move quickly, but he must make no mistakes.

He listened, and at last he heard them. Voices. Down a dark corridor, behind a door. Slowly, slowly, he crept toward it. Slowly, noiselessly he turned the doorknob and cracked the door. He listened.

John Rathburn was laughing. "Arrest him?" he was saying, humor tingeing his voice. "Arrest him, when 'twas I who hired him to kill ye and yer maid in the first place."

"You? But step-uncle, you're my guardian. You have cared for me all my life."

"Cared for ye? As long as ye had worth for me, I cared for ye. But ye abused it. Ye brought this on yourself. Ye threatened me. Me. Because of that Pennsylvania deal, which has, by the way, been quite lucrative. And ye told yer maid. Yer maid. Unforgivable. Well, what was I to do? Submit to yer blackmail? When 'twas pure treason ye offered me?

"But I had one better for ye. While appearing to submit to yer request, I hired Thompson here to do away with ye and yer maid. I am only disgusted with Thompson that he has left the job undone. But he shall not fail now. Indeed not. I'm afraid I will require ye to write a note, dear. One stating that ye could not envision life without yer dearly beloved Indians. Therefore, ye have had no choice but to take yer own life. Here is pen and paper. Write it."

"I will not."

"If ye won't do it, then I'll see that cook is quietly done away with in as terrible a way as possible. Do ye think I was not aware of your plans?"

Marisa remained silent.

"Now write it. That's a fine lass. There ye go, now. Let me read it. Good. Good. Thompson, shoot her in the head. Now."

But Thompson never had a chance. Black Eagle's knife whizzed through the air, hitting Thompson's shooting hand square. The gun fell to the floor.

With a loud war whoop, Black Eagle shot into the room,

and taking his tomahawk in hand, he hurled himself at Thompson, making a swipe at him. But Thompson ducked and the offense did no greater damage than tear his clothes at the waist.

But wait, what was that? Blood oozed through his clothes. As though only now aware of what had happened, Thompson glanced down, gazing back up at Black Eagle in disbelief.

The two men stared at each other, challenging each other, then Black Eagle, executing a hundred-degree turn, shoved his tomahawk into Thompson's side, next to his neck. Thompson went down. Thompson was dead.

Black Eagle turned to John Rathburn. "I'll take that note," he said.

"I think not." Rathburn made a dash for the gun that Thompson had dropped, but he was too late. Perhaps it was being on the trail with Black Eagle that had done it, maybe it was something else, but Marisa's instincts were swifter than her guardian's. Marisa beat him to it. She held the gun in her hand, steady. Black Eagle was proud of her. Very proud.

She said, "Give him the note."

John Rathburn was not a fool. He acted accordingly.

"I'll give ye ten thousand dollars in gold if ye let me go." He was speaking to Black Eagle. "Here, the gold is in my desk."

"Don't move." It was Marisa speaking. Then to Black Eagle, "He has a gun in his desk."

"I think you should come away from there," said Black Eagle, his musket aimed toward Rathburn's head. "I am a good shot, especially at close range."

"You had better do as he says," said Marisa. "He's only looking for a good reason to do it."

Rathburn stopped midstride.

"And now, step-uncle," said Marisa. "I think there is a confession to be made. 'Tis yours. Here is pen and paper."

"You can't make me do it."

"Perhaps not," she said. "As I said, my husband is only

waiting for a good reason to kill you. I, too. Perhaps both of us will do it."

Rathburn shook his head at her.

"Which is it? Confession or death?"

Presented with no other choice, John Rathburn, at some length, sat and wrote, while both Marisa and Black Eagle watched.

At last it was done. Marisa read the note with care.

She said, "I think there is more for you to confess. But perhaps the Pennsylvania incident is a good start. If I remember correctly, however, there is a maid you took into service, whose parents you killed, whose land you took and who you enslaved. That will be part of this confession, as well."

With a deep sigh, Rathburn again put pen to paper.

When it was done, Marisa said, "And now for James. Where is James? I have something to say to him, too."

"James is no longer with me," Rathburn confessed. "Of all the insolent, ugly men. And a bad butler he was, as well. He had the gall to go to a preacher and confess his sins."

"Did he?" Marisa smiled. "I am glad to hear that at least one man has a conscience."

At last the note was signed and sealed. John Rathburn turned to Marisa. He said, "And now what? Are you going to kill me anyway?"

"No," she said. "I won't let you take the easy way out. I think we are going to escort you and your written confession to the town constable. I think we'll do it now."

"'Tis the middle of the night."

"So it is," she said, and she smiled. "So it is."

# Twenty-four

It was done. At last John Rathburn was to face a jury of his peers for the crimes he had committed. At last Marisa was free.

There would be the Rathburn home and estate to dispose of properly. But upon further thought, Marisa decided she would leave even that for the authorities. There was nothing here for her. She had become Mohawk, and she wanted to return home.

But they wouldn't be staying there. She and Black Eagle were going to take Sir William's advice and go west. It was true, the Mohawk village was too close to Albany. There would always be trouble. So why stay?

Instead, they would make their own life elsewhere, away from all this. Away from the prejudice and war. It was possible. Even in this war-torn world, they could and they would find happiness.

# Epilogue

It was Spring. The woods were alive with new life, and there was a scent in the air of hope. Of hope and happiness. The winter in the Mohawk village had been long and happy. But it was time to move west.

Black Eagle led the way down the Iroquois long trail. Marisa followed, but there was one other with them this day. Pretty Ribbon skipped along before Marisa, who pulled up their rear.

"Do you think there will be Seneca children for me to play with?"

"There will be many," said Marisa. "No doubt. And they'll love you, as I love you, too."

Pretty Ribbon smiled. "I am glad that you let me come with you, sister. I'll go back and visit the rest of the family, but I'm glad to be with you."

"How could we have left you behind?"

"*Nyoh*," said Black Eagle, as he turned back to them. "How could we have left you behind?" He smiled at them both. "Look there," he said, pointing west. "Do you see the hill? Do you see the river? We are almost there."

Marisa gazed in the direction that he indicated. It was

another strong, fortified village. "What if they don't like me?" she asked.

"They will love you. But it matters little. I think we will seek our happiness beyond even Seneca country. I hear there is a beautiful plain country further west. Would you like to go there with me?"

"I will follow you anywhere. For you see, I love you."

"As I love you, my wife. As I love you." He took her in his arms and hugged her, kissing her with a passion that would serve them all their life through. Pretty Ribbon stood between them, her arms encircling them, and on her countenance was a smile that was a beautiful thing to behold.

# Historical Note

I hope you will bear with me as I take a moment to impart a bit of history that is, I think, important for a clear understanding of this period in our nation's history. If you are at all like me, in order to visualize scenes well, it is necessary to have an understanding of the forces at work in the world at this time.

Long ago, before the white man ever stepped foot on the North American continent, there was a Native American confederation that was established for the purpose of bringing peace to the land they called Turtle Island (the known world at that time), and to abolish war forever. That confederation was and still is called the Iroquois confederation or the League of the Five/Six Nations.

The confederation was composed of five—and eventually six—Nations who were related by custom, language and blood. These Nations were the Mohawk, the Oneida, the Onondagas, the Cayuga and the Seneca. In the early eighteenth century (sometime around 1722) the Tuscaroras joined the confederation, making the league six instead of five nations.

What is called the Great Peace of the Iroquois came about because of two men, Deganawida and Hiawatha (the real Hiawatha, not the Hiawatha of Longfellow's poem). Both of these men had a vision of ending war and the fear associated with war, and bringing peace and unity to a people that would not only make the people strong, but would allow the people to live their lives in freedom.

The Council of the Great Peace was an extraordinary government, unparalleled in European culture. It made each man, woman and child free of government rule, and provided strong provisions to ensure that the chiefs remained responsible to the people. So strict and astute were these laws that if any chief began to serve his own needs, instead of those of the people, the offending chief was at once removed by the elder women of the tribe. That such men lived the rest of their lives in disgrace was evident.

Within the council a majority could not force the minority to their will. All had to agree before any law or action came into being, thus debate and oratory were highly valued. The Great Peace was a government truly of, by and for the people, and it influenced Benjamin Franklin, Thomas Paine and Thomas Jefferson. When it came time to set up our own government and constitution, Benjamin Franklin studied the Iroquois confederation in detail. This is a fact that I didn't learn in school, and in case you didn't either, I thought I would bring the information to your attention.

There truly was a spirit of freedom and independence that filled Native America long before the white man "discovered" America. This was so much the case, that it was unwittingly written into James Fenimore Cooper's books. In his prose, one can lay witness to a taste of this spirit. In fact, if one were to watch Michael Mann's most recent rendition of *The Last of the Mohicans* (1992), and listen to our hero, Nathaniel, one can hear him state that he is not *subject* to much at all. Such was the attitude prevalent throughout Native America. It was a country of free men and free women, and no "subjects" were to be found.

From my studies I have come to believe that it was this
concept of freedom and independence that met and influenced the first European settlers. Indeed, the European
people who came to the shores of America had not been
indoctrinated in the idea of freedom of thought. Instead,
the Europeans came to America to escape oppression, and
a government that considered people little more than chat-
tel; the right to have an individual thought was almost non-
existent. Instead the "Divine Right of Kings," where the
King owned everything and everyone, ruled England and
Europe.

Although the doctrines of Greece influenced our
Founding Fathers considerably, not even in Greece was
the concept of equality and the idea of being beholden to
none better embraced than in Native America. This was
particularly so amongst the Iroquois, who gave our founding country so much.

So remember, when one conceives of the idea of American freedom as we have come to know it, those roots grow
deep in Native America.

It is also a truth to say that without the Iroquois's covenant chain that bound them to England, and England to
them, the French and Indian War would have very likely
ended with a different ruling body over the American
continent. It was the Mohawks who guarded our northern
borders against French invasion. It was the Senecas who
guarded the western borders against the French, for French
reign included not only Canada at that time, but much of
the Ohio Valley, leaving the English and the American settlers choked on the Eastern coast, unable to go West.

Sandwiched on land situated between the French and
English settlements sat the Native Americans on ground
they had owned for centuries. Because the Native Americans were also a people who had raised some of the finest
warriors in history, the English and French vied to obtain
the loyalty of the Iroquois, often spreading fear and rumors,
one against the other in the attempt to gain their support.

The French and Indian War was called such because

several Canadian Indians did side with the French. Many of those Indians were of Algonquin stock, but some were Christian Mohawks who had come under the influence of French Jesuits, and who had left their homeland in what is now New York for Canada. That this pitted Mohawk against Mohawk, brother against brother, was not forgotten by the Iroquois, and is one reason why, during the Revolutionary War, many Iroquois people were determined to remain neutral.

During the time period when this book takes place, the French and Indian War was in full swing. The Iroquois—specifically the Mohawk living along the Mohawk River in upper New York State—were aligned with the English and the Americans.

I am happy to have shared this journey back in time to a period in the history of Turtle Island (the world at that time) that was most heroic.

Gen Bailey

# One More Historical Note

In the beginning to this book, Sir William Johnson is escorted to the Water-that-runs-swift by members of the Mohawk Nation. Although this is a true historical event, it didn't happen at the Battle of Lake George. It happened later, in 1767 when Sir William was suffering from gout, and also from the effects of the bullet he had received in the Battle at Lake George.

He was at that time taken by boat to Schenectady and then carried across the Iroquois trails by the Mohawks, arriving at the Water-that-runs-swift in late August.

I hope you will bear with me as I took a little literary license and changed this bit of history.

Among the children who had been carried off young, and had long lived with the Indians, it is not to be expected that any marks of joy would appear on their being restored to their parents or relatives. Having been accustomed to look upon the Indians as the only connexions they had, having been tenderly treated by them, and speaking their language, it is no wonder that they considered their new state in the light of a captivity, and parted from the savages with tears.

But it must not be denied that there were even some grown persons who shewed an unwillingness to return. The Shawanese were obliged to bind several of their prisoners and force them along to the camp; and some women, who had been delivered up, afterwards found means to escape and run back to the Indian towns. Some, who could not make their escape, clung to their savage acquaintance at parting, and continued many days in bitter lamentations, even refusing sustenance.

William Smith,
*Historical Account of Bouquet's Expedition
against the Ohio Indians in 1764*
Cincinnati: Robert Clarke and Co., 1868, p. 80.